"HER WOMEN HAVE DIGNITY AND STRENGTH!"

—Marge Piercy

ELIZABETH A. LYNN has lived in New York, Cleveland, and Chicago and is now happily settled in San Francisco where, she says, she belonged all along. A DIFFERENT LIGHT, published by Berkley in 1978, was her first novel. Since then she has published the critically acclaimed and very successful *The Chronicles of Tornor,* a fantasy trilogy: WATCHTOWER, THE DANCERS OF ARUN and THE NORTHERN GIRL. At the 1980 World Fantasy Convention, Lynn was awarded two World Fantasy Awards—one for WATCHTOWER and one for her short story, "The Woman Who Loved the Moon." Her new novel, THE SARDONYX NET, will be published by Berkley in 1982. Ms. Lynn teaches in the Women Studies Program at San Francisco State University.

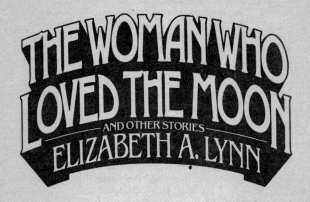

THE WOMAN WHO LOVED THE MOON

AND OTHER STORIES

ELIZABETH A. LYNN

BERKLEY BOOKS, NEW YORK

"Wizard's Domain" first appeared in *Basilisk* (1980) edited by Ellen Kushner. "The Gods of Reorth" first appeared in *The Berkley Showcase I* (1980) edited by Victoria Schochet and John Silbersack. "We All Have To Go" first appeared in *Tricks and Treats* (1976) edited by Joe Gores and Bill Pronzini. "The Saints of Driman" first appeared in *Antaeus*, Spring/ Summer 1977. "I Dream of a Fish, I Dream of a Bird" first appeared in *Isaac Asimov's Science Fiction Magazine*, Summer 1977. "The Island" first appeared in *The Magazine of Fantasy and Science Fiction*, November 1977. "The Dragon That Lived in the Sea" first appeared in *Other Worlds 1* (1979) edited by Roy Torgeson. "Mindseye" and "The Man Who Was Pregnant" first appeared in *Chrysalis 1* (1977) edited by Roy Torgeson. "Obsessions" first appeared under the title "The Fire Man" in *Dark Sins, Dark Dreams* (1978) edited by Barry Malzberg and Bill Pronzini. "The Woman in the Phone Booth" first appeared in *New Dimensions 12* (1981) edited by Marta Randall and Robert Silverberg. "Don't Look At Me" first appeared in *Chrysalis 2* (1978) edited by Roy Torgeson. "Jubilee's Story" first appeared in *Millennial Women* (1978) edited by Virginia Kidd. "The Circus That Disappeared" first appeared under the title "Circus" in *Chrysalis 3* (1978) edited by Roy Torgeson. "The White King's Dream" first appeared in *Shadows 2* (1979) edited by Charles L. Grant. "The Woman Who Loved The Moon" first appeared in *Amazons!* (1979) edited by Jessica Amanda Salmonson.

THE WOMAN WHO LOVED THE MOON AND
OTHER STORIES

A Berkley Book / published by arrangement with
the author

PRINTING HISTORY
Berkley edition / September 1981

ISBN: 0-425-05161-7

A BERKLEY BOOK® TM 757,375

PRINTED IN THE UNITED STATES OF AMERICA

The author would like to thank the two people most responsible for the appearance of this collection: Winifred N. Lynn and Robert W. Shurtleff.

This book is for Richard Curtis

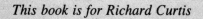

• Table of Contents •

•*Wizard's Domain*•

This story is first in the collection, although it was published in 1980, because it is the first piece of fiction I completed. Before this, everything I began ended in the middle. I was living in Chicago; it was 1971. I can still recall the sense of intense satisfaction that filled me when I wrote the final sentence and realized that yes, it was done. I started submitting the story to markets in 1972. It was rejected everywhere for four years. (Ted White lost it.) In 1977 David Hartwell accepted it for *Cosmos*, but the magazine folded before it could appear.

It had gone through several rewrites by this time. In 1979 Ellen Kushner, then assistant editor at Ace, read it and liked it. After requesting some revisions, which were made, she bought it for the fantasy anthology *Basilisk*.

It is a story about power, and is set in the imaginary country of Ryoka.

They tell this story in the Eastern Counties of Ryoka. The house by Kameni Bay is gone, covered by the restless sand. If Shea Sealord lives, he is old, and his power gone. But the bay remains, gray and cold. Froth-white curls rise from it and ride to shore again, and again. Wind whips the surface of the vagrant sea, and if you stand on the rocks that breakwater the bay, you will hear that it does, indeed, make the sound of a man sobbing.

At the time of the making of this tale, there were wizards in Ryoka, greater wizards and lesser. Some had names that folk could say. Others were nameless. Some lived in caves, and fields, and mountains. And some lived in houses, wearing the guise and speaking the language of mortals. One of these was Shea. No one is quite sure when he first appeared, riding his ship *Windcatcher*, sailing up to the harbor in Skyeggo, not tall, not small, a silent man dressed in gray. He built a house on the shore of Kameni Bay, and hired servants to tend it, and commissioned a ship to be built in Skyeggo harbor, and when it was built he hired sailors to sail it. He paid in gold that did not melt. The ship sailed south, and there were those that swore it would not return. But when it did, laden with spice and timber and silver ore and all manner of precious things, the whispers ceased. When Shea built a second ship, and a third, the merchants of Ryoka wondered. The second ship sailed, and the third, and they both returned. In this manner Shea Sealord drew people to his service, and they say few regretted it. Thieves and knaves found no place with him, but honest folk were well-rewarded. In time there were a few such folk who could, if asked, call Shea "friend."

One of these was Rhune. He had captained the first ship, not knowing where he was going or what he would find, trusting the word of the wizard. (What he found, in the southern lands, is not a part of this tale.) He was a big man, silent, slow to anger, but feared on the docks for his skill in combat. He was often seen walking through the city or on the shore of Kameni Bay with Shea. No one on the docks was surprised when Shea named him master of his fleet.

But one autumn Rhune was gone—vanished overnight, they said—and it was whispered through the city that he had somehow offended his wizard master, and had paid an unnameable and terrible penalty for that offense. Folk said he was dead, or worse, that he was not, but prisoned somewhere, in some hell known only to magicians. The whispers swelled until they seeped through the Eastern Counties. But they stopped wherever Shea turned his cool, sea-gray eyes. Folk learned not to say Rhune's name where the Sealord might hear it, and Birne, another of Shea's captains, was named the new master of the fleet.

But memories fade, and human loyalties are fickle. New tales filled the marketplace and docks of Skyeggo. One autumn afternoon Shea said to his servants: "I shall be walking by the bay. Do not disturb me." And the servants bowed, and did not wonder at the order, for they had heard it many times, though (to tell the truth) not so often of late.

Shea walked to the edge of the sand. He watched the rush and retreat of the waves. They swirled around him, never touching him, always leaving him a clear space in the wet sand. He stepped forward. They retreated.

He spoke aloud. "Rhune?"

In his mind the water answered. *Come to gloat, Shea? Does it give you satisfaction to know me imprisoned here?*

Shea said nothing, but he gestured with one hand. The sea changed. The wind stormed and sang and scraped the waves. They flung themselves against the rocks.

He calmed them. "You are still angry."

Have I not cause? cried the voice only he could hear.

"Had I not cause?" Shea responded.

A long time passed before the answer came into his mind. *You had cause.*

Shea half-smiled. "Rhune, would you be free?"

Silence.

"You will never ask it, though," he said softly. "I know you. Will you buy it from me. Rhune? I will free you now, for a price."

What price?

"I need your help."

My help?

"I need your skills, and your strength. I need your knowledge of men. I need your guile, my traitor, and your deceit."

The water sobbed. For a long time there was no reply. Finally the words came. *I will help you, Lord.*

Shea smiled truly, and lifted his hands to call the winds.

In the bay, a great whirlpool of water rose, like dark and liquid smoke, sucked out of the ocean by the wind. It was huge, and black. It sank lower, and lower. When it reached the height of a tall man a head emerged from it, and when as it sank further there appeared shoulders, chest, waist, until a naked man stood knee-deep in the waves. Slowly he waded to shore. He was tall and broad, with fair hair that fell past his shoulders. He was breathing hard, and shivering.

Shea took off his gray cloak, and swung it over those muscular shoulders. "Come."

Together, neither looking back, they walked across the beach to the house.

The morning sun came through the eastward windows: also came in the sound of the sea. Rhune sat by the window, listening to the sound of the waves. He had not heard that sound for a year: the sea does not hear its own music.

There were clothes laid out for him at the foot of the bed. He remembered, with some amusement, the look on the faces of the servants when he walked into the house, naked, dripping. Shea had given a few orders and vanished into the back of the house. Servants, all of whom he knew, brought Rhune a towel, clothing, food. He had almost forgotten the taste of bread, the feel of silk.

With sunlight streaking the colored floor tiles, he dressed now and went out through the terrace doors to find the master of the house. As he had expected, Shea was sitting on the beach.

The Sealord turned as Rhune padded across the sand. "Good morning," he said politely. "Did you sleep well?"

Rhune smiled. "Yes. Thank you." Quietly he settled himself beside the wizard.

Shea said, "Your reappearance has somewhat shaken my household."

"Where did they think I was?" Rhune asked.

"They do not think about such things," said the wizard.

Rhune looked down at his hands. They were no different than when he had last seen them, a year back. *As I should not have thought about wizardry and the things of wizardry,* he thought.

He held his anger silent, and said, "They are wise. I'm sure the sailors and captains on the docks will be equally surprised."

"I did not bring you back to be captain, or sailor," said Shea.

"Why did you bring me back?" said Rhune.

Shea said, "To be a warrior. To join me—if you will—in a task of great import and high adventure."

Rhune cocked his head and glanced at the wizard somewhat quizzically. Shea was not wont to speak dramatically, except in jest. But the gray, changeful eyes were serious. Shea pointed at the water.

"Look," he said.

Rhune looked at his prison, and saw a volcano, all green and gray and moving, rise from the waves, spewing wet fire.

It fell into the bay again, and the waves made by the fall surged up the beach, detouring around the two seated men.

"Of what does that remind you?" said Shea.

Rhune said slowly, "That's easy. The Firemountain."

Four days' journey off Ryoka coast the great volcano sat. It was ruled by the Firelord, Seramir. The volcano lay quiescent now, its fire seeming spent. Yet once Seramir had been very powerful. Seventy years back his ships had sailed from the Firemountain, black ships with red sails and brightly painted dragons on their bows. Grim men with weapons had tramped from the ships to strip the wealth and beauty from the towns of the eastern shore.

Khelen the Sorceress, greatest magician of her day, had come from the west to pit magic against magic. Tales of that battle are still told from one end of Ryoka to the other. It was a terrible fight. But Khelen prevailed. Ships smashed, men beaten, drowned, or buried, Seramir had begged peace. By the terms of that peace he was confined to the Firemountain, forbidden to sail or to cause others to sail beyond a day's journey from its shores.

Yet he was still feared in the coastal counties. People spoke with fear of the red-eyed lord of fire. And trading ships sailing to and from Skyeggo paid a toll in gold to the captains of the tall dragon ships.

"The Firemountain, yes," said Shea. "Where Seramir Firelord lives, and watches—and hates."

"Hates?" said Rhune, who knew something of hatred.

"Hates—the land, its cities, its people. He ages now. His power wanes, and so he loves it more, and craves its increase. Yet the only power he has over all Ryoka is the power of the toll—he who is lord of Fire! It galls him. He does not need gold, what is gold to a wizard? I can make gold out of sand. So can he. He craves mastery."

The certainty in Shea's voice made Rhune shiver. "Is he mad?" he asked.

"A little. Even magicians were born human."

I can understand him, then, Rhune thought. I was mad, once. "You spoke of war," he said. "I thought, when Khelen bested him, Seramir swore never to make war upon Ryoka again."

"He swore never to send ships or men to burn cities and plunder the land. He keeps that oath. Only"—Shea shifted, and sand slid down the side of the dune—"it seems that the fires of earth itself have of late grown restless. From all over Ryoka, out to the very edge of the Western Counties, come reports of crevices opening in the earth, rocks shifting and falling, streams steaming. The cliffs at Mantalo erupted a month ago, drowning ships and men in spouts of liquid fire. Forty died. A little firemountain grows now in the harbor."

Rhune remembered the harbor of Mantalo, blue and white and gold, filled with tall-masted ships bobbing in the sun. A horror filled him. "Seramir has done this?"

"I believe so."

"How can his power reach so far?"

Shea half-smiled, as if in approval of the question. "Some device or tool which he has found or bought or made permits him to extend his will even to the Western Counties. There are tales of such things in the lore books."

"Can he be stopped?"

"He must be," said Shea. "But Khelen is dead, and there are few with the power to thwart him. Malice—the will to twist and ruin—drives him now."

Rhune looked across the bay. "You are Sealord," he said. "Can you drown his island in ocean?"

"*I* have no device with which to reach across distance. To best him I must go to him."

Rhune blinked. "Would he not know you?" he said doubtfully.

"I would not go alone, nor as myself. You are right, he will be expecting me, or someone like me. But what if Rhune—friend, servant, and traitor to Shea Sealord—were to be freed by him in a moment of mercy—or weakness? *He* might sail to the Firemountain. And with him, naturally, he would take *his* servant." Shea folded his hands in his lap, and his gray-green eyes gleamed, unfathomable as ocean.

Rhune closed his own eyes against their power, listening to the lift and fall of the sleepless, ever-patient sea.

I can't, he thought. I can't play such a part.

"If I refuse to do this thing," he said, "will you prison me again?"

"Look at me," said the Sealord.

Rhune opened his eyes. Shea's gray glance searched his face. "If in truth," said the wizard, "the ocean has washed from you your ability to charm, to deceive, and to lie, then I will find some other way to counter Seramir, and you may go from here. But if you say so, be sure you speak truth." Shea's voice grew very soft. "It is no longer in your power to lie to me."

Rhune bowed his head. "Please," he said, "let me think."

Shea left him. He sat alone (as he had not been for many months—the ocean is never alone) smelling the salt air. Gulls rode the currents, calling to one another. He tried to picture the harbor at Mantalo as it must look, broken and dark with soot. It made an ugly image.

He dug his bare feet into the sand. His head felt thick and sluggish. The wind ruffled his hair, and he turned his face to the east to watch the rising sun coat the sea with light.

Once he had had guile and treachery aplenty. He remembered Osher, who had thought himself a wizard, and had been only a vicious, flattering fool. But he had not seemed foolish. He had measured his victim well, and his flatteries and baits had worked.

He said, "Without you, Shea is nothing. You build and stock his ships. You choose his captains and crews. You are his fleetmaster, and his chief counselor. Am I right in this? Yet you name him *Lord*. Lands, ships, lordship—it is through your effort that he keeps them. Only in his magic is he your master. Do you not resent it? You ought to. You call him 'friend,' but I will give you what he has never deigned or dared to give you—magic. Surely he fears you, and is no true friend, or else he would have offered it to you long ago."

With these words and others like them Osher fueled Rhune's ambitions. Two words from Shea would have ended it. But Shea seemed not to notice. One moonless autumn night, Rhune himself had opened the gates of the house, this house, and broken the neck of the guard who tried to shout a warning. Puffed with the desire for magic, he had let Osher and his soldiers in, to capture and dungeon Shea.

But Osher died, and Shea sent the raging sea into his house and tore it to rubble. Frightened, as he had never been before, by that power, Rhune fled, traveling west and north, away from the sea, hoping that Shea's power would fade. But everywhere he ran streams, rivers, lakes, springs, the very water in the wells rose to bar his passage. Chilled, hungry, refugeless and raging, he surrendered, and Shea bound him with chains cold as ice, and brought him to the bay.

His hands twisted against each other. A year he had rested in it, not eating, not sleeping, part of the ocean and the tides, but conscious, and human, if one can be human and still be ocean. In it his ambitions and his pride had dissolved, washed away by the endless rocking of the earth. He *thought* they had dissolved.

But the anger, like a lump of iron in the earth, remained. (Two words from you, Sealord, and it might never have happened. But you saw nothing, said nothing. Only at the end did you speak.)

At last, with memories crowding his mind, he rose, and went to look for Shea.

He found him in the library, holding a rolled scroll.

"I will do it," he said.

Shea nodded. Gently he fingered open the brittle paper. "I thought you would." His face was unreadable, but his voice held a subtle mingling of sadness and relief.

It took Shea some three weeks to make preparation for the journey. Some of his tasks were practical and some were magical.

During that time, Rhune stayed near the house. Shea had asked him to, saying, "It will be best if your coming is a surprise to Seramir, if he does not even know that you are free. If you go into the city there will be talk, and he has agents in the city."

Rhune agreed. There was no one he wished to see in Skyeggo. The terms of his old life had been washed out of him. By day he walked in the sunlight, or swam in the bay, delighting in the feel of the sun and water on his skin. In the afternoons, he practised weaponry and combat with the house guards.

In the evenings, he sat with Shea in the library, listening to the magician speak about the Firelord. "The island is his domain," Shea said, "and all that lives on it is his. Trust no one. The most guileless-seeming scullion may be a spy, or worse, a creature made by Seramir out of fire. He has that skill, as do all the element-lords." He spoke casually, as if he were not one himself. "Eat no food that has been prepared with fire unless you see others eating it. The fire-folk do not eat. Any food made with fire may be spelled to trap you."

"But you will be with me," said Rhune. "Can I not watch what you eat?"

"We may not always be together," said Shea.

The last few days before the journey, Birne, the fleetmaster, came to the house. Rhune spent most of those days on the beach. One morning he was walking when Shea called to him. Rhune went to the Sealord's side. "Walk with me," said the wizard.

Obediently, Rhune followed him into the meadow west of the bay. The grass was lush, well-watered, as all Shea's lands were. Once more, the wizard began to speak of the Firelord.

"I desire him to trust you," he said. "If he trusts you, he will boast to you of his powers. He may even tell you about the device with which he wreaks such destruction upon Ryoka. But I do not think he will tell you where it can be found. I shall have to search his rooms for it. If I cannot find it there"—Shea paused, and with a deliberate, studied gesture, snapped the head from a daisy—"I will have to make him tell me where it is." A yellow bee buzzed up angrily from his fingers, circled him once, and flew away.

Rhune said, "Can you not destroy this device at a distance, from the harbor?"

Shea shook his head. "Seramir guards his mountain well," he said. "Once he is bound and weakened, it would be possible. But I cannot bind him from a distance. Even face to face, the task is difficult. It is not easy to capture a wizard in his own domain."

Rhune said, "I know."

Shea half-smiled. "You are a strong man," he said. "But the chain with which I bound you was common steel, locked with a binding spell. It would not hold Seramir. Anything made with fire is subject to his command."

They continued to walk across the meadow. Finally Shea halted, beside a bare circle, brown and hard and strange amid the luxurious grass. "Therefore we will forge a chain," said Shea. Again he looked at Rhune. "You wished once to do magic, did you not?"

Rhune set his teeth. "I did."

Shea knelt by—not on—the bare spot. Rhune copied him. "You shall. Hold one hand out to the center of the circle, and wait."

Rhune obeyed. Soon he felt a vibration, as if the earth itself were soundlessly humming. The sensation was unpleasant, though not painful, and it was weakening. "Pull back!" said Shea.

Rhune pulled his arm back. It trembled with tension, as if he had been holding a heavy weight. "What is it?" he asked.

Shea said, "A place of power. They are sometimes called witch's circles. As a lens can focus sunlight, so this spot can focus the power of mind that we call magic."

Rhune rubbed his arm. "I don't understand."

"As a volcano is a pool of the earth's unseen fires, and a spring the release of underground waters, so this circle is a pool, a well, a spring—whatever image suits your mind—for magic. They can be used, by those who know how to use them."

As I do not, Rhune thought. He gazed with some trepidation at the circle of power.

Shea said, "It will not hurt you."

The reassurance stung. Rhune said, "What do I do?"

"Put both hands in the circle." Shea put his own hands forward as he spoke. "Choose from one of those pictures, pool or well or spring, or make another in your mind from what I told you. Make the picture clear and strong, and then see yourself as drawing substance out of it."

Rhune extended both hands into the barren place. For a moment he was at a loss. Finally he visualized beneath the bare earth a huge magnet. It was old, brown, heavy rock, and it pulled as the pole pulls at the compass. Rhune felt the pull. "I thought it would be easy," he said.

"No," Shea said, "it isn't easy. Don't stop."

Rhune clenched his eyelids shut and pulled against the rock. It dragged back at him, pulling strength from him, pulling thoughts, loves, fears, hopes, pulling senses and nerves, pulling heart and lungs—his breath burned in his throat—pulling legs and arms and fingers, pulling blood and bone and brain . . . "Feel," said Shea. He guided Rhune's shaking hands to something so fine it felt no thicker than an eyelash. "Do you feel it? That is our chain."

"I feel it," said Rhune. The words came in grunts. He opened his eyes. Shea's fingers were shaking, too, and his arms and shoulders were trembling. His face was streaked with sweat.

Rhune's fingers crooked. He felt as if he were being drawn into the earth. The top of his head was white-hot.

"Take your hands from the circle!" snapped Shea.

Rhune withdrew his hands. Lying back in the cool grass, he crossed his arm over his stinging eyes, and waited for the world to cease spinning like a manic top.

"Good," said Shea.

Rhune struggled up. "Show me."

Shea held out his palms. They looked empty. "Extend your hands," he said. Rhune held his hands out, palm up. Shea laid—something—over them: four strands, as light as gossamer. Rhune stroked them. They were fine as human hair.

"This is all?" he said.

"Try to break them," said Shea.

Rhune felt along the length. They were long enough to tie a man down, provided there was something to tie him to. Wrapping them around his hands, he braced and pulled, until the muscles stood out in his throat. His shoulders and wrists knotted and cracked. Blood roared in his ears.

The invisible chains did not break.

"They—they're strong," he said.

Shea took them, with a gesture that seemed to sling them around his neck. "They cannot be cut, and they cannot melt. The only thing which will undo them once tied, is our thought, woven in the breaking as it was in the making." He smiled. "Thus Seramir, once bound, is unlikely to attempt to harm us, because he will never then be free."

"I hope he knows that," Rhune said.

"He will," Shea said. Standing, he held out his hands and walked once around the bare spot, singing.

"What is that?" Rhune asked when he had done.

"I laid a warding spell on the circle. There is power in it now deadly enough to kill any unwary animal or a child. The spell will keep anyone from blundering into it until the effect fades."

They returned to the house. At the door to the library, Shea said, "Will you be practicing in the pavilion this afternoon?"

Few magicians are warriors. But, watching Rhune break up a sailors' fight on the docks, Shea had grown intrigued with the arts of weaponry and wrestling. He had asked Rhune to show him what he knew, and over the years it had become a pastime between the two men. At Rhune's suggestion Shea had had a practice pavilion built near the house on Kameni Bay. It was in the garden, and was not, strictly speaking, a pavilion, but a square of lawn protected by a light awning, and walled on three sides with trellises. Flowers dangled from the trellis rungs, so that the smells of sweat and oil mingled with the scent of roses.

"I had thought to," said Rhune.

"I should like to join you," said the wizard. "I have neglected it, in the past year."

Something bitter twisted inside Rhune's mind. He bowed. "As you will, lord," he said.

Crouching, right hand knife-edge out to protect his face and throat, Rhune circled. His feet shifted in tight short steps. His body was slick with oil. Two arms' lengths from him, Shea matched his movements, gray eyes watchful. This was their fourth encounter.

Around the perimeter of the pavilion, the guards watched. Shea had not ordered them there; they had wandered by, casually it seemed. Rhune wondered if they thought he was a threat to Shea. It was an ironic but, he concluded, not a stupid suspicion.

The first two matches had been with wooden knives. Shea had won them both. He was deadly with knives. The third match had been wrestling, which Rhune had won, as he was about to win this one.

Shea feinted a punch, and followed it with a true one. Rhune seized the extended arm and twisted it in a circle. Shea's whole body spun with the motion. Rhune yanked the arm upward until the wizard's thumb touched his shoulder blade and scythed the wizard's legs out from under him. Shea dropped, free arm curling to protect his head as he fell. Rhune followed him to the grass and held him there, arm locked, his knees on Shea's spine.

"Two and two," he said, and let go.

Shea rolled upright. He was breathing hard. "Winner's choice."

Rhune flexed his fingers. "Staves."

With staves they were even; Rhune was taller, with a longer reach, but Shea was swifter. Nodding, Shea beckoned a guard to throw down two staves from the rack. "The red one," he directed, as the man hesitated. "And any other." The red staff was the sturdy oak one that Rhune had cut and polished himself, three years ago. No, Rhune reminded himself. Four years ago. A year had passed since he'd touched it. He picked it from the grass, feeling the familiar slant and warp and pattern of the grain.

"You kept it," he said.

Shea half-smiled. "I don't throw things away."

He dropped into stance, one foot forward of the other, hands spaced evenly on the cudgel. They circled slowly, feinting and withdrawing. Rhune struck twice but Shea was ahead of him both times. *I don't throw things away.* Am I a thing? Rhune thought. His hands tensed on his stick.

Slowly, and then faster, Shea began to push the attack, whirling his staff in jarring blows that Rhune was hard put to it to block, to the head, the groin, the stomach, the legs. The guards murmured approval. Rhune twisted and blocked and countered, feeling himself pressed. Suddenly he saw an opening as Shea, careless in victory, swung his staff at an almost horizontal angle to Rhune's ribs. Rhune stepped inside the blow and swung his own staff into the pit of Shea's stomach.

The shock of the strike went into Rhune's hands and up to his elbows. He had not meant to hit that hard. Shea doubled and fell, gasping, fighting for breath.

Rhune dropped his own stick and knelt. "Shea?"

"All right," whispered the wizard. He gestured with one hand. Rhune glanced around. Three guards had crossed the border of the practice space, their eyes worried. At the gesture, they halted. Rhune put his hands under Shea's arms and helped him to sit.

"I'm sorry," he said. "I didn't mean that."

Shea took a deep breath. He coughed. "I swear there's a hole in my spine," he said. "Your match, I think." Standing, he stretched. Rhune rose. Suddenly Shea whirled, swift as a cat, and his right hand, knife-edged, slashed Rhune's neck.

Rhune rode the blow back, shaking his head to clear it, falling into a defensive posture automatically—but Shea did not follow up.

"You're recovered," Rhune said. "I wish I had your recovery time."

"You don't need it if you don't get hit, and *you* don't, very often." Shea started for the house, then changed his mind. "I'll come in a while," he said. Rhune could not tell for whom he was speaking, Rhune or the guards. "I'm going for a swim."

Rhune put the staves back on the rack himself. He smelled his own stink. The sigh of the spray on the breakwater rocks seemed inviting. Finally he followed Shea's footprints east. He scrubbed himself clean of the oil with sand, and ducked in and out of the surf a few times. The westering sun laid a red track over the surface of the bay. Rhune closed his eyes, wondering how much more Shea had to do before they could leave.

He found himself listening, and laughed at himself. Shea was agile and silent in water as if he had been born in it. All he could hear was the hiss and moan of spray.

Suddenly a green wave rose up and up like a wall, and Shea came sliding down the curl like a dolphin riding a wake.

Beckoning, the Sealord said his name. Rhune rose from where he had been sitting. "Come walk," said Shea. They walked, stitching a path of prints down the wet sand.

Fear began to grow in Rhune: fear of the future. Finally he could no longer stand the silence. "Shea, I don't want to go."

He felt Shea look at him. "Afraid?"

"Yes! Not of Seramir."

"Of what?"

Rhune clenched his fists. "Of myself, and what I might do."

"Go on."

Rhune looked at the bay. "I broke faith with you. I—you were right to name me traitor. Might it not happen again?"

There. He had said it.

"It might," said Shea. He sounded very calm. "I think it will not. Besides, I broke a kind of faith with you."

"How?" Rhune said. It was not what he had expected Shea to say.

"Do you not know?" said the wizard. Rhune shook his head, unsure of the Sealord's meaning. "Strange. But you are still angry. Surely you must have wondered why, of everything the ocean took from you, the anger remains."

He sat on the sand. Rhune sat beside him. "I always had a temper," he said. The clinging sand made him itch; he brushed it off, watching the shadows move and slide over Shea's face.

Shea said, "We built the fleet together, you and I, Rhune. It took ten years."

"Yes," said Rhune. The rush of memories made his heart twitch with pain.

Inexorably the quiet voice went on. "You loved that life—the life of the docks and the ships. You were the best fleetmaster this coast has ever seen."

Rhune bowed his head. "I thought I was."

"We only lost one ship. It was *Waverunner*, do you remember? She foundered in the fourth year, in the autumn gales. The other ships wore black sails for a month. All the hands were lost."

"I remember it."

"That was the first year I thought of giving up the fleet," said Shea.

Rhune jerked his head up. "You never spoke of it."

"I know. I should have. I blamed myself for those deaths."

"Could you have prevented them?" Rhune asked.

Shea shook his head. "No. But it was my ship they sailed, my route they followed—my will that kept them in the water. For that I am responsible. Power over wealth, over lives—that is not always a good power to give to a sorcerer. It's too easy for us to abuse it."

Rhune said, "You did not abuse it."

Shea sighed. He lifted a handful of sand from the beach, and let the grains slip through his fingers. "I think I did. Remember the day we sailed *Windcatcher* to Mantalo, to ride the waves?"

Rhune smiled. "I remember." He recalled the feel of the wave cresting under his thighs, and the great green hole it carved in the sea before it fell. He had ridden it down, without even a piece of wood to hold, with death a thunder in his ears, and Shea's laughter ringing through his veins...

"It was good," Shea said. "Terrible, and beautiful, and you trusted me to keep you safe..."

"Yes," Rhune said.

"Yet I could not—did not—spare a thought to keep you from Osher's whispers and his greed. If you needed wealth, I should have given you wealth."

Rhune's heart lurched. "*Given* me wealth? I killed a man

last year to try to take that fleet from you—and now you say you should have given it to me?" His voice rasped. He stood, legs shaking. He stared at Shea's upturned, shadowed face. "I'll see you dead before you give me anything!"

Two days later, they sailed for the Firemountain.

Shea called a wind into the sails to speed them on their way, but it was still past sunset when they saw to the northeast the red glow of the Firemountain against the blackening sky. As they sailed nearer, they saw red streamers reflecting off the water. "What is that?" Rhune whispered.

Shea said, "The mountain's heart is restless."

Three lengths offshore they were intercepted by a ship. It had red sails, and painted on its black hull was the golden image of a firedrake. Lanterns glimmered along its prow.

"Halt," came the call from the ship.

Rhune repeated the order to Shea, who was handling the boat. Like an obedient servant, Shea furled the sails and bent to oars to hold *Windcatcher* in her rocking trough. The name on the little ship was not *Windcatcher*, nor did she look as she usually did, trim and sleek and white, nor did Shea look like Shea. All these things he had changed, with magic. Only Rhune looked himself. It made him feel exposed.

"Who are you?" cried the voice from the big ship. "By what right do you trespass into the domain of the Firelord?"

Rhune filled his lungs. He saw Shea's nod of encouragement and trust. "My name is Rhune," he called. "I enter by right of refuge!"

From the pause that followed his announcement, Rhune guessed that his name was not unknown to the voice. Finally the answer wafted down to them. "Follow us." Shea shipped the oars and raised sail. Slowly they tacked in toward the docks, keeping as far back as they could from the dragon-ship's long white wake.

The harbor was lit with great red torches. By their light, Rhune could see along the docks and into the interior of the island. Shea had not told him what to expect, and as he gazed he felt the muscles of his face slacken in surprise. Built up the sloping side of the volcano was a mighty stone city. The streets were wide and smooth, paved with stone. Red banners with the dragon device waved everywhere. It was night, but all through the myriad streets and alleys people moved. Rhune counted thirty ships anchored in the harbor. Over all, the mountain rumbled softly, like a sleeping dragon.

The master of the ship that met them directed them to a berth amid the boats, and waited for them to leave the craft. He bowed to Rhune. "Welcome to the Firemountain," he said. "Come with me." They followed him (Shea at Rhune's back, as was proper) to a great stone palace. Its sides were smooth as water, and they shone like scarlet glass.

Guards barred their passage. But the master of the ship drew them aside. Rhune heard his name, and then Shea's. He kept his face impassive. Finally the guards moved from the door. It swung open, into a long dark hall.

A silent man beckoned them into the darkness. "Come," he whispered. They paced after him through an immense, windowless corridor. Torches flickered in the silence. He opened yet another door, and pointed. "Go." Rhune swallowed, and went in. Shea came afterward. He had changed his face and coloring and also the way he walked. Rhune kept having to glance twice at him before he remembered that this was Shea.

The room was hot, and rich with tapestries, rugs, heavy, polished furniture, and red-gold ornaments. Rhune paced. He did not want to sit down. He itched for a bath and some cold water to drink, feeling dirty and rough from the journey.

A small door popped open in a wall. Rhune stiffened. A man walked toward him. He wore red and black. His hair was gray. His face was white, and his eyes deep ebony. In them a steady red flame seemed to burn. "Good evening, traveler," he said. His voice was deep. "I am Seramir, Lord of this mountain."

Rhune bowed low. His palms were clammy with sweat. "Lord, my name is Rhune."

"Rhune, who once served Shea Sealord?"

"That is right."

Seramir signalled. A servant entered, carrying a golden tray. She set it on the table and pulled two chairs to the table's edge. The Firelord sat. "You are welcome to my kingdom," he said. "You are no doubt hungry and thirsty from your journey. Let us eat, and then talk. Your servant"—the dark, burning eyes found Shea, where he stood silently against a wall—"may find food and drink in my kitchens."

Rhune tensed, remembering Shea's admonition to him, that he should eat nothing prepared with fire. "I am not hungry, lord. Thank you."

"But after so long a journey you must be thirsty," said the Firelord. He poured something from a golden pitcher into a golden cup. "It is a tiring sail from Kameni Bay." He pointed to the velvet-backed chair. Gingerly, Rhune seated himself at its edge. The Firelord held out the cup. Rhune took it. "Dismiss your servant, Rhune Fleetmaster. Drink, and be refreshed—if it is not discourteous of me to offer liquid to a man who has so recently been an ocean."

There was no help for it. Rhune gestured to Shea to depart with the Firelord's servant, and took the cup. He hoped the goblet held water but no, it held wine. He sipped it. It was red and rich, a Ryokan vintage, flavorfully spiced. "I am not a fleetmaster, lord."

"You were once," said Seramir. "Perhaps you will·be again. How do you like the wine?"

"It's very good," said Rhune. "It tastes like a Mantalo vintage."

Seramir nodded. "It is. We grow no grapes on the island." He filled his own cup and drank. Rhune swallowed a little more of the liquid. He wondered whose ships had carried the casks from Mantalo, and if its sailors lay buried in the ash of the ruined harbor.

"You are certain you are not hungry," said Seramir.

"I am certain," Rhune said firmly. He sipped more wine, glancing with unfeigned curiosity round the room. The furniture was ebony, the tapestries fine woold, and the table-top—he rubbed his fingertip across it—was a thin smooth slab of pale green jade.

Seramir said softly, "Well, Rhune-who-is-not-a-fleetmaster; is my house fine enough for you?"

Rhune said, "Lord, I have never seen anything like it."

"Does not Shea live in such luxury?"

"Not like this," said Rhune. He gazed at his host. The wizard was dressed in fine silks. A gold brooch of a dragon rode his right shoulder. "Thank you for admitting me to your kingdom, lord."

The wizard lifted his golden cup. "Shall I spurn what Shea

valued?" he said. "Though I am very curious to know what brings you here."

"Lord, I will tell you," Rhune said. It seemed strange to be naming this man 'lord.' Yet it seemed to Rhune that Seramir and Shea had something—he was not sure what—in common. It was nothing so simple as the habit of command. He wondered if the mere possession of magic could change a woman or man's face and eyes...The flame in Seramir's dark eyes gleamed like Shea's sea-green ones. The resemblance was suddenly so acute that Rhune had to look away.

Staring into the wine in the cup, he told the story he and Shea had devised. It poured out of him easily. At the end of it, Seramir pursed his lips. "Having served one wizard ill," he said, "you still desire to serve another?"

Rhune swallowed. "In serving one wizard ill," he answered, "I learned a harsh lesson. I swear I would serve you well, lord. Give me a ship under my feet and I can ask no more of you." He let bitterness steal into his voice. "There is nowhere else for me to go, lord, except out of the Eastern Counties. No one of Skyeggo would employ me now. If you cannot trust me on a ship, let me chip barnacles off the hulls of rowboats. But I beg you not to send me away!"

The wizard nodded. "I see why Shea Sealord valued you," he said. "I will not send you hence. Tell me—what do you feel for him?"

Rhune drank. "I hate him," he said, and was not surprised to hear the words surge out with real truth.

"You have cause," said Seramir. "Would you do him ill, if you could?"

Rhune said, carefully, "I came here to leave an old life behind, lord."

"Well said," said Seramir. "So, you would be a sailor, a captain, and not a traitor?" His tone sang with irony. "Do you like the taste of the spices in the wine? We mull it in our own kitchens."

Rhune's throat constricted. Mulled wine was heated. He set the cup down quickly.

"Is your thirst quenched?" said the wizard. "Mine is not. Drink, Rhune-the-traitor!"

Rhune's right hand grasped the golden cup and lifted it to

his lips. Helpless, he drank.

"That is excellent," said Seramir. "Now, tell me truly why you have come to my island."

Rhune began to speak, then stopped. His mouth felt full of cotton. His head ached. Then slowly, thickly, he told the Firelord exactly why he had come to the mountain, as the wizard's dark eyes raked his face with flame.

It was dark; a soft, cool, safe darkness.

Hand in hand with Marisa, Rhune climbed the mountain paths. Breaking from him, she ran ahead of him, but he found her again lying in a hollow in the earth, waiting for him. Her hair burned red as fire. Above them the Firemountain hissed, a many-headed python whose tongues were made of smoky flame.

After their lovemaking, Rhune strained to hold Marisa at his side, but she broke his weak grip easily. "It is near dawn," she said, "and I must go. So must you. Meet me tomorrow night under the Tower." She ran, red hair shining, up the stony slope toward the red mouth of the volcano. A great weariness came over Rhune. He rubbed his eyes. He needed to sleep now, to sleep and sleep until midnight, when he would wake and leave his bed and find Marisa again.

He spent most of his waking hours with her. Rarely did he see the other inhabitants of the house. Sometimes his servants woke him and dressed him in rich clothes and led him through the halls of the house to a great room, and there he would see the Firelord. He dreaded those times, though he did not know why. The Lord always spoke gently and kindly to him, and gave him good things to eat and drink, and did not keep him long.

He stared at the sky. The light was growing. Low in the east the morning star faded, flickered, and vanished. Worry nagged him like a sore. He thought, I should be home in bed. They will not like my being out after dawn.

Rising from the hollow their bodies had warmed, he began to stumble slowly down the mountainside to the house. He was higher up and farther away from it than he had ever been before. The path was not clear to him; in the brightness of the morning he lost it several times. He had to wander higher along the slopes to find it. Finally he lost it altogether. Disturbed and exhausted, for it was now way past sunup and the sun lay full upon him, he thought of a way to find his path. He climbed with difficulty to a ledge, and looked from there for the cool, regular shapes of the Tower and the Hall.

He saw them, but he was very high, and he saw beyond them the glittering, swinging, blue-green coil of the ocean.

He sank down to the rock, and stared at it.

When his anxious servants found him, he was stumbling on the lower ridges of the mountain, far from his original trail. They took him down the mountain by the shortest way, and brought him, dazed as he was, directly to the Firelord. He seemed to hear and see them through a haze or dream.

"A touch of sunstroke, Lord," said one of the servants, trembling. "He has been a night creature for so long that he cannot face the sun."

The Lord sat in his great stone chair on a dais. "Bring him here," he said.

Two men led the unresisting Rhune up the dais to the chair upon which the Firelord sat. "Kneel!" they said. He knelt. Dark eyes searched his face, and a hand came out to hold his chin. The touch burned like flame.

"You are weary, are you not?" said the soft, deep voice. "Where have you been? Your clothes are scratched and torn. Why are you back so late?"

"I lost the path—could not see—the sun—" Rhune slumped in the arms of the servants.

The fingers lifted from his chin. "Put him to bed and let him sleep. Which of you is responsible for permitting him to wander alone on the heights?"

There was anger in the question. The guards shivered and looked at one another. Finally one of them stepped forward. "I am, Lord."

Seramir stood up, and someone cried out. In his hand swung a bright coil. The man who had spoken said nothing, but he shook on his feet.

Twice the length of a man, of searing flame, the lash beat at him. He flung up a hand to guard his eyes. Four times it struck him The fourth blow drove him to the floor. With a snap, Seramir coiled the fiery whip. "Help him up," he directed.

"Tend him until he is healed." Gingerly the men took their

fellow from the hall. Rhune they took to his own room with the heavy black curtains across the windows They pulled off his boots and put him to bed, and went away. As usual, they left one of their company to stand guard outside his door.

Rhune heard them whisper awhile, and finally leave. Slowly he sat up. He rubbed his eyes with his fists, like a child. He was very tired, his eyes hurt, but he willed himself to stay awake a little longer. He wanted to think.

The room was hot. He wondered if they kept it so to keep him sleepy. He could hear his guard whistling through the door. His dazed condition had been an act, and false. He had seen the path to the house at once, and had seen, too, a plausible place to wander and be lost in. His faint upon the dais had been false as well, and he had seen what, if he had seen it before, he had never remembered: the Firelash. He thought, Seramir does not know that I saw it, that I am awake. He does not know I saw the sea. I am Rhune. That is my name. I remember that now. I remember, too, that I sailed here across that sea from somewhere else, in a boat, with a design...

Need for rest numbed him. He did not know what kept him mindless and happy in Seramir's power. Something in the food or drink...? He could not remember. But he *had* seen the sea. He remembered his name. He remembered, too, that he was a man accustomed to the light and air of day. Yet here on the Fire-mountain he slept all day, and lived at night.

He bit his lip, hard. The pain helped him stay awake. He was afraid that after he slept he would return again to mind-lessness and play. He thought, I do not want to do that. He wondered why he was here, shut in this little room with no windows and a guard outside. He could not remember, and it was important that he *did* remember. Maybe it was indeed something in the food which kept him stupid. He had to sleep. He yawned. He could not stay awake any longer. He swore to himself, he would remember about the food. He would remember that he *had* seen the sea...

He slept, and woke, and slept again.

The first time he woke, the guard came in with a golden goblet filled with hot, spiced wine. "Drink this," he said.

Rhune feigned sickness. "Please," he whispered, "may I have some water?" The guard frowned and muttered, and brought him some. "Thank you," Rhune said.

When he woke for good, they brought him more hot wine, and food. He poured the wine (a little at a time, so that they would think he drank it) behind his bed. He did not eat the food, but wrapped it in a cloth and hid it in his pockets, to toss to the owls and foxes that night.

At midnight, as was his custom, Rhune went out to meet Marisa. She came smiling to him, red hair glowing, body deft and quick as flame, and pressed herself against him. He kissed her, but he knew now what she was: no true woman, but an illusion, a being created out of magic and fire, and given shape and purpose by the Firelord. She had no soul, and daylight withered her, so that she had to run at dawn away from him, up to the fiery heart from which she came.

He could no longer trust her. Still, she was wild and beautiful, and it gave him pleasure to be with her in the starry night. Again as day began she broke away from him with a whispered promise to return.

When he woke from sleep again, he drank only water. His head cleared as his body grew hungrier. Maybe, he thought, something in this house can tell me who I am and what I am doing here. With some trepidation, he said to his guards. "I wish to walk around the house tonight, and see its wonders."

They laughed at him. "What might a lackwit like you see?" said the one who was supposed to guard him that night.

"Oh, take him," said a second. "We're supposed to keep him happy, remember."

The guard snorted. His name was Hraki; he was a smaller man than Rhune, and overquick with his hands. "I'll keep him happy," he said. "I'll take you."

"But I want to go by myself," Rhune said petulantly.

"You? You'll get lost. You'll go where I take you."

Rhune nodded, pleased. He had thought to be thwarted in his request, and it was being half-granted.

That evening he set out to learn the secret places of the house, and to look for traces of his mission in its halls. In the kitchen he sat on a stool, and watched the cooks and kitchen-maids at work. His guard grew bored, and went to talk with one of the girls. Rhune made sure that no one was looking at him, and then snatched meat and fruit from a table. He gulped it quickly, before Hraki returned. With this wholesome food, strength seemed to flow through his bones.

Hraki came back, scowling. "What are you doing?" he demanded, straightening his clothes. He did not look happy, and Rhune wondered if the girls had teased him.

"Nothing," he answered hastily. He guessed that the drugs which suppressed his memory had also suppressed his strength. He recalled that once he had been counted a very powerful man, knowledgeable in the ways of weaponry and war. When he rose from the stool he was careful to look no different to his guard, but he moved with greater surety. He wondered again what it was that he had come to the Firemountain to do. He thought, They must fear me if they drug me to keep me weak.

Hraki dragged at his shoulder. "Come on," he said impatiently, and Rhune wondered why the man was so impatient. They climbed a stairway to the second floor. Rhune went slowly, pretending to be weak. But his sharpening eyes looked at everything, and forgot nothing. He began to build up a picture of the great house in his mind, like the drawing of a map within his head.

All the windows were obscured by dark heavy curtains. Rhune tried to push one aside. Hraki backhanded him away from it. "You know you aren't allowed to look out!" he said. Rhune stepped back, but as he did so he lost his footing and fell against the curtain, knocking it aside with his shoulder.

Hraki seized it and pulled it closed. "Clumsy fool!" He slapped Rhune, harder. Rhune kept his face unchanged, and as if emboldened by his silence, the guard hit him again. Rhune did not react, though his shoulders tensed. But through the crack in the curtain he had seen the reflection of fire and starlight on the surface of the sea. Ignoring Hraki's brutality, he wandered along the corridor, smiling within the vacancy of his face.

On the third floor Hraki would not permit him to enter any of the chambers. "These are the Lord Seramir's own rooms," he said. "If we should enter them—" he shuddered. "Come on."

"Where are we going?" Rhune said.

The man licked his lips. "To the Tower," he replied. At the end of the hall there was a staircase which led up, where all the others now led down, and he pointed toward it. Something furtive and ugly entered his voice and eyes. "You said you wanted to see wonders. I will show you wonders, up there. But you must speak of this to no one. You are not supposed to visit the Tower."

"What is there?" Rhune asked.

Hraki said, "You'll see." He pushed Rhune. "Go on, climb!" He made Rhune go ahead of him. The stair was narrow, and made of stone; their steps echoed from it. Rhune grew apprehensive, and sweat began to coat his sides. He pictured the Firelord waiting for him in the Tower, with punishment for his presumption, and drugs to put him once more to sleep, never to wake again. The thought weakened him so that he sagged against the wall.

Hraki hissed viciously at him. "Dolt! Fool! Don't stop!" He pushed Rhune from behind. Mastering himself, Rhune straightened. Heart pounding against his ribs, he climbed the stair to its end. The guard came after him, eyes gleaming with a strange delight.

The top of the Tower was square and cold. Three doors led off, in three separate directions. There were no rugs on the stone flags, and no tapestries on the grim dark walls.

The guard pointed at one of the doors. It was slightly ajar. "You may go into that room," he said. "But you must promise to touch nothing."

"I promise," said Rhune. Swallowing his terror, he went into the room. Hraki came after him. It was empty. A fire burned in a grate. By its light Rhune made out strange shapes. After a while he began to see what they were. In one corner of the little chamber sat a rack, its hideous machinery silent, and in another corner a wheel. A third corner held a table with instruments of torture laid out carefully on it: pincers and irons and screws. Rhune swallowed back the bile that rose in his throat. He said, "I do not like this place."

Hraki chuckled evilly. "No one does." But he beckoned Rhune to leave. Outside, he pointed to a second door. "You may look in this room." But when Rhune reached to open the door the smaller man struck his hand from the knob. "No!" He pointed to a sliding panel, set in the door. "Look through this." Rhune thrust the panel back. Stooping a little, he gazed through the opening.

This room was a small stone cage, bare but for three things. The first was a set of chains to go about a person's wrists and ankles and stand him up against a wall. The second was another set of chains, this one set in the floor, so that a man within their hold would have to lie spread upon the cold stone, unable to move save to lift his head.

The third thing in the room was a great nest of coiling snakes, their bodies living flames. They hissed langourously at each other. Fire dripped from their tails and scales and tongues. Hraki chuckled. "Beauties, eh?" He struck Rhune's shoulder. Rhune schooled his face to vacancy. But his mind was cold with rage and horror as he pictured a man or woman chained to the wall, or worse, to the floor, unable to escape the serpents' touch.

His guide's eyes now had an eager look in them that Rhune did not like. "And there is the third room," he said. He dragged Rhune across the corridor, opened the third door, and practically shoved Rhune in.

In this room there was a man.

He lay locked onto the floor in the center of the room, arms and legs spread taut. Rhune could not see the chains that held him. Around him, out of the air, red fire lunged. It burned without consuming, touching his face and belly and groin, it burst from beneath his back, it ran along his legs and arms. His muscles contracted and strained with agony. Soundlessly he twisted and writhed in the invisible chains.

"The fire will not hurt us if we do not touch him," said Hraki. He pushed Rhune again. "Go closer. Look at him."

Rhune moved closer to the tortured captive. Green eyes from the floor watched his face.

"Who is this man?" he asked softly.

The guard grinned. "This was a great enemy of our Lord's. He came here with magic chains, seeking to bind him, and now he lies bound, the fool! This is his punishment for such presumption."

"How long has he been here?"

"Three months," said the guard. He laughed. "Just as long as you."

"How is it that the fire burns him, but he is not burned up?" Rhune asked.

"It is magic fire," said Hraki. "But it is real, and it is even hotter than real fire. While it burns him he cannot eat or sleep or rest."

"How long will he stay here?"

Hraki grinned. "Forever, I suppose."

Rhune looked down, and saw the marks of the Firelash lacing the man's body. "Three months," he repeated. "Do you know his name?"

Hraki smiled, as at a cunning jest. "When he had a name, it was Shea."

"Yes," said Rhune. Reaching out, he fastened his hands on the sadist's neck.

Hraki struggled, but he was no match for Rhune's strength. Rhune cast the broken-necked body aside. Kneeling down, he said. "Shea. Tell me what to do to break the chains."

Shea's lips twisted with pain. It was clear that he could not speak. The fire weaved over his flesh. Rhune took a deep breath. Then he lifted himself up and lowered himself over Shea, covering him, taking the flames on his own body. They seared through his clothes. It hurt. Tears ran out of his eyes. He groaned, and laid his face against Shea's.

"The spring drying—the well empty—then pull—"

"I heard," Rhune whispered. He sat up, away from the flames. Hastily he made a picture in his mind, of a magnet weakening, dying, losing its power, till it was no more than a limp of tired rock in the ground . . . Then he reached again through the fire.

He felt for the chains. Finally he found them, light and thin as a child's hair, hard and strong as iron. Rage and pity and love rose in his mind. He seized and wrenched until they shattered in his hands, first right, then left, arms, then legs. Then he lifted Shea from the fire as a man might lift a lover, and carried him from the room.

With stealth and speed he ran down the stairway and out a side door. If he was seen, he was not recognized. The thick velvet drape that he had ripped down to conceal his burden made it unrecognizable as human. He made his way through the grounds of the great stone palace to the water. Flinging the drape away, he waded out, and then knelt in the cold sea, lowering Shea into the ocean.

He propped Shea's head against his shoulder. "Shea—can you hear me?"

"I hear you," whispered the wizard.

"I've been drugged and dumb for three months, living at night, charmed by a fire creature, barely knowing my own name. I saw the sea. It woke me. I stole wholesome food and came searching through the house, not even knowing what I was looking for—" His voice broke. "Had you left me in the ocean I would have served you better!"

"No," whispered Shea. His voice was stronger. "We both failed. And paid."

"You paid for us both."

Somehow, Shea laughed. "I had hope, where you did not. I knew you would come. He told me you were alive, taunting me with it. But I always knew that was a mistake." The Sealord's voice was almost normal. He stirred in Rhune's grasp and then moved to stand naked in the sea, his body shining red in the light of the volcano. "My strength returns. Rhune, don't torment yourself. It's done. Now we have our task to do."

"No!" protested Rhune. "Shea, you're weak as a child. You cannot fight Seramir now. Let us leave."

Shea glanced at the stars. "It is six hours to dawn. In six hours Seramir will climb the stairs to that room, whip in hand. He will find a dead man on the floor, and me gone. He will rouse the mountain and all his power to find us. If he finds us, we will never escape him, and if he does not find us, he will wreak such havoc upon Ryoka that we will wish we had never set out upon this errand. We must return to the house, and do what we came to do."

"Can't you just tear the mountain apart, and drown him?" Rhune demanded.

"I do not think I could kill him. Even if I could, I have no right."

"No *right*!" Rhune shivered with rage. "I will do it, if you will not."

Shea smiled. "If I cannot, you certainly will not be able to. But you will not try, Rhune. Swear it." His voice sharpened, and Rhune had to look away from the power in his eyes.

"I swear it," he said.

"Good."

"But, damn it, Shea, you cannot go back into that house. You've spent three months in chains. You're too weak to confront Seramir within his own domain."

Shea's smile broadened. He said, "But I have you." He

turned to walk to shore. Rhune cursed. Then he caught Shea's wrists from behind, locking them behind the whip-marked back, holding him.

The ocean reached out a giant paw and tore his fingers loose. Water roared around him, deafened him, blinded him. His lungs burned. Darkness pounded its fist against his skull. Then he was free. He sat gasping in shallow water. A few lengths away, Shea watched him.

"Coming?"

"Damn you," Rhune said. He stood up. "Tell me what I have to do."

They silenced and bound two livery-clad servants, and took their clothes. Dressed, they moved like men on an important errand up the back stairway past the ground floor, past the second floor, to the third. Shea strode down the hall to a shut door. "He is here," the wizard said. "Go in swiftly, Rhune, and do not look into his eyes. He is offguard, unsuspecting, and that is our advantage and our weapon."

Rhune nodded. He walked to the door, flung it open, and stood swaying in the doorway. "Lord—" he said, and then crumpled to the floor.

"What—?" Seramir hurried to him, and knelt, reaching for the throat pulse. With the speed of one of the Firelord's own serpents, Rhune lunged upward and closed his hands around the wizard's neck. Seramir flapped, but Rhune thrust his thumbs against the great arteries that lead to the brain until the man went limp. Rhune hoisted him to his shoulder. They went down the stairs, out a door (not the kitchen door) and into the grounds. Rhune kept a hand on Seramir's throat as they moved. They went over the lawn, across the rocks as before, and into the sea.

"He wakes," Rhune warned. He tightened his grip on the Firelord's wrists.

Seramir moaned and opened his eyes. He looked at Rhune from pupils that seemed all red flame.

But Shea looked into them and his own eyes were cold as the winter seas. He touched the guard's knife to Seramir's throat. "If you move or speak without permission," he said, "you are dead." Catching Seramir's hair in his left hand, he jerked the older man's head back, baring his throat wholly to the blade. "I owe you much, tormentor." The water touching Seramir grew icy. Rhune felt him shudder. "You are in my element, Seramir, as I was in yours. Can you name a reason why I should let you go? Speak."

Seramir swallowed, and spoke. "I have something you want."

"What, Lord of Fire?"

"Power."

Shea laughed. "The power of the sea can master the power of fire. The ocean is deep and strong and never sleeps. Your mountain is only a little volcanic island. Find me another reason. I grow impatient, and my memory is sharp—sharper than this knife. Perhaps you will discover a reason if I feed your eyes to the fish." Shea rested the point of the knife lightly, very lightly, on Seramir's closed left eyelid.

"No."

Again Shea laughed. "No, you will not speak, or no, I must not take your eyes? Look at me!" He moved the knife.

Seramir opened his eyes, and the flame in them was almost gone. "I will give you the thing you came for—the tool that lets me call the fires of Ryoka from their resting-place."

"Where is it?"

"In my room, the room you took me from. Take me there, and I will give it to you."

Shea laughed a third time, and Rhune trembled at the fierceness of the laughter. "Fool you think me, Seramir Firelord. Shall I indeed go with you to your chambers, the heart of your kingdom? For that alone I should bind you living to the seabed." His hands moved. "Watch!"

And the ocean behind them lifted from its rest and fell upon the cone-shaped mountain. Inexorable and unbreachable, it grew into a tremendous wave, higher than their heads, higher than treetops, higher than the Tower of the Firelord's house. The wave raced like a hurricane toward the shore, and the water screamed as it poured upon the stone, and so did the people of the house, cowering with terror as the wall of water crashed over them. Down it fell, like the sundering of the sky. Then it sucked back, and with it came the palace: stones, rugs, drapes, furnishings, and people, in a great vortex of ruin. The debris swirled by them and out to sea.

Seramir stared at the scar in the earth where his home had been.

"It is gone," said Shea softly. "All your devices of magic are gone. While I live the sea will not give them up. No more of your power have I ever desired, than this. Your servants and all the folk of your house live, and are swimming back to shore. Your palace you may rebuild. Your ships I have not touched. Still will the dragon-ships ride through the waters, and the merchants of Ryoka will pay their toll." He sheathed the knife. Rhune released the Firelord's hands. "And if you can, Seramir, you may still bind men into your dungeons of fire, or drug them to oblivion in your tapestried halls."

A small sailboat came scudding round the rocks from the harbor. It was *Windcatcher*, sleek and trim. Rhune caught the rocking ship and steadied it.

Sealord and Firelord matched gazes in silence.

At last, Seramir turned away. "Ryoka has again defeated me," he said. "O Shea, you have grown strong. But you will bear my marks on your body for as long as you wear it, and, when you sleep, your nightmares will be of fire."

Under the turning stars, pushed by an enchanted wind, *Windcatcher* rode steadily and surely westward.

Shea sat in the stern. Rhune lay in the bow. His head felt light with exhaustion, and his belly with hunger. Over him the winter stars played their patterns against the night. Three months I have been captive in Seramir's halls, he thought. Damn all wizards!

Querulously he said, "How long will it take us to reach land?"

Shea answered, "Current and wind will have us home within ten hours."

Rhune scowled.

"Is that so slow?" said Shea.

"No."

"Then tell me what it is that makes you look so discontent."

Rhune raised his eyes to the Sealord's face. "I have no home," he said.

Shea said, "I will give you one."

Rhune said, between his teeth, "I will take nothing from you."

Shea pursed his lips. That look, part sadness, part relief, brushed over his face. He said, very gently, "Rhune—tell me, if you can and will—what did Osher offer you to tempt you to turn traitor, beside wealth, lands, fleet?"

Rhune said, "Don't you think those are sufficient?"

Shea said, "Was there something else?"

Rhune sighed. "He told me he would teach me magic." A hope he had thought was gone quivered inside him. He lifted on an elbow.

Shea said, "Ah." The soft syllable sighed like the sea-wind. "He lied to you, Rhune. He could no more do that than he could call the sea. The power cannot be taught, and it is not in you."

The hope died. Rhune bowed his head, staring at the planks of the sailboat. Finally he said, "I am not your fleetmaster now, nor am I traitor, or ocean—what am I, Shea? What is left of me?"

Shea said, "You are what you have always been. You still have the strength to break a man's neck between your hands. You have the guile to fool a sorcerer face to face. You spent a year as an ocean, and rose from it stronger. You have the courage and love to reach through fire to save a friend." He smiled. "And when we reach shore I will show you another thing."

They came into the bay before noon. Leaving *Windcatcher* to make her own magical way to her anchorage, they waded to shore. They were just south of the house. Rhune shaded his eyes from the bright glare of the daylight. "I'm not used to this," he muttered.

Shea strode a few steps up the tight-packed sand of the beach, and then halted. "Here," he said.

"Here what?" Rhune said.

Shea tugged his shirt up over his head. Red scars stood out clearly on his chest. "Take your shirt off." Puzzled, Rhune took his shirt off. The sun felt delicious on his bare skin. "Now, fight me, Rhune."

Rhune stared at the wizard. "You're mad," he said. "We're both weak and tired—and anyhow, you'll lose." He whirled and began to walk in the direction of the house.

A wet hand pulled him down. The surf tumbled him in its froth and washed him up, choking, at Shea's feet.

He sprang up, enraged.

"You will," said Shea. "Or we shall see what more the ocean can do to you."

The threat was totally infuriating. Rhune rushed at the Sea-lord, but light as the sea breeze Shea moved and was not there. Rhune whirled to face him, hands outstretched to grip.

Shea smiled. The gray-green eyes gleamed sardonically. "Keep your temper, my friend. You'll never win that way."

"You asked for this," Rhune growled. He clamped his rage still and moved forward. They circled, feinted, and struck: had Rhune been truly able to grip and hold he would have won ten times over, but each time he came close Shea's speed spun him just out of reach.

But Shea was tiring. His reflexes, almost imperceptibly, were slowing. Rhune slowed, too. At last Shea's block to a kick was just a tiny bit too low and too wide.

Rhune moved in fast. He punched Shea's belly, caught the wizard's right arm as he staggered, and snapped it up high behind his back. Shea's knees buckled. Still he fought to pull away. Rhune dug his knuckles into the nerves of Shea's wrist, until the arm muscles leaped in involuntary spasm.

Then anger, long held in, flooded Rhune's mind. The man he held down seemed to him to be not a man he knew, but an enemy, someone to break. He ground his knee into the other's spine and, with his powerful right hand, probed rigid fingers into the pain center of the collarbone. The stranger's back muscles roiled inside his skin. Rhune marveled at his endurance, wondering that no sound, no plea, came from the stranger's lips, forced from them by the dreadful pain.

Something slipped into—or out of—his head. The body beneath his hands was no enemy's. Rhune stopped breathing. Then, setting his teeth, he lifted his fingers. He looked at the ocean, wondering why it had not risen from its bed and torn him into half a hundred pieces. Very gently, he took the twisted arm and straightened it. He stretched Shea out on the sand, head toward the sea, and carefully, without pressure, stroked the muscles of his shoulders and spine until the deep-down muscle tremors ceased.

Shea rolled over. His face was very white, but he was smiling.

"Now that you have beaten me," he said, "will you take the

fleet? I have no wish to become, like Seramir, an aging tyrant, desiring only wealth or possessions, or power over other human lives. *Windcatcher* alone I reserve as mine; she will take me where I want to go. There are lands and shores our ships have never seen, but I have seen them. It is time for me to visit them again."

Rhune swallowed. "I will," he said.

"It will be yours, Rhune—to keep, and hold, and lose if you are cruel or careless!"

"I won't lose it."

Shea stood up. "I believe you," he said. He stretched his arms to the sun. "Get up, my friend. We have much to do. And you cannot be half as weary now as I am!"

It took through the end of winter, past spring, past summer, before all that they had to do was done. But on a clear, cool autumn morning Shea and Rhune walked to the beach; to where *Windcatcher* waited. The breeze stiffened her sail in the sunlight. Shea called her; like a sentient thing she came and hovered in the shadows.

Shea fastened the gray cloak around his shoulders. "Look for me when the storms rise," he said. "If I come back it will be on a hurricane. And if ever you have need of me, come to this place and speak your need aloud, and the winds will bring your words to me, wherever I am."

Rhune nodded. "I will. And if ever you need a companion in your travels, Shea, get word to me by any means you can, and I will come to you."

They embraced. The bay reached in, and a wave wrapped Shea in a gray-green fist. He rode it to the little ship, and boarded her, and turned her outward. The current took them. The sail winked in the sunlight once and then grew small: a white wing skimming a green sea.

"Farewell. Sail well," called Rhune. The wind caught his words and tossed them into the brilliant air. For a while he lingered on the beach, till he could no longer see the ship. Then he turned, and, without looking back, walked across the beach to the house of Kameni Bay.

•The Gods of Reorth•

This story is the second story I finished. It too was written in Chicago. I started submitting it to markets in the summer of 1972, and it came right back to me with encouraging little notes saying that although the editors didn't want that story, she/he/they liked the quality of my writing. Vonda McIntyre and Susan Janice Anderson wanted to buy it for *Aurora: Beyond Equality*, except, they said unhappily, it didn't really fit their theme. A few editors, all but one male, returned it to me with snarly comments about wanting to kill men. I thought they'd missed the point...

This is the story of a goddess Who had once been a woman named Jael, and what She did.

She lived in a cave on an island. Around Her island of Mykneresta lay others: Kovos and Nysineria, Hechlos, Dechlas, and larger, longer, fish-shaped Rys, where the Fire God lived within his fuming, cone-shaped house. She was the Goddess. From Her cave sprang the vines and grains that women and men reaped from the fertile ground; from the springs of Her mountain welled the clear water that made the ground fertile, and gave life. Her mountain towered over the land. When She grew angry the lightning tore from the skies over Her cave, and the goats went mad on the mountainsides. *"Hard as frost, indolent as summer rain, spare us, spare us. O Lady of the Lightning,"* Her poets sang. Sometimes the music appeased Her, and then She smiled, and the skies smiled clear and purple-blue, as some said Her eyes must be. But they were not: they were dark and smoky-green, like the color in the heart of a sunlit pool, touched to movement by a summer shower.

They smoked now. Above Her cave lightning reached webbed fingers to the stars. "The Lady is angry," whispered the villagers. Inside the vast cavern that was Her home She stood staring at a pulsing screen. It burned and leaped with pinpoints of light. She read the message from the screen as easily as a scribe reads writing, and Her fingers sent a rapid reply out to the waiting stars.

> WHY DO THE MEN OF RYS ARM FOR WAR?
> MYKNERESTA IS A PEACEFUL AND FRUITFUL PLACE.

A moment passed, and the patterns answered, scrolling lines of amber fire on the dark, metallic screen.

> PROBABILITIES PROJECT RYS AN EMPIRE.
> THIS IS DESIRABLE. DO NOT IMPEDE.

Jael stared at the fading pattern, and swept a fierce hand across the board. The message vanished; above the cave's roof, fireballs rolled and then disappeared down the sides of the mountain.

This is desirable. In her mind, the silent screens retained a voice, a cool, sardonic, male voice. War! She scowled across the room. An ugly, evil thing she knew it was—though she had never seen a war. She did not desire war on Mykneresta. Yet it was "desirable" that Rys become an empire. Were the worshippers of the Fire God to rule, eventually, all of the planet Methys? She snorted. The Fire God had once been only a man, named Yron. Long ago, when they had been much younger, they had used the lumenings, the lightscreens, to talk with one another across the planet. But that had been an age ago, it seemed. She did not want to talk to Yron now.

Are you jealous, she asked herself, because his children will rule a world, and yours will not? She caught herself thinking it, and laughed. What nonsense to be feeling, that she, who had seen five worlds, and governed four, should care who or what ruled on a little planet round a little sun, whirling on an arm of a vast galaxy, a galaxy ruled by Reorth. Yet—Methys was important. Long-term assignments to undeveloped planets were not made unless they were important. Somewhere on a probability-line Methys was a key, a focus of power. Somewhere on Reorth, in the great block-like towers that held their machines, a technician had seen this world matched to a time within a nexus of possibilities, and had decided that, changed thus and so, moved in this or that direction, Methys could matter. *Do not impede*. Reorth wants a war.

Jael stepped away from the cavern which held the lumen-ings, the spyeyes, and all the other machines that made her Goddess. She walked along passageways, grown with fungus that glowed as she passed it, and ducked through a door cut into the rock. Now she was outside. Above her the night sky gleamed, thick with stars. Wind whipped round the granite crags with words hidden in its howls. She rubbed her arms with her hands, suddenly cold. It was autumn, drawing close to winter. I wonder how Yron likes living in his volcano, she thought, all smoke. That made her smile. With the bracelets on her slim wrists she drew a cloak of warmth around herself, and sent ahead of her, along the hard ground, a beam of yellow light. Slowly she walked down the mountainside, listening, smelling, tasting the life that roamed in the darkness. Once a cougar leaped to pace beside her, great head proud. She reached to stroke it. It sprang away, regarding her with widened eyes. She could compel it back—but even as she thought it, she rejected the thought. It was part of the night, with the wind and the starlight. Let it run free.

She came at last to the path which led to the villages—a worn and hidden path it was, and even she could not remember when it first was made. One bright star shone through the tree trunks. She stared at its flickering yellow light. It was not a star, but flame. Curious, she dimmed the light from her brace-lets and walked toward it. Who would dare to come so far up the mountainside? It was almost a sacrilege. Perhaps it was a poet; they did strange things sometimes. Perhaps some traveler, lost and tired and unable to go on, had dared to build a small fire almost at Her door, praying Her to spare him in his hour of need.

But it was more substantial than that; it was a house, a rough-hewn cabin, and at the side of the house was a rain barrel, and there was a yellow curtain at the window. Marveling a little, Jael went up to the curtain and put her eye to the gap where it flapped.

She saw a small room, with a neat pallet on the floor, a table, a chair near the hearth, a candle on the table. From the low rafters, like bats, hung bunches and strings of herbs, roots, leaves, a witchwoman's stock. A woman sat on the chair, bending forward, poking at the fire with a long forked stick.

Jael understood. This was a woman who had chosen, as was her right, to live alone; to take no man and bear no children; to be, instead, wise-woman, healer, barren yet powerful in her choice, for did not the Goddess honor those who chose to be lonely in Her service? She watched. The woman rose. She went to a chest beside the bed, took out a sheepskin cape, and began to pick the burrs from it.

Suddenly she turned toward the window. Jael drew back instinctively, and then caught herself and used the bracelets to blur the air around her, so that she could stand still and not be seen. Gray eyes seemed to look right into hers; gray eyes like smoke, framed by the smoke of long dark hair.

Then the dark head bowed and was covered by the cloak's hood. She walked to the door. Jael blurred herself wholly to human eyes and waited as the witchwoman opened the door and closed it behind her. She wondered (even She) where, on the Lady's mountain, even a witch would dare to go.

She walked along the path that followed the stream bed. Jael followed behind her, hidden and silent. At the pool by the waterfall, she knelt. Jael smiled. This was one of Her places; it was not so long ago that She had showed Herself, under the glare of a harvest moon, to an awed crowd. Now the stream bed was clogged with fallen leaves, but it was still a holy place. The waterfall was a small but steady drip over the lip of rock to the clear dark pool below.

The witchwoman knelt on the flat stones that ringed the pool's edge, staring into the fecund depth of water. Her face was grave and still. At last she rose, and made her way to the path. Her silent homage made Jael hesitate. But she decided not to follow the witchwoman to her cabin. Instead, she returned to her cave. Stalking to the lumenings, she lit them with a wave of her hand, and then, irresolute, stood thinking what to say.

She decided.

EXPLAIN NEED FOR EMPIRE AT THIS TIME.

The lights pulsed and went dim. She waited. No answer appeared. Oh well—they might answer another time. The question would surprise them. Jael remembered years of famine, of drought, of blight. Once She had sent a plague. It had hurt, watching the inexorable processes of disease and death sweep over Her people. She had not asked reasons for that.

War is different, she thought.

But how can I know that? I have never seen a war. Perhaps it is just like a plague. But plague is natural, she thought. War is made by men.

What's this? she asked herself. That plague was not "natural," *you* made it, with your training and your machines. What makes this different? Woman of Reorth, she said sternly, naming herself in her own mind, as she rarely did, how are *you* different from a war?

The next day brought no answer from the lumenings, nor did the one after that, nor the one after that.

Autumn began the steep slide into winter. Round the Lady's mountain it rained and rained, gullying the fields, now stripped of grain, and washing the last leaves from the thin trees. The waterfall sang strongly for a time.

Then one morning the ground was white and cold and hard, and ice spears tipped the trees and fences, and hung from the eaves. Village children drove their herds into barns, whooping and shouting, snapping willow switches from the dead branches of the willow trees. Men gathered wood; women counted over the apples and dried ears of corn that filled the storerooms, and prayed to the Goddess for a gentle winter. Mountain goats watched the stooping wood gatherers with disdainful eyes, their coats grown shaggy and long, for in winter the hunting stopped. In Rys and allied Hechlos the mining ceased. Only in the smithies the men worked, forging swords and knives and shields and spear and arrowheads. In the smithies it stayed warm.

Sometime during the winter procession of ice, snow, and thaw, Reorth answered. The lumenings lit, held a pattern for a few moments, and then went dark.

It was the outline of a machine, sketched in light. For weeks Jael could not think what it might mean. She had decided to dismiss it as a misdirected transmission, meant for someone, when one night she dreamed. It was a dream of Reorth, of home. She woke, weeping for a world she had not seen in three hundred years, and, in the darkness of her cave, heard herself say aloud the name of the machine.

It was a chronoscope, one of the great machines that scanned the timelines. She had not seen one in—in—she could not remember how long. Rage filled her. Was she a child, to be answered with pictures? The contemptuousness of the response brought her in haste to the screen, fingers crooked, ready to scorch the sky with lightning.

But she caught her hands back in mid-reach. The folk who had sent her here would not be impressed with her anger. The answer was plain, as they had meant it. The need is there, seen in the timelines. You know your job. Do as you are told.

Do. not impede.

The year moved on. The waterfall over the pool froze into fantastic sculpted shapes, thawed, fell, froze again. The pool did not freeze. Only its color changed, deepening under stormy skies to black. The villagers did not visit it, but the witch-woman, Akys, did, coming to kneel on the icy, slippery stones once or twice each week.

The witchwoman's cabin by the streambed was as far up the Lady's mountain as the villagers would venture. They came reluctantly, drawn by need: a sick child, a sick cow, an ax wound. The women came first, and then the men. This was as it should be, for men had no place on Her mountain.

More rarely, the witchwoman went to the villagers, down the steep pathway from her home to the rutted village streets. How the knowledge came she was never sure, save that it did come, like a tugging within her head, a warning that something was amiss in wood-or village. Once it was a girl who had slipped gathering kindling and wedged her legs between two rocks. Akys had gone down to the village to fetch the villagers and bring them to the child. Once a fire started in a storeroom; they never discovered how. Had Akys smelled the smoke? She could not tell, but with knowledge beating like the blood in her temples against her brain, she came scrambling down the path to call the villagers out from sleep, and helped them beat the flames out in the icy, knife-edged wind.

In the thick of the winter, trying to gather twigs on the stony slope, the witchwoman would find firewood outside her door, or apples, cider, even small jugs of wine, to warm her when the ashes gave no warmth, and the wind thrust its many-fingered hands through her cabin's myriad chinks. After the fire they left her a haunch of venison. She was grateful for it, for the hares and sparrows grew trapwise, and her snares often sat empty.

To pass the shut-in days in the lonely hut, the witchwoman cut a flute from a tree near the Lady's pool, and made music. It floated down the hillside, and the village children stopped their foraging to listen to the running melodies.

Jael heard them, too. They drew her. The quavering pure tones seemed to her to be the voice of winter, singing in the ice storms. Sometimes, on dark nights, she would throw on her cloak of green cloth—a cloak made on Reorth—and go past the pool, up to the shuttered window of the witch's house, to listen.

The music made her lonely.

On impulse one night, she shifted the lumenings to local and called across the islands to Yron. She called and called. Then she called Reorth.

YRON DOES NOT ACKNOWLEDGE TRANSMISSION

The reply came at once.

YRON RECALLED 20 YEARS AGO, LOCAL TIME.
NEW ASSIGNMENT ACCEPTED. COORDINATES
FOLLOW.

There was a pause. Then a set of planetary coordinates flashed across the screen.

Jael shrugged. The transmission continued.

YOUR RECALL UNDER CONSIDERATION.
WOULD YOU ACCEPT REASSIGNMENT?
TAKE YOUR TIME.

Akys did not know when she first began to sense the presence of a stranger near her home. It came out of nowhere, like the gift of warning in her head. Especially it came at night, when clouds hid the moon and stars. At first she thought it was the wild things of the mountain, drawn by her music. But beasts

leave signs that eyes can read. This presence left no sign—
save, once, what might have been the print of a booted foot
in snow.

On a day when the sun at noon was a copper coin seen
through cloud, she heard a knock at her door. She thought,
Someone in trouble? Her gift had given her no warning. She
stood, laying the flute aside, moving slowly with weariness
and hunger, for her snares had shown empty for three days.
She went to the door and opened it.

A woman stood under the icicled eaves. She wore a long
green cloak, trimmed with rich dark fur. From her fingers
dangled two partridges.

"Favor and grace to you," she said. Her voice was low and
gentle. "My name is Jael. We are neighbors on the mountain.
I have heard your music in the evenings; it gives me much
delight. I wished to bring you a gift." She held out the birds.
Her hair, escaping from its hood, was the bright auburn of a
harvest moon.

Akys stepped back. "Will you come inside? It's cold on the
doorstep."

"Gladly," said the stranger. She dropped her hood back,
and stepped into the small, smoky house.

Taking the birds from the slim hands, Akys said, "I didn't
know I had any neighbors."

Her quick eyes caught the tint of gold as the cape shifted.
Who was this woman, dressed so richly and strangely, who
called her "neighbor" and brought her food?

"My name is Jael," said Jael again. "I am new come to this
place. I lived before in"—she seemed to hesitate—"Cythera,
west of here. Now I live near the Lady's well."

"I do not know that place, Cythera," said the witchwoman.
She began to strip the feathers from the birds. "Are you alone?"
she murmured.

Jael nodded. "I have no man," she said.

"Then will you eat with me tonight?" said Akys. "It is hard
to come to a new home alone, especially in winter. And they
are your birds, after all."

Jael came to the hearth, where Akys sat cleaning the birds.
Kneeling, she stretched out her hands to the warmth. Her fingers were slender, unscarred by work. On her wrists wire brace-

lets shone gold in the firelight. The flame seemed to leap toward them.

She glanced up, into Akys' gray eyes. "Forgive my silence," she said. "I may not speak of my past. But I mean you no harm."

"I can see that," said Akys. "I accept your gift and your silence." *She has a vow,* she thought. *Perhaps she has left wealth and family behind, to serve the Lady. That is noble in one so beautiful and young.*

She picked up the bellows and blew the fire up, and dropped the cleaned partridge in the pot. "I am alone, too," she said matter-of-factly.

"So I see," said Jael, looking around at the one room with its narrow pallet, and single chair. "You've not much space."

Akys shrugged. "It's all I need. Though I never thought to have visitors. I might get another chair."

Jael tucked her feet beneath her and settled beside the fire. "Another chair," she agreed quietly, "for visitors—or a friend."

Through the rest of the short, severe winter the two women shared food: birds, coneys, dried fruits, nuts, and clear water. In the thaws, when the snow melted and the streams swelled, they made hooks and lines to catch fish. They hunted the squirrels' stores from the ground, and gathered wood for the hearth. Jael's hands and cheeks grew brown, chapped by wind and water.

"Akys!" she would call from the house, flinging wide the door.

And Akys, kneeling by the stream, water bucket in hand, felt her heart lift at that clear, lovely call. "Yes!"

"Can I stuff quail with nuts?"

"Have we enough?"

"I think so."

"Slice them thin." She brought the bucket to the house. Jael was chopping chestnuts into bits. She watched warily over Jael's shoulder, wondering as she watched how the younger woman had managed, alone. She did not know the simplest things. "Be careful with that knife."

"If I dull it," Jael said, "you'll have to get the smith to sharpen it for you again."

"I don't want you to cut yourself," said Akys.

Jael smiled. "I never do," she said, "do I?"

"No."

Jael set the knife down and pushed the sliced nuts into the cavity. She trussed the bird with cord, held it, hefted it. "It's a big one. I'm glad you got that new pot from the village."

"I hate asking for things," said Akys.

Jael said, "I know. But you can't build an iron pot the way you can a chair." Crossing the room, she dumped the bird into the cauldron. "And tomorrow I want to fish. I'll bring some metal hooks with me when I return in the morning."

Akys said, quietly, "Why don't you stay the night?"

Jael shook her head.

During the days she became a human woman. She learned, or relearned, for surely she had known these skills before, to chop wood, to skin, clean, and cook animals, to fish, with coarse strings of hemp she had twisted herself, and a willow pole. She got cold and wet, went hungry when Akys did, and climbed to her cave tired and footsore. But she always went back at night. Fidelity had made her set the lumenings to Record, and she turned them on each evening, awaiting—what? Sometimes she told herself she was waiting for her recall. Touching her machines, she was once more the Goddess. But in the morning, when she went back down the slope to Akys, the reality of Reorth receded in her mind, and all its designs became bits of a dream, known only at night, and she did not think of recall.

Akys never asked questions. The brief tale told at their first meeting remained unembroidered, and Jael had half-forgotten it. She felt no need to have a past. Sometimes Akys looked at her with a stir of inquiry in her gray eyes. But if questions roiled her mind, they never reached her tongue.

Spring broke through winter like water breaking through a dam. They measured time by the rise and fall of the river. In spring the fish came leaping upstream, and if you held out a net—ah, if you just held out your hands—they would leap to the trap, bellies iridescent in the sunshine. In the white rapids they looked like pieces cut from rainbow.

"I want to bathe in the river!" cried Jael.

"It's too cold now," said practical Akys. "You'll freeze."

"Then I want summer to come." Jael pouted. "Why does

the year move so slowly?" she demanded, flinging her arms wide.

Yet in the cavern at night, she saw the year moving swiftly, and wished that her power extended to the movement of the planet in its course around its sun.

The spyeyes set to Rys told her that armies and ships were gathering. They will be coming in the fall, she thought. They will be ready then. Spykos, king of Rys, was drawing men from all his cities and from the cities of nearby Dechlas. He cemented his alliance with Hechlos by marrying his daughter to Hechlos' king's son, and the goddess within Jael-the-woman raged, that these men could see women as so many cattle, bought and bred to found a dynasty. Spykos raided the harbor towns of Nysineria and Kovos—in winter!—distracting them, frightening them, keeping them busy and off guard. Jael watched the raids with a drawn face. It hurt, to see the villages burn.

What will you do?

This was the question she did not allow herself to hear. If she heard it, she would have to answer it. It kept her wakeful at night, walking through her caverns, staring at the dark, unspeaking luminings.

Akys scolded her. "What's wrong with you? Your eyes have pits under them. Are you sleeping?"

"Not very well."

"I can give you a drink to help you sleep."

"No."

"Won't you stay here? It tires you, going home at night."

Jael shook her head.

Summer came to the mountain with a rush of heat. The children herded the beasts up to the high pastures again. The crags echoed to their whistles and calls and to the barking of the dogs. The heavy scents of summer filled meadows and forests: honeysuckle, clover, roses, wet grass steamy after a rainstorm.

Akys said, "You could bathe in the river now."

They went to the river, now strong and swift in its bed. Jael flung off her clothes. Her body was slim, hard and flat, golden-white except where weather had turned it brown. She dipped a toe in the rushing stream. "Ah, it's cold!" She grinned at

Akys. "I'm going to dive right off this rock!"

Akys sat on the bank, watching her, as she ducked beneath the flowing, foamy water, playing, pretending to be a duck, a salmon, an otter, a beaver, an eel. Finally the cold turned her blue. She jumped out. Akys flung a quilt around her. She wrapped up in it, and rolled to dry. The long grass, sweet with the fragrance of summer, tickled her neck. She sat up.

"Hold still," said Akys. "You've got grass all over your hair." She picked it out with light, steady fingers.

Jael butted her gently. "Why don't you go in?"

"Too cold for me," said Akys. "Besides, I'd scare the fish." She looked at Jael. "I'm clumsy."

Jael said, "That's not true. You move like a mountain goat; I've watched you climbing on the rocks. And you're never clumsy with your hands. You didn't pull my hair, once."

Akys said. "Yes, but—you look like a merwoman in the water. I'd look like an old brown log."

Jael said, "I'm younger than you. I haven't had to work as hard."

"How old are you?" Akys asked.

Jael struggled to see her face through timebound eyes. "Twenty," she lied.

"I'm thirty-two," said Akys. "If I had had children, my body would be old by now, and I would be worrying about their future, and not my own."

Jael let the ominous remark pass. "Are you sorry that you have no children?" she said.

"No. A promise is a promise. For the beauty I lack—a little."

"Don't be silly." Jael bent forward and caught Akys' hands between her own. The quilt slid from her shoulders. "You *are* beautiful. You cannot see yourself, but I can see you, and I know. Do you think you need a man's eyes to find your beauty? Never say such nonsense to me again! You are strong, graceful, and wise."

She felt Akys' fingers tighten on her own. "I—I thank you."

"I don't want your thanks," said Jael.

That night, Jael lay in Akys' arms on the narrow, hard, straw-stuffed pallet, listening to rain against the roof slats, pat, pit-pat. The hiss of fire on wet wood made a little song in the cabin.

"Why are you awake still," murmured Akys into her hair. "Go to sleep."

Jael let her body relax. After a while Akys' breathing slowed and deepened. But Jael lay wakeful, staring at the dark roof, watching the patterns thrust against the ceiling by the guttering flames.

Autumn followed summer like a devouring fire. The leaves and grasses turned gold, red, brown, and withered; the leaves fell. Days shortened. The harvest moon burned over a blue-black sky. The villagers held Harvest Festival. Like great copper-colored snakes the lines with torches danced through the stripped fields, women and children first, and then the men.

Smoke from the flaring torches floated up the mountainside to the cabin. Akys played her flute. It made Jael lonely again to hear it. It seemed to mock the laughter and singing of the dancers, and, as if the chill of winter had come too soon, she shivered.

Akys pulled the winter furs from her chest, and hung them up to air out the musty smell. She set a second quilt at the foot of the pallet.

"We don't need that yet," said Jael.

"You were shivering," said the witchwoman. "Besides, we will."

One night they took the quilt out and lay in the warm dry grass to watch the stars blossom, silver, amber, red, and blue. A trail of light shot across the sky. "A falling star!" cried Akys. "Wish."

Jael smiled grimly, watching the meteor plunge through the atmosphere. She imagined that it hit the sea, hissing and boiling, humping up a huge wave, a wall of water thundering through the harbors, tossing the Rysian ships like wood chips on the surface of a puddle, smashing them to splinters against the rocks. I wish I could wish for that, she thought.

"What are you thinking . . . ?" said Akys.

"About Rys."

"The rumors . . ."

"Suppose," said Jael carefully, "suppose they're true."

Akys lifted on an elbow. "Do you think they are?"

"I don't know. They frighten me."

"We're inland, a little ways anyways, and this village is so close to Her mountain. They wouldn't dare come here."

Jael shivered.

"You dream about it, don't you?" said Akys. "Sometimes you cry out, in your sleep."

Later she said, "Jael, could you go back home?"

"What?"

"To that place you came from, in the west, I forget its name."

"Cythera."

"Yes. Could you go back there? You'd be safer there, if the men of Rys do come."

"No," said Jael, "I can't go back. Besides, I know you won't leave this place, and I won't leave you."

"That makes me happy and sad at the same time," said Akys.

"I don't want to make you sad."

"Come close, then, and make me happy."

They made love, and then slept, and woke when the stars were paling. The quilt was wet beneath them. They ran through the dewy grass to the cabin, and pulled the dry quilt around them.

Jael went back to the cave the next night.

This is madness, she told herself on the way. You cannot be two people like this; you cannot be both the Goddess and Akys' lover. But around her the dark forest gave no answer back, except the swoop of owls and the cry of mice, and the hunting howl of a mountain cat.

She went first to the lumenings, but they were dark. In all the months she had stayed away, no messages had come. Next she checked the spyeyes. Ships spread their sails across the water like wings, catching the wind, hurrying, hurrying, their sails dark against the moonlit sea. She calculated their speed. They would reach the coast of Mykneresta in, perhaps, four days. She contemplated sending a great fog over the ocean. Let them go blundering about on reefs and rocks. If not a fog, then a gale, a western wind to blow them back to Rys, an eastern wind to rip their sails and snap their masts, a northern wind to ice their decks . . . She clenched her teeth against her deadly dreaming.

She waited out a day and a night in the cave, and then went back to Akys.

The witchwoman was sitting at her table with a whetstone, sharpening her knives.

"You have some news," said Jael. "What have you heard?"

Akys tried to smile. Her lips trembled. "The runner came yesterday, while you were gone. They have sighted ships, a fleet. The villages are arming." Her face had aged overnight, but her hands were steady. "I walked down to the forge and asked the smith for a sharpening-stone. I have never killed a man, but I know it helps to have your knife sharp."

"Maybe they will not come here," said Jael.

"Maybe." Akys laid down one knife, and picked up another. "I went to the Lady's pool yesterday, after I heard the news."

"And?"

"There was nothing, no sign. The Lady does not often speak, but this time I thought She might . . . I was wrong."

"Maybe She is busy with the fleet."

Akys said. "We cannot live on maybes."

"Have you had anything to eat today?" said Jael.

Akys stayed her work. "I can't remember."

"Idiot. I'll check the snares. You make a fire under the pot."

"I don't think I set the snares."

Jael kissed her. "You were thinking of other things. Don't worry, there'll be something. Get up now." She waited until Akys rose before leaving the little hut.

She checked the snares; they had not been set. I should never have stayed away, she thought. She stood beside a thicket, listening for bird sounds, keening her senses. When she heard the flutter of a grouse through grass she called it to her. Trusting, it came into her outstretched hands, and with a quick twist she wrung its neck.

She brought the bird to the table and rolled up her sleeves. Akys was poking up the fire. "I chased a fox from a grouse," Jael said. "Throw some herbs into the water."

In bed, under two quilts, they talked. "Why do men go to war?" said Akys.

"For wealth, or power, or lands," said Jael.

"Why should anyone want those things?"

"Why are you thinking about it? Try to sleep."

"Do you think She is angry with us, Jael, for something we have done, or not done?"

"I do not know," Jael answered. She was glad of the darkness, glad that Akys could not see her face.

"They have a god who lives in fire, these men of Rys."

"How do you know?"

"The smith told me. He must like blood, their god."

"Hush," said Jael.

Finally Akys wept herself into an exhausted sleep. Jael held her tightly, fiercely, keeping the nightmares away. So Akys had held her, through earlier nights.

In the morning they heard the children shrilling and calling to the herds. "What are they doing?" wondered Akys.

"Taking the cattle to the summer pasture."

"But why, when it is so late—ah. They'll be safer higher up. Will the children stay with them?"

Jael didn't know.

That night, when she wrapped her cloak around her, Akys stood up as if to bar the door. "No, Jael, you can't go back tonight. What if they come, and find you alone?"

Jael said, "They won't find me."

"You are young, and beautiful. I am old, and a witch, and under Her protection. Stay with me."

Under her cloak Jael's hands clenched together. "I must go," she said. "I'll come back in the morning. They won't come at night, Akys, when they can't see, not in strange country. They'll come in daylight, if they come at all. I'll come back in the morning."

"Take one of the knives."

"I don't dare. I'd probably cut myself in the dark."

"Don't go," pleaded Akys.

"I must."

At last she got away.

At the cave, she would not look at the spyeyes. She had told Akys the truth, they would not come at night, she was sure of that. But in the morning . . . She twisted her hands together until her fingers hurt. What have you chosen, woman of Reorth?

She couldn't sleep. She sat in the cavern with her machines, banks of them. With them she could touch anyplace on Methys, she could change the climate, trouble the seas, kill. . . . The bracelets on her wrists shimmered with power. She dulled them. If only she could sleep. She rose. Slowly, she began to walk, pacing back and forth, back and forth, from one side of the cave to the other, chaining herself to it with her will.

You may not go out, she commanded herself. Walk. You may *not* go out. It became a kind of delirium. Walk to that wall. Now turn. Walk to *that* wall. Turn. Do not impede. Walk. This is desirable. Walk. Turn. You may not go out.

In the morning, when the machines told her the sun was up and high, she left the cave.

She went down the path toward the hut. The smell of smoke tormented her nostrils. She passed the pool, went through the trees that ringed it, and came out near the river. The cabin seemed intact. She walked toward it, and saw what she had not seen at first: the door, torn from its hinges, lying flat on the tramped-down, muddied grass.

She went into the cabin. Akys lay on the bed, on her side. There was blood all around her, all over the bed and floor. She was naked, but someone had tossed her sheepskin cloak across her waist and legs. Jael walked to her. Her eyes were open, her expression twisted with determination and pain. Her stiff right arm had blood on it to the elbow. Jael's foot struck something. She bent to see what it was. It was a bloody knife on the stained floor.

Jael looked once around the cabin. The raiders had broken down the door, to find a dead or dying woman, and had left. It was kind of them not to burn or loot the tiny place, she thought.

She walked from the hut. Smoke eddied still from the village below. She went down the path. She smelled charred meat. The storehouses were gone. They had come burning and hacking in the dawnlight. She wondered if they had killed everyone. There was a body in the street. She went to look at it; it was a ewe-goat with its throat slit. A man came out of a house, cursing and crying. Jael blurred Herself to human eyes. She went in through the broken door. There were dead women in here, too: one an old lady, her body a huddled, smashed thing against the wall, like a dead moth, the other a young woman, who might have once been beautiful. One could not tell from the things they had done.

Had they killed only women, then? She left the house. No,

there was a man. He lay against a wall, both hands holding his belly, from which his entrails spilled. Flies buzzed around his hands.

Around Her the sounds of weeping rose and fell.

She walked the length of the street, and then turned, and walked back again, past the dead man, the dead ewe, the granaries smoking in the sunlight. They had left enough people alive in the village to starve through the winter. She followed the river past the cabin, past the pool. Just below the cabin She hesitated, drawn by a change in the mutter of the stream. The raiders had tossed a dead body into the clear water, and wedged it between two big rocks, defiling it.

She returned to the cave.

She lit it with a wave of Her hand. The light flamed and stayed, as if the stone walls had incandesced. Surrounded by bright, bare, burning stone, Jael walked to Her machines. She flung a gesture at the lumenings: the points of light whirled crazily, crackled, and died. The screen went blank. She passed Her hand over it; it stayed blank, broken, dead.

She smiled.

She turned to a machine, setting the controlling pattern with deft fingertips. She had not used this instrument since the plague time, when She had had to mutate a strain of bacteria. Meticulously She checked the pattern, and then tuned it finer still. When She was wholly satisfied, She turned the machinery on.

It hummed softly. A beam went out, radiation, cued to a genetic pattern. It touched Spykos of Rys, where he lay in his war tent outside the walls of Mykneresta's capitol, the city of Ain, with a twelve-year-old captive daughter of that city whose home and street his soldiers were busy burning to ash. It touched the guard outside his door. It touched the soldiers pillaging the city. It touched the little bands of raiders raping and killing in the countryside.

It touched the nobles of Rys. It touched Araf, Hechlos' king, where he lay with his third wife, and Asch, his son, where *he* lay with a slave girl whose looks he'd admired, that morning. His new wife slept alone. It touched the nobles of Hechlos, the high families of Dechlas.

It touched every male human being over fourteen on the six islands. It did not kill, but when it encountered the particular genetic pattern to which it had been cued, it sterilized. The men of Kovos, Nysineria, and Mykneresta it ignored. But on Rys, Hechlos, and Dechlas, and wherever it found men of that breed, it lingered. No seed, no children; no children, no dynasty; no dynasty, no empire; no empire, no war.

At last She shut it off. Around Her the stones still burned with light. She looked once around the cave that had been Her home for three hundred years. Then, using the bracelets, She set a protective shield around Herself, and summoned the patient lightning from the walls.

To the remaining villagers who saw it, it seemed as if the whole of the Lady's mountain exploded into flame. Balls of fire hurtled down the mountainside; fire-wisps danced on the crags like demented demons. Stones flaked and crumbled. "It is the Fire God of Rys," the villagers whispered. "He has come to vanquish the Lady." All through the night they watched the fires burn. By morning the flames seemed gone. That day some brave women crept up the path. Where the Lady's pool had been was a rushing stream, scored by the tips of jagged rocks like teeth. Above it the mountaintop was scoured into bare, blue ash. The Lady had fled. The grieving women stumbled home, weeping.

No seed, no children.

With the coming of the first snow, word came to Mykneresta, carried by travelers. "The women of Rys are barren," they said. "They bear no children." And in the villages they wondered at this news.

But in the spring, the singers one by one came from their winter homes, to take their accustomed ways along the roads. They told the news a different way. "The Fire God's seed is ash," they cried, "He burns but cannot beget," and they made up songs to mock Him, and sang them throughout the marveling countryside. No children, no dynasty. They sang them under the walls of the brand new palace that Spykos of Rys had built in Ain. But no soldiers emerged to punish them for this temerity, for the brand new palace was empty, save for the rats. No dynasty, no empire. There was war in Rys over the succession, and Spykos had gone home.

It was the women who brought the truth. They came from Rys, from Hechlos, from Dechlas. Leaving lands, wealth, and kin, they came to the islands their men had tried to conquer.

They came in boats, wives of fishermen, and in ships, wives of nobles. Wives of soldiers and merchants, kings and carpenters, they came. "Our men give us no children," they said. "We bear no sons for our fields, no daughters for our hearths. We come for children. Have pity on us, folk of Mykneresta; give us children, and our daughters will be your daughters, and our sons, your sons." No empire, no war.

Then the whole world knew. The poets sang it aloud: "The Lady is with us still, and She has taken vengeance for us." In Ain they rebuilt Her altar, and set Her statue on it, and they made Her hair as red as fire, and set hissing, coiling snakes about Her wrists, so real that one could almost see them move. Even on Rys the poets sang, and under the Harvest Moon the people danced for Her, keeping one eye on the Fire God's mountain. But it stayed silent and smokeless.

On Mykneresta the trees and bushes grew back on the Lady's mountain. One day in late summer, when the streams were dry, some rocks slid and fell. After the rain a pool formed, and it stayed. The old women went up the path to look. "She has returned," they said.

In spring the next year a woman came to the village. Her face was worn and weathered, but her back was straight, and though her red hair was streaked with gray, she walked as lightly as a young girl. "I am vowed to the Lady," she told the villagers, and she showed them the bracelets, like coiled snakes, on her slim brown wrists. "I am a healer. I have been in many lands, I have even been to Rys, but now I must come home. Help me build a house."

So the villagers built her a cabin by the curve of the stream, below the Lady's pool. They brought her meat and fruit and wine, when they had it, and she tended their sickness and healed their wounds. They asked her name, and she said, "My name is Jael."

"Have you really been to Rys?" they asked her.

"I have," she said. And she told them stories, about cities of stone, and tall men with golden hair, and ships with prows like the beaks of eagles, and streets with no children.

The children of the village asked, "Is it true they killed their king, because they thought he brought the Lady's Curse?"

"It's true," she said. "Camilla of Ain rules in Rys, and she is a better ruler than Spykos ever was or ever could be."

"Will they ever come again?"

"No, they never will."

A girl with brown braids and a small, serious face, asked, "Why did they come before?"

"Who knows? Now, be off with you, before night comes."

The children ran, save for the brown-haired girl. She lingered by the door. "Jael, aren't you ever afraid, so close to Her holy place?"

"How could I be?" said the healer. "This is my home, and She is good. Go on now, run, before the light goes."

"May I come back tomorrow?" said the girl.

"Why?" said Jael.

"I—I want to learn. About herbs, and healing, and the Lady."

"Come, then," said Jael.

The girl smiled, like a coal quickening in the darkness, and waved, and ran like a deer down the path beside the stream. Jael watched her go. Above her the clouds spun a net to catch the moon. She stood in the cabin doorway for a long time. At last the cold wind blew. Turning from the night, she pulled her green cloak close about her throat, and closed the cabin door against the stars.

•*We All Have To Go*•

This is the first of my short stories to be published. It has a remarkable publication history, most of which was created by one publisher's monumental bad faith. The story was accepted in 1974 by Scott Edelstein for an anthology called *Future Pastimes*, which he was editing for Aurora Publishers. Supposedly, *Future Pastimes* was to be the first of a series of anthologies; other titles in the series were *Outpost*, *Black Holes*, *Thanatos*, *The Universe Within*, and *Future Professions*.

It soon became clear that Aurora had no knowledge of and no real interest in science fiction. God only knows how Scott managed to talk them into publishing anything. It took about eighteen months before I was paid. The anthology was actually published in 1977, long after Aurora's rights—to the original stories, at least—had expired. None of the other anthologies ever appeared. A number of the contributors never got any money, and Scott had to sue Aurora to get it. His letters got progressively stranger.

Now to back up: in 1975, Bill Pronzini and Joe Gores were editing the annual anthology of the Mystery Writers of America. I knew Bill slightly. In a conversation over lunch, he discussed the volume and asked me if I had written anything that could possibly be called a crime story. I mentioned "We All Have To Go," rather diffidently.

Bill asked to see it. I brought it to him the next week. Some weeks later he informed me that, pending revisions, he and Joe wanted to buy it. Technically it would be a non-professional sale; the money which would normally be paid to contributors to the MWA anthology goes into MWA's coffers. I was of course delighted, but explained that I didn't know if I could let him have it: Aurora owned the first publication right, and *Future Pastimes* had not come out. I queried Scott

Edelstein, who said rather wearily that he had no idea when *Future Pastimes* would appear. Since my contract was with him, as editor, he gave me formal permission to let Bill use the story. It was published in *Tricks And Treats* in 1976, well before the publication of the Aurora anthology, but after their right to publish the story had expired.

Got that?

I think of this as my Chicago story. The version here is the original version which appeared in *Future Pastimes*. The revisions Bill asked me to make undoubtedly tightened the prose, but they eliminated several passages about the city which I enjoyed writing and I thought you might enjoy reading. Anyone who asks, "Where did you get your idea?" for *this* story has obviously never lived in Chicago.

Eight A.M., Friday morning in Chicago, Jordan Granelli sat at his desk, reading the Corpse Roster. High above the street, on the two-hundreth floor of the Daley Tower, he escaped the noise of city sirens and the chatter of voices: here there was only the rustling paper and the click of computers, and a blue, silent sky. He read the print-outs slowly and carefully, making little piles on the desk top. Out on Madison there was an old wino dead; they named him King of the Alkies—he never let a man go without a drink if he had a drop in his flask . . . the bums are sobering up for his funeral today . . . On Sheridan Road, in the heart of the Gold Coast, there was a crippled girl whose rich family bankrupted itself to keep her alive; she died this morning, 4 A.M. . . . On Kedzie the hard-working mother of three just died of DDT poisoning . . . All good, heart-breaking stories. In Evanston, a widower's only son just got killed swinging on a monorail pylon, 10 P.M. last night . . . He frowned and tossed that one aside. They'd done a dead child Tuesday. He flipped back and pulled a sheet out, and buzzed for a messenger.

"Take this to the director's office," he told the boy, and swiveled his chair towards the window. He gazed out at the light-filled sky, at the lake, at the morning sun. There was no place in the world he felt more alive, unless it was in front of

the camera's eye. "In the midst of life we are in death," he
said to the sky, rolling the words like honey on the tongue.
They loved it, his idiot public, when he poured clichés on their
ears. He wrapped the dead round with sweet words, and the
money came tumbling in. Power rose in his blood like fever.
Noon was his hour. He waited for the earth's slow turn to
noon.

Noon, on a Friday in Chicago: means it is 1:00 in New
York, 11:00 in Denver, 10:00 in Los Angeles. In L. A. the
housewives turn off their vacuums and turn on the TVs, and
the secretaries in San Francisco and in Denver take their morning half-hour break in a crowded lounge. In New York clerks
and tellers and factory workers take a late lunch, and the men
in the bars, checking their watches, order one last quick one.
And in Chicago the entire city settles into appreciative stillness.
On the lunch counters and in the restaurants, up on the beams
of rising buildings jutting through dust clouds and smog like
Babel, even inside the ghastly painted cheerfulness of hospitals,
mental homes, and morgues, TV sets glow.

Jordan Granelli looked out at them all through the camera.
"It's a sad thing," he said, his voice graceful and deep, "when
the very young are called. Who of us has not, would not, mourn
for the death of a child? But it is doubly sad when young and
old join in mourning for one they loved, and miss. Today, my
friends, we talk with Ms. Emily Maddy, who has lost her only
daughter, Jennifer. Jennifer was a woman in her prime, with
three young children of her own, and now they and her own
mother have lost her."

The camera swung slowly around a shack-like house, and
stopped on the face of a bent, tired woman looking dully up
at Jordan Granelli. "The kids don't understand it yet," she said.
"They think she's comin' back. I wish it had been me. It should
have been me."

A woman in a factory in Atlanta rubs her eyes. "She looks
like my mother. I'm voting my money to her."

"Look at that hole she's living in!" comments a city planner
in San Diego, watching the miniature Japanese set on his secretary's desk. "Mary and I just bought our voting card last

week. I wonder if we'll get to see the kids?"

A man on a road construction crew in Cleveland says, "I'm voting for her."

"You said Tuesday you were gonna vote for the guy whose son was killed by the fire engine," his neighbor reminds him.

"Well, this old lady needs it more; she's got those kids to look after."

"I don't know how you can watch that stuff," a third man says fiercely. "It makes me puke." He walks ostentatiously out of earshot of the TV. They stare at him in wonder.

"His wife died in June," someone volunteers. "Left him with two kids. He hates to be reminded."

"Jealous?" the first man nods. "He would have liked a little cash himself, I bet. He's got no feeling for other peoples' troubles, that guy. I wouldn't vote a cent to him, not a cent."

On their big wall screen in Chicago, the network executives watch the woman's tears with pleasure. "That son-of-a-bitch sure knows how to play it," says a vice-president. "I'm damned if I know why no one ever thought of it before. It's a great gimmick, death. He'll top last week's ratings."

"Ssh!" says his boss. "I want to hear what he says."

The woman's sobs were at last quieting. She bent her head away from the bright lights, and they touched the white streaks in her hair with silver. One shaky hand shaded her eyes. Jordan Granelli took hold of the other with tender insistence. The camera moved in closer; the button mike on Granelli's collar caught each meticulous word, and resonated it out to eighty million people.

"Let your grief happen," he said softly. It was one of his favorite remarks. "Ms. Maddy, you told us that your daughter was a good person."

"Yes," said her mother, "oh yes, she was. Good with the kids and always laughing and sunny—"

"There's nothing to be ashamed of in tears for youth and grace and goodness. In all your pain, remember—" he paused histrionically, and she looked up at him as if he might, indeed, comfort her with his precisely rounded sentences, "remember, my friends, that we are all in debt, and we pay it with our sorrow. Ms. Maddy, there are millions of people feeling for you at this very moment. We live by chance, and Dame Fortune, who smiles on us today, cuts the thread of our lives tomorrow. Mourn for those you love—for you may not mourn for yourself—and think kindly of those that death has left behind. In life we are in death. And we all have to go."

Poetic, smooth, slimy bastard, Christy thought. She moved even closer in, catching his craggy expressive hand holding the woman's worn one, the dirty dark furniture, the crinkled photograph of the dead daughter on the table, the stains on the floor—push that poverty, girl, it brings in the money every time—and, as the light booms drew back, the play of moving shadows across white hair. That ought to do it. The sound had cut out at Granelli's final echoing syllable. She cut out and stepped back; simultaneously, Leo, the set director, standing to her left, sliced his long fingers through the air. The crew relaxed.

Granelli stood up briskly, dropping the old woman's hand. He brushed some dirt off his trousers and walked towards the door. As he passed Christy he inclined his head: "Thank you, Ms. Holland."

She ignored his thanks. She would have turned her back, except that would have been too pointedly rude, and even she, his chief camerawoman, could not be rude with impunity to Jordan Granelli. One word from him and the network would break her back down to children's shows. She simply concentrated on taking her camera from its tripod and storing it in its case. Her arms ached. Ms. Maddy, she saw, was looking after Granelli as if he had left a hole in the air. Christy hated it, that look of beaten bewilderment. Did you think that sympathy was real, lady? He fooled you, too. He's a ghoul. We're all ghouls.

Zenan, the second cameraman, strolled over to her, from his leaning place behind her on the wall. She could smell the alcohol on his breath. He stayed drunk most of the time, now. "You okay?" she asked him.

"Another day, another death, right, Chris?" he said.

"Shut up, Zen," she said.

"Tell me, Christy, how much do you think the great-hearted American public will pay the lady for her sterling performance? Friday's death has an edge, they say, on the ones at the beginning of the week. If ten million people vote a dollar a week, take away the network cut, and Mr. Granelli's handsome salary, and what you and I need to pay our bills—hell, I was never very good at arithmetic in school. But it's a lot of money. Weep your heart out for Mr. Death, and win a million!" he proclaimed. "Does *she* know it's a lot of money?" he asked, jerking his thumb at Ms. Maddy.

"Zen, for pity's sake!" She could see Jake leaning towards them from his place near the door, listening, with a concentrated, big cat stare. Is there danger? those eyes asked. She caught that directed gaze and shrugged. After six years working for "We All Have To Go," I'll be a drunk too.

"For pity's sake?" he repeated. He looked down at her from his greater height. "Here am I, a sodden voice crying in the wilderness, crying that when Jordan Granelli walks, in the dark nights when the moon is full, the deathlight shines around him!"

And Jake was there, one big hand holding Zenan's arm. "Come on, Zen, come outside."

Leo came striding in. "What the hell happened?"

She smiled. "He called Granelli 'Mister Death.'"

"You think it's funny? Some day Granelli's going to hear it and frown, and his guards are going to take Zenan to an empty lot and smash his windpipe in."

She was jolted. "Jake wouldn't do that!"

"You like Jake? Well, Cary or Stew. That's what he pays them for—that's what the network pays them for," he amended. "Ah, Christ. He's got seniority. They can't fire him. He's our reality check." He scowled. "I've been here too long myself."

Have I really only been here two years? She lugged her case and tripod over to Willy, manager of Stores. "See you Monday," he said cheerily. He'd been there eight years, longer than anybody. But nothing seemed to touch him.

She ducked out of the tiny house to get a breath of air. Granelli's big limousine, pearl-white with its black crest on the side, sat parked at the curb. Around the house, in a big semicircle kept back by the police, a crowd had gathered to watch. She heard the whispers start. What are they waiting for? Granelli? But they could all see him, he was there in the car, and besides, they all knew his face. They saw him five afternoons a week on their TV screens, much closer than they would ever get to him in reality. They're waiting for death, she thought morbidly. The Grim Reaper himself, striding out of the house with jangling fingers, hoisting his scythe on his clavicle.

Jake came round the corner. "What'd you do with Zenan?" she asked him.

"Locked him in the crew trailer," Jake said. "It doesn't matter who he talks to, in there." He looked worried. "Christy, you a friend of Zenan's? Tell him to shut up about Mr. Granelli. If he starts upsetting people, Mr. Granelli won't like it, and the network won't either."

"I don't know what he has to complain about—Zenan, I mean," Christy said. "Any TV show that gets eighty million people watching it every day, can't be wrong."

He started to answer, and then the car motor rumbled and he ran for his seat, riding shotgun next to Cary, who drove. Stew sat in the back next to Jordan Granelli. Does he ever talk to them? Christy wondered. Does he know that Jake used to be a skyhook and Cary paints old houses for fun? Or are they merely pieces of furniture for him, parts of the landscape, conveniences bought for him by the grateful network, like the cameras and the car?

Leo came walking out of the house as the long white car pulled away. "Another week gone," he said.

"Jake stuck Zenan in the crew trailer," Christy said.

Leo wiped a big hand across his eyes, and shrugged. "I don't want to deal with it," he said. "I think I'll just go home. It's Friday. Want to walk to the subway?"

"I'd love to!"

"Good. Let me tell Gus to go without us." He strolled down the uneven sidewalk to where the crew trailer was parked, and leaned his head in to talk to the driver. The engine was idling softly, like a patted drum, as Gus played with it. Gus was nineteen, born thirty years too late, he said. His Golden Age was the world of the sixties and early seventies, before the banning of private cars from cities all over the world, when the motor was king, and all you needed was three dollars for a license to drive a car. His childhood memories were an improbable nostalgia of freeways and shiny beetle-like cars with names like Pinto and Jaguar and Matador. He even owned a monster old car ("We were born the same year") and raced it, for pleasure, along the old Lake Shore Drive. The club he belonged to paid terrific sums to keep the unused roadway in repair. Right now its current project was to convince a skeptical city government to let them use Wrigley Field for something called a Demolition Derby. In it you smashed cars against each other until they all broke down.

"All right," said Leo. "Come on."

They walked down Kedzie Street to Lake and turned east. The sun was hot; Chris felt her shirt starting to stick to her back. She hummed. The show was behind her now, and with all her will she would forget it; today was Friday, and she was going home, home to two days with Paul. Leo's head was down, as if he were counting the cracks in the broken concrete. She could just see his face. He looked tired and bothered. I wouldn't want his job, she thought, not for all the world. Maybe he was worried about Zenan. We've been friends for a long time. Maybe he'll talk to me.

He surprised her. "Do you ever think about Dacca?"

I never forget it, she thought.

Once, she had tried to tell Paul about it, what it had been like for her, for them all, that summer in Bangladesh. For him it was barely remembered history; he had been fourteen. He stopped her, after five minutes, because of what it did to her eyes and mouth and hands. But Leo remembers it just the way I do. Scenes unreeled at the back of her mind. Babies, crawling over one another on slimy floors, dying as they crawled, and bodies like skeletons with grotesque distended bellies, piled along dirt roads, the skitter of rats in the gutters like the drift of falling leaves, and flies numerous as grains of rice—and no rice. No food. The Famine Year: it had killed fifty million people in Bangladesh. And she and Leo had met there, on the network news team in Dacca. "I remember it. I dream about it sometimes."

He nodded. "Me, too. Thirteen years, and I still have night-mares. The gods like irony, Christy. When I came home, all I wanted to do was to get the smell of death from my nostrils. I *asked* for daytime TV, to work on soap operas and childrens' shows and giveaways. And here I am working for Jordan Granelli. Mr. Death."

"You too?"

"I sound like Zenan. I know why he drinks. We are the modern equivalent of a Roman circus. Under the poetry and Granelli's decorum, the audience can smell the blood—and they love it. It titillates them, being so close to it, and safe. Death is something that happens to other people. And when it happens—call an ambulance! Call a hospital! Tell the family, gently. And be sure to bring the camera close, so we can watch. And don't, don't even try to help. You'll spoil the scene—and we all have to go." He mimicked Jordan Granelli with a bitter smile.

"I have Paul," Christy said. "What do you do, Leo?"

"I take long walks," Leo said. "I read a lot of history. I try to figure out how long it will take for us to run ourselves into the ground—like Babylon, and Tyre, and Nineveh, and Rome."

"Are we close?"

He shrugged. "I own a very unreliable crystal ball."

They had reached the subway line; Christy could feel beneath her feet the secret march of trains. "I'll take the subway here, Leo," she said. "See you Monday."

"I shall take a long walk and contemplate the city. See you Monday."

As she went down the stairs to the subway, Christy looked with curiosity at the people around her. Was there really such a thing as a mass mind? The faces bobbing by her—some were content, some discontent, thin, fat, calm or harried, bored or excited—what would they do, each of them, if she were to collapse at their feet? Observe, in an interested circle? Ignore it? Call the police or an ambulance, maybe—the professionals who know how to deal with death. Death is something that happens to other people. All we, the survivors, need to do is to mourn.

Damn it, I don't want to think about it! She interposed Paul between her mind and the faces, and it quickened her breathing—two days! Two days with Paul. Fool woman! Grown woman of thirty-four, no adolescent, so suffused with plain physical passion that people waiting near you are staring at you! She raised her chin to meet their eyes. Under her shirt her nipples were stiff. I wonder if Paul ever thinks of me, and gets a hard-on riding home from work. The thought delighted her.

She quivered like an antenna to the presence of the people around her, and to the city. She was riding on the city's main subway line. It ran from south to north under the city, passing beneath its vital parts—city hall, business district, the towering apartment complexes of the rich, the university—like a notochord. East of it lay Lake Michigan, with its algae and seaweed beds, like green islands, set in a blue sea. West of it the bulk of the city sprawled, primitive and indolent in the summer heat, a lolling dinosaur.

And Paul was out there, high in the smoggy sky, a mite on the dinosaur's back. She had first seen them through a camera's eye. She'd been shooting a documentary on new city buildings, six years back. He had been walking the beams of a building sixty stories up, dark against the sun, his hair blazing gold, his hooks swinging on his belt. She had asked one of the soundmen, "What are those hooks they carry?"

"Those are the skyhooks. They're protection. See the network of cables on the frame?" Through the camera she could see it, like a spiderweb in the sun. "If a worker up there falls, he can use those hooks to catch the cables and save himself. Experienced workers use the cables to get around. They swing on them, like monkeys, hand over hand. The hooks don't slip, and the cables are rough, so they fit together like two gears, meshing." He made a gear with the interlocking fingers of his two hands.

"But I thought the name for the *people* was skyhooks," she said.

"It is."

Human beings, she thought, with hooks to hold down the sky . . .

She opened the door to the apartment. Paul was sitting in a chair, waiting for her.

He jumped up and came to her across the room, fitting his hands against her backbone and his lips to hers with the precision of anticipation. His lips were salt-rimmed from a morning's sweating in the sun. She leaned into him. At last she tugged on his ears to free her mouth. "Nice that you're home. How come?"

"Monday's Labor Day. Dale gave us the afternoon off. Said to get an early start on drinking, so we'd all get to work Tuesday sober."

"That was smart of her." Dale was the crew boss on the building.

"So we have three and a half days."

"No," she said sadly, "only two and a half."

"Why?" he demanded sharply, pulling away from her as if it were her fault.

"The show doesn't stop for Labor Day. Think of all those lucky folks who could be home to watch it! Makes more money. Christmas, New Year's, yes. Labor Day, no."

He grunted and came back to her arms abruptly. "Then let's go to bed now."

They went to bed, diving for the big double bed and turning to each other with the hunger of new lovers. They rode each other's bodies until they lost even each other's names, calling in whispers and groans and laughter, and ending half-asleep in each other's arms, soaked and surfeited with loving.

Christy woke from the drowse first. Paul's head lay against her breasts. She tongued his forehead gently. He stirred. The camera eye in her came alive: she saw him curled like a great baby against her, looking even younger than his twenty-seven years, chunky and strong and satiated, his skin dark red-bronze where the sun had darkened it, fairer elsewhere, his hair red-gold . . . How brown I am against him, she thought. A thin beard rose rough on his cheeks and chin, his chest was hairless and well-muscled, his hands work-callused . . . He opened his eyes. He has blue eyes, she completed, and bent to kiss his eyelids.

"What do you see?" he asked her.

"I see my love," she answered. "What do *you* see?"

"I see *my* love."

"Thin brown woman."

"Beautiful woman."

It was an old dialogue between them, six years old. It amazed Christy that, in their transient world, they had survived six years together. I love you, she thought at him.

Suddenly, as if someone had spliced it into her mind, she heard Zenan, drunk and sardonic. "If Jordan Granelli had a lover," he said, "and that lover collapsed in front of him, dying, he'd first call the ambulance, and then call the cameras."

What the hell? Angry, she thrust Zenan, the show, Granelli, from her mind, and like a shadow on a wall they crept back at her. "What is it?" Paul said.

"Ah. Come with me to work Monday," she said suddenly.

"Why?"

"So that I can see you sooner." So I can hold you in front of the shadows, she thought, like a bright and burnished shield. "Please."

Sunday night, the shadows turned to nightmare black.

She was in Dacca, standing in front of a wretched yellow brick tenement. It was falling apart; there were even gaping holes in the shoddy walls, and it stank. The dust stung Christy's eyes. She looked around for a landmark, but all she could see clearly was this one building; the dust clouds obscured the rest. I want to go back to the hotel, she thought, but, impelled, she went towards it. I don't want to go in.

Close to the entrance something moved. Dog pack? She looked around in haste for a brick or a stone to pitch. But the dust drew aside for a moment and she saw: it was a woman, bending or crouching, close to the open door.

Her thin flowing robes were mud-stained, and she hunched like a flightless withered bird on the ground, holding something protectively to her breasts. The whites of her eyes were as yellow as the building. Jaundice. She stared at Christy and then turned her head away, making a crooning wail. A fold of cloth fell away from her, and Christy saw that she was holding a baby. With terrible feeble movements of its lips it tried to suck, and then it cried, a whimper of sound. The woman's breast was a dun-colored rag. She has no milk, Christy thought. The mother wailed again, and looked at Christy with huge imploring eyes.

I must have something. Christy reached for the little pack she carried at her hip. She pulled out a small can of goat's milk with triumph, and pried it open with her knife. Hunkering down beside the woman, she held out the can. "Here."

The woman sniffed at the milk. Then she took the can from Christy's hand and tipped it towards the child's mouth. The infant coughed, and the milk ran out, down its cheek and neck. The woman tried again. Again the baby coughed, a minute weak sound like a hiccough, and gave a gasp, and was still. The woman peered at it and let out a moan. "What is it?" Christy said, and then she saw that the child was dead. It had died as they tried to feed it. She touched its forehead with one finger and pulled her hand away quickly from the ferocious heat.

She started to cry, and with tears on her face, she stood up and stumbled away from the mother and the dead baby. She turned away from the building, and not three feet away from her, directly in her path, stood Jordan Granelli. He was carrying a tripod and a camera, and his face was the face of a skull. It grinned at her, and his hand patted the camera. "Thank you, Ms. Holland," he said.

When Paul woke her, she was making small crying sounds in her sleep. He rocked her and stroked her. "A Dacca dream?"

"Yes—no. Come with me tomorrow, Paul, please!"

"I'll come," he promised.

"Love me. I need you to love me." In the dark morning they made love, like two armies battling for a hilltop, intent on the same desire; sighted, grasped for, won.

They woke late that morning. It was hard to dress: they kept running into one another in the way to the bathroom. Paul shaved, standing naked in front of the mirror. When he pulled on his pants, he stuck his skyhook sheaths on his belt, like a badge of office, and thrust the hooks into them.

Christy glared at him. "You're coming with me."

"I said so. But I want to make damn sure that nobody asks me to do anything. I won't look like a cameraman in these."

That's for sure, Christy thought. He looked like an extra from a set. She suspected, with envy, that he was going to visit his building, later, just for the fun of swinging around it. *I wish I could love my job like that.*

They arrived late to the studio. The equipment van, which carried the cameras and the lights, the cable wheels and the trailing sound booms, was parked outside on the roadway, its red lights flashing. The trailer sat behind it. Christy and Paul stepped up into it. "Sorry we're late," she said to Leo.

"Hello, Paul."

"Hello."

"Okay, Gus. Let's go."

Gus played race car driver all the way to the South Side, flinging them happily against the sides of the crew van like peas in a can. "Christ," muttered Zenan, "it's a good thing I didn't eat my breakfast."

"Why don't you let Gus drive the equipment van tomorrow?" Christy asked Leo plaintively.

"Because he'd break all the lenses doing it," Leo said.

Zenan added, "Us he can break."

They stopped at last. Jordan Granelli's limousine was parked up the street. He was standing outside it, with his three guards around him, waiting for them. "Next time," Leo suggested gently, "maybe you could go a little slower? Even if we are late. Tom doesn't seem to know Chicago as well as you do, even though he's forty-seven and has lived here all his life."

Gus mumbled and bent over his steering wheel as if it were a prayer wheel. Jake walked across the street to them. "Mr. Granelli's getting impatient," he said. Leo shrugged. Jake looked at them uncertainly. He eyed Paul.

Christy said, "Jake, this is Paul; he's a friend of mine," Christy said. "Paul, this is Jake. He's one of Jordan Granelli's bodyguards."

They nodded at each other. "Skyhook," Jake said. "So was I."

Paul was interested. "Were you? Where'd you work?"

"Lot of buildings. I worked on the Daley Towers."

"Did you! I didn't," Paul said with regret. That massive building, Chicago's monument to its most famous mayor, was still the tallest in the city, though it was six years old.

"Last year I was working on the new City Trust building when a swinging beam hit me—so." He made a horizontal cut with the edge of his hand against his right side. "Knocked me off. I hooked the cable—but it cracked some ribs, and my back's been bad ever since. I had to quit."

"Tough luck," said Paul sympathetically.

They waited. "Which house is it?" Christy asked. Leo pointed to a white frame house across the street. Christy saw the flutter of curtains in the house next door. A woman with a baby on her hip was standing at her window, staring out at the black van, and at the white car with its black device.

She shivered suddenly. Paul put an arm around her shoulders. "Cold?"

"No—I don't know," she answered, irritated.

"Goose walking on your grave," commented Jake.

The equipment van came screeching around the corner then. Tom pulled it up past them, and backed with a roar of his engines. "Cars," Zenan muttered. "Oh, watch it!" Paul caught Christy's arm. The doors of the van, jarred by the forceful jerky halt, came flying open, and something black came careening swiftly out.

For Christy the events resolved suddenly to a series of stills. She sprawled where a thrust of Paul's arm had put her. The cable wheel bounded high in the air as it hit a projection in the ill-paved road. The thick cable unwound like a whip cracking. Paul seemed to leap to meet it. She heard the sound as it struck him, saw him fall—and saw the wheel roll past him, stringing cable out behind it, to hit the curb, where it shattered and sat. Cable uncoiled like a snake around the jigsaw wreckage of wood.

She stood up slowly. Her palms and arms and knees and chin hurt, and the taste of gravel stung her lips. She walked to Paul. It took her a long time to reach him, and when she did her knees gave out suddenly, so that she sat thudding to the ground.

The cable had lashed him down; there was a black and purple bruise across his right cheek. His eyes were open, but he looked up at the sky without seeing it. She interposed her face between his eyes and the sky. Nothing changed. In one hand his fingers were clenching a skyhook. He tried to hook the cable, she thought. She touched his hand. The fingers lolled loose. The hook rolled free with a clatter. She reached for it, and used it like a cane, prying herself up off the street.

Leo came round in front of her, hiding Paul from her. He took hold of her shoulders. "Come away, Chris," he said. "We've called the ambulance."

"He doesn't need one," she said. "And I don't either." They circled her: Leo, Zenan, Jake, Gus.

"Christy," said another voice, a stranger's. The circle broke apart. Jordan Granelli stood in front of her, his fine hands extended to her. "Christy, I'm so sorry."

"Yes," she said.

He stepped up to her and took her hand. "Don't be afraid to mourn for him, child," he said. "I know what grief is. We all do. Chance takes us all, and she gives nothing back. There's no way to make the weight any lighter. We feel for you." He stepped back, spreading his arms in supplication and sympathy. Christy felt the first tears thicken in her eyes. She stared at him through their distorting film.

Behind him, in macabre mime, Zenan cranked an ancient

imaginary camera. From a distance came the high keening of the ambulance.

Granelli turned his back on her as one of the sound men approached him. The man asked him something, pointing at the loose cable. She heard his answer clearly. "Of course we'll shoot! Get someone to help you move that thing back. And wipe it clean, first." Leo turned, his face whitened with anger. Jake looked shocked.

"Mr. Granelli," Christy whispered, to herself, to Paul. "Mr. Death, who always happens to other people." She walked towards him. The metal skyhook was cold and hard and heavy in her palm. She swung it: back, forth, back, forth—and up.

At the last minute Jake saw her, but Zenan was in his way. Jordan Granelli turned around, and screamed.

They reached her by the third blow—too late.

•*The Saints of Driman*•

When I wrote this story, a friend of mine had recently died. His name was David Mason, and he was a science fiction and fantasy writer. He'd written five novels for Lancer, none of which is in print today. He lived on a houseboat in the San Francisco Marina. He was an irritating, irascible, difficult man, and I liked him very much. After he died, I wrote this. It went to a number of magazines and anthologies. They rejected it. Finally my newly acquired agent sent it to the New York literary magazine, *Antaeus*, for their "Popular Fiction" issue. They published it.

David would have laughed...

Ares-Ak
Kimbel 15

How easily I write that designation on the page!

After four years, the names of the months of Driman seem natural to me. I mark our survey records with the changing dates and months. There are no seasons here. There is only the omnipotent, omnipresent heat. Kimbel 15—and in Ares-Ak they give names, not numbers, to the years—and Mary is still sick. This will be The Year the Strangers Go Home.

She is feverish, dehydrated, and partially delirious. We've never been sick here, before. It began two days ago. Morgan has already sent a message capsule. He curses the heat, and stamps around his room muttering to himself. I leave. I escape to the shops, to the cool white tile of Pir's temple, to the dry green of the succulent gardens. The people of Ares-Ak are used to seeing me in their streets. Only children sometimes trail after me, to stare at my foreign dark hair and skin. Morgan they follow in procession, as if he were the Pied Piper. He hates the city. He leaves it to me.

Mary keeps calling for water, water. Her forehead, throat, chin, and nose have a waxy, yellowish sheen. Her lips are purplish-red. Her cheekbones and eyelids are flushed. She drinks in gulps, like a baby. She sweats desperately. I gave her an alcohol rub this morning: that lowered the fever a little, but it rises, as the heat rises, and breaks at night. It's 38.8 now.

She keeps calling. I just went in and bent over the bed, but there is nobody behind her staring eyes. Just Fever.

I have to get out of here. I'm going for a walk.

Mary is better. She knows me when I come in, but the fever dries her throat out so that she can barely talk. We are giving her fluids intravenously. Her mouth is sore, but she drinks uncomplaining the water and cactus juice I bring her. The Drimanese doctors gave us some supplemental drugs: an antihydrotic that we can't match in our medikit, and an antipyretic that seems to work faster than our own Old Reliable, aspirin. Morgan is useless. His hands shake when he helps me lift her. She noticed it this morning and her poor mouth made a moue of laughter at me. But we are still going home, Morgan says. "Our work's done," he said to me at lunch. He's never asked me if my work is done. He disapproves strongly of my interest in the Saints. Religion makes him nervous; he prefers politics. "We can make a report on the data we have," he growled, as if he thought I would argue. I didn't. I know better than to fight with Morgan when Mary is sick and cannot calm him down. And—I want to go home, too. I want to see a waterfall, an ocean, a field of green grass, a mountain. Driman has none of these. Oh, there is an ocean of sorts—a green, sluggish pond that stirs dimly to the sun's pull. I want to see a hurricane. And god, what I wouldn't do for a moon! I would dance naked in the moonlight, shamelessly lunatic.

I saw a Saint today. She was sitting in the dust in the marketplace. She was gaunt as an old stick, and glowing, with that crazy joy that wells from them. I squirmed my way across the square and planted myself in front of her. No one looked at me. It was hard to notice anything but her. She exhaled calm and peace. It's hard to believe she's slowly starving to death. When Mary saw her first Saint, she said to me in mock Scots, "'Tis no' canny, lass," to make me laugh. I find the Saints awesome, and infuriating, and I am angry at myself for having ignored them for so long. Soon we will leave—and dragging information out of Pir is like pulling one's own teeth!

Ares-Ak
Kimbel 19

They are sending a ship for us.

A capsule came today, dropping into the desert like a spent bullet. Morgan rode a chorn out to get it. I hate those beasts, ugly fat things like giant armadillos. Feet and chornback are Driman's means of transport. The planet is hideously short of fuel. In an emergency you can obtain an electric vehicle from the city government, but it must be a real emergency, not a personal or ceremonial one. When our ship came falling out of the sky, the Drimanese met it with chorns. Their planet has taught them to be tightfisted with what they have.

Morgan accepts this. He dislikes the city; he enjoys riding into the desert on an armored pig. He would be snugly happy in a tower in the dunes, while I would go mad there. And yet— he cannot bear to be truly alone, and I hug my privacy to me like lust.

What odd people we are!

The ship must make two stops before it can land on Driman. Morgan is seething. "She could die in a week!" But he doesn't really think Mary will die, though her fever spikes and subsides, spikes and subsides, making palisades on the chart we keep at her bedside. She's eating again: the soft pulp of the pinwheel cactus, and a few meager mouthfuls of soup. Last night, she says, she dreamed of a red fruit, and woke with the taste and texture of apple on her tongue.

I wonder— do the Saints dream of food, as their bodies waste away? Does hunger ever fight its way through holiness into unholy dreams?

Ares-Ak
Kimbel 20

I asked Pir about the dreams of Saints today. I couldn't tell if he was amused or shocked. I know him better than any other

Drimanese, he taught me his language, and I still can't read his expression. Sotoko, his disciple, definitely disapproves of me; I can read *his* face like a book. He thinks Pir wastes too much time talking to me. Pir's accessibility sometimes accentuates the mishaps in our conversations, when I forget the "yes" is not a vertical nod, but a toss of the head. I translate to myself each time he does it: *That means "yes," Lex.*

"Do Saints dream?" I asked him.

"I don't know. It seems likely. But I know very little about the Saints." He is a priest, yet he claims ignorance of the Saints. I have asked him several times where the Saints come from, and what kind of spiritual training they undergo to achieve their transcendent state. I told him the story of the Buddha. He looked surprised, and then gave that brisk negative shake of his bald skull. I presume he meant that their training does not parallel the story at all.

Where *do* the Saints come from? The word I translate as "saint" is related to the word for sacrifice. It might better be translated "one who sacrifices." Why? But this mystery I won't have time to solve. The ship will be here in eight days.

                                              Ares-Ak
                                              Kimbel 21

Mary asked me today, in her new hoarse voice: "What are you working on, Alexa?" I sat on the bed and deluged her with my speculations about the Saints. Morgan doesn't want to hear it. I exhausted her, and broke off in mid-spate, feeling like a rat. She was all whited out. Morgan came in. He smelled of chorn. Chorns smell like shit.

"The ship will be three days late," he said.

Mary said: "Good! I'll have time to get so much stronger, they won't believe I've been sick." Morgan said something trivial, and pulled me out the door. He yelled at me in a whisper for having gotten her tired. I told him to go fuck a chorn. I am not responsible for Mary to *him*. He has left her white and tired enough days and nights on Driman.

I am tired of Morgan.

The Saint came back to the marketplace today.

She is noticeably weaker. My fingers itched for a veni-puncture kit, for tubes and needles and slides and a centrifuge and my microscope. The Drimanese might honor that desire. Their own biochemists have done some stupefying work. But I suspect they would not like me to apply it here. I want to *know*—what is going on in that emaciated golden body? This holiness is devouring; it eats up its bearers like flame. I asked Pir: "Is it forbidden to the Saints to eat?"

He said, "No. They no longer want to."

"Do they want to die?"

He didn't answer. It was a foolish question. The symbol of his religion, which they name The Path, is a circle with a line bisecting it north and south and extending out beyond the poles. It resembles the Terran mathematical symbol for the empty set. In the temples it is elaborated: a huge wheel, with many lines through it, and standing at top and at bottom, two human figures. It's the Wheel of Fortune. We who are on it only see half of it, living as we do within the limits of time. But Death is just the underside of the Wheel, and the Wheel is forever turning. Saints know that Death and Life are equal turns of the Wheel. They go beyond our human uncertainties; it's a seductive fate.

But where do they learn their fiery happiness? The monasteries attached to the temples are for priests. Where are they taught to smile, and cease eating, and gaily starve into death? I'll ask Pir again tomorrow. Maybe he'll tell me. Ares-Ak has been generous to us, letting us prick and poke and probe and pack away specimens, holo records, observe what we please. They accept us with astounding equanimity. Could it be that suspicious curiosity is *not* the normal emotional reaction of the universe?

Maybe it's just mine.

Ares-Ak
Kimbel 28

Sotoko told me!

We went to the Great Temple. I wanted to see it again before leaving. Terra has nothing left that's old. The Great Temple of Ares-Ak is four thousand years old. It's attended by priests, and visited daily by throngs of devotees who come to question the Wheel. Pir could not take me, and Sotoko, with more sensitivity than I have come to expect from him, offered to be my escort.

The Temple is a cavernous mandala of a building. It has eight long hallway entrances, like octopus arms, to lead the visitor inward towards the center. In the center, under a dome, is the Oracle Wheel. It is eight feet in diameter, brass, and polished bright with constant touching. Sotoko studies how to divine the future from its intricate glyphs. Pir is a master at it. He says: "All that can be known of the universe is contained here." It looks to me like a giant roulette wheel. I've seen it work. The comparison is apt. First, you tell the priest your question. Then you stand at one of the eight compass points, and the priest spins the Wheel. Where it stops is your answer, its meaning modified by the meaning of the compass point you chose. There are obvious possibilities for abuse in the system. The priests could get fat selling answers. They don't. It has happened—I have read it in the histories—but at this time, whatever corruptions attach to the Wheel are temporarily out of order.

Sotoko said to me, as we walked away from the Wheel, "I asked the Wheel a question about you."

I was surprised.

"It said you should be told what you want to know."

I looked at him, not yet understanding.

He said: "You want to know about the Saints. You want to know how they become Saints."

I said, "Yes. I do."

"It is a drug."

I managed not to stop conspicuously dead in the hallway. A drug! I know of substances that simulate physiologically a spiritual condition: peyote, DMSO, certain forms of Base-LSD. Their enlightenment fades. This drug is much more potent.

It also seems to be immensely toxic.

I wonder where they get it.

I'll talk with Pir at sunset tomorrow, when I go to tell the old man good-bye.

**Ares-Ak
Kimbel 29, Midnight.**

Mary is dead.

She collapsed at dinner, convulsing, febrile, scorched like a piece of fluff in a candle flame. She went swiftly into coma. She died in three hours. We have just finished burying her, shoveled into the treacherous alien sand with haste. Bodies decay fast on Driman. The ship will be here tomorrow. I have never before understood the true meaning of the word "irony." It is like iron—a barbarous weight, too heavy to bear. I *must* write about this evening at the temple—but the weight is too heavy. If Morgan walks in on me now I will throw this book at him—or else I will cry. I have not yet been able to cry.

The seed of my act lies within me now, ripening, ripening...

**The Daffyd ap Llewellyn
Ship's time: night.**

The ship is in Hyperspace, hopping around in the Hype like a busy mechanical flea. We have been to three other solar systems, and are just now heading for home. My sense of time is wrecked. It doesn't matter.

I couldn't eat dinner, again. Occasionally I'm thirsty; but 50 cc. of water is enough to quench my thirst. I've lost three kilograms. I itch. It doesn't matter.

Morgan said to me this morning, over the breakfast I didn't eat, "You've changed, Lex." I know to what he attributes it. I am mellow, like a melon—I am ripening. I ripen into death.

I had expected it to be a pill, or a sacramental wafer. But what Pir handed me was a little rectangle of cake, brown at the edges, like shortbread. "Do what you wish," he said to me, and then he went away. I took out the sterile tube I so carefully saved out of my last-minute packing. I thought of Alice with a piece of mushroom in her fist. I thought of Marie Curie, studying the radiation burns on her own hands. What strange symbols imagination uses to speak with consciousness! I ate the cake. It tasted bitter. I put a crumb of it into the tube. Were Sotoko and Pir peering out from behind a pillar, watching their experiment walk down the hall? I didn't see them. I left.

I have a list of questions written down. I will try to remember to answer them. I will try to keep records of how much I drink, how much weight I lose, what my symptoms are. There are tiny scaly lesions on my torso and my upper arms. My mouth is always dry. I sweat a lot. My heart pounds. I smile. I hope the crumb, safe in its labelled tube, contains enough of the drug for analysis. I suspect it acts on the central nervous system, rather like our amphetamines. I'll never know for sure.

I just had a thought. Will my body remain uncorrupted for weeks after I die? The lab won't have to pickle the remains. That should confuse them.

The Daffyd ap Llewellyn.
Another time.

I cannot tell how much time has passed since my last set of notes. My temperature is normal. I do not eat. I do not drink. I smile. My skin is paper-dry: my body withers. I hold the pen with difficulty; my fingers forget. What is my name? My mind cannot recall. What am I doing this for? Oh yes—I know. I wanted to record the change. Within me something is working. I am being drained of life: How do I record that? Hold me up to the mirror of other faces and my life like light reflects in them: I am their sun.

I burn. Like a smiling sun I burn away.

I am alone in a room. They do not talk to me anymore. They have taken away my thermometer and my charts, and stuck a long needle into my arm. They visit me—like a sacred relic.

I am empty, and I burn. My face in rictus smiles, and they smile back. They give names to what I am becoming, never seeing truly what I am. I am their sacrifice.

How much longer can this go on?

Until there is nothing left.

Now I know the answer, if anyone is asking: the Saints of Driman dream of death.

It is dark.

The center is emptied. The center is emptied.

The Light . . . !

•*I Dream of a Fish, I Dream of a Bird*•

This was the first story I sold to an sf magazine. I was inordinately proud of it. It appeared in *Isaac Asimov's Science Fiction Magazine* in the summer of 1977. Originally it had been a rather unwieldy novella, but after that was rejected a few times I took it back, cut it to bits, and entirely restructured the story.

The imagery of the story came from two specific sources. It's rare that I can pinpoint the creative moment so precisely. The first source was a dream I had. I had just read Robert Silverberg's novel *The World Inside*, and that night I dreamed about his 1000 storey towers, the urban monads. But in my dream, the towers were set in the sea.

The second source was a song written by David Crosby and Stephen Stills, and recorded by them and by The Jefferson Airplane: "Wooden Ships." I liked the Airplane's version better, and listened to it constantly. There is a line in it which goes "Silver people on the shoreline, leave us be..." and though the sense of the line in the song is very different from what the image became in my story, that is where the image of Illis originated.

It's one of the few stories I've written about the doings of science, and it's been pointed out to me that it's misleading: most discoveries in science are made when the discoverer was looking the other way. I know that researchers rarely find what they are looking for (though they often find something else); nevertheless it has happened. We don't, by the way, have an artificial skin, yet, and when we do it probably won't be made of fish scales. But the chemistry is not impossible, only unlikely, and I want to thank Katherine MacLean (thanks, Katie!) for suggesting it.

Forty miles off the coast, anchored in the sea floor, Vancouver stood.

It had been designed and built before the Change, for bored, rich land-dwellers to play in. Sixty years after the Change, it was a tower filled with refugees. Pictures in the library showed the abandoned land: brown, bleak, and ruined, with skeletal steel buildings twisted and broken across it, like the torn masts of wrecked ships. War, disease, famine, and madness had created that.

The names of the lost cities—New York, Boston, Ellay, Tokyo, Cairo, Capetown—and the burnt lands, were a litany of lament in their history lessons.

Where the radiation levels let them get to it, the shards of steel engraving the gullied lands were City salvage—a needed, dangerous harvest.

Illis swung on the handle of the door, and pushed. It opened grudgingly, silently, as he thrust his weight against it. Smooth metal felt cold on his palms. He slipped through the narrow space into the dark hallway. This made the fifth time he had sneaked out into the sleeping skyscraper, to climb the webway. He was not supposed to go out of the Children's Floor at night.

But it was hard to stay still in bed, when dreams left him with a dry mouth, twitching muscles, and visions winging through his brain.

He ran to the window at the end of the corridor, and looked out—and down. Waves beneath him humped and bumped in dark, endless circles.

Nose against the cold glass, he looked east, towards land. On clear bright days he saw it, or thought he saw it. He dreamed about it: only in his dreams it was green, and there were birds. He had never seen a bird; there were none, but in his dreams they soared against the clouds in graceful spirals, making odd mewing sounds. *I want to be a bird.*

He had told his mother Janna about the birds in his dreams. "Maybe there is memory in your blood," she'd said. "I dream of birds, too."

"Have you seen one!"

But no, she had shaken her head.

He walked back down the hall. Set in the wall, like a mosaic or a painting, was the round, rainbow-colored webway door.

Illis wiped his palms on his jumpsuit. "A climbing fool," Janna called him. She was one, too; she had taught him to climb. He liked sailing. He was good at handling the boats, careful and attentive, though he was only ten, and uncomfortably small for his age. But he was a City child, and his delight was in climbing.

Even on tiptoe, he couldn't hold down the release set at the top of the door. It was there on purpose, he well knew, so that small children could not finger it curiously and by mistake open the door. There was no one in the shadowy hall to stop him. He took a breath, and jumped for the release, holding with both hands, hanging from the handle, pulling it sideways with his weight. The door slid back. He looked down.

Imagine a spider, trapped in a long vertical pipe, spinning web after web at regular intervals from the bottom to the top of the pipe. Look down the pipe. You will see layer upon layer of web, until the layers blend to your eyes. Look up. It looks the same. Illis checked to see that there was no one at the net beneath him. Then he hooked his fingers over the rope that dangled from just inside the entrance.

He swung out, twisting around to touch the red button that opened and closed the door from the inside. Then he set his feet against the lip of the doorway and kicked off into the center of the web.

Falling—falling—sproong! He landed bouncing, curling his body like a ball to take the shock. The net bucked and quivered. He balanced on it and looked around for a "hole." There was one, a meter away. He slid easily through it, hung one-handed from the rope next to it, and dropped. SPROONG.

The webway was playground, gymnasium, and stairway to the skyscraper city. Illis couldn't see why anyone bothered to use the lifts, except for going up. Climbing up on the webway, going up the knotted ropes, hauling himself back up through the holes, made his arms ache. But going down was like flying! He dropped again. That was three. The farther he got from his floor, the harder it was for him to get back there. The danger of being caught excited him almost as much as the webway itself.

Above him the door slid back.

Illis looked up, counting. Go in! he thought at the net-obscured form. Be lazy. Take the lift! But the person was not being lazy. Illis's jumpsuit felt suddenly tight and hot. He scuttled for the webway door and punched the inside button. The door opened and he swung through it. He pressed against the wall by the hole in the wall, listening to the steady descent. I'll wait till there's no one there, he thought. Then I'll get back on the web and I'll climb home, to the Children's Floor.

"What are *you* up to?" asked an amused voice above his intent head.

Illis looked up. Leaning over him was a very tall woman, with black hair and brown skin and amber eyes. She looked exactly like his mother. "Nothing," he said, and ducked under her arm. He ran down the hall. A door came slapping in front of him. He hauled on the handle with all his strength, and scooted inside. It smelled of soap, and fish. It was cold. He heard water running. Around him the tall bulk of machinery gleamed metal. He searched for a corner to hide in, careful as he went scrambling to keep his elbows in.

"Hey!" He shrank against a door. "Did you see a kid?"

A man's voice answered, through the sound of rushing water: "What would a kid be doing in here?"

"I chased one down the hall," said the woman. "Take a look around, will you? I'll check the refectory."

"Sure." Illis, crouching very still, heard her open the door. He looked cautiously for the source of the other voice. There he was—hosing down the floor. He doesn't look in a hurry to find me, Illis thought. Where am I? Around him, above him, hanging from pegs on the wall, were pots, pans, knives, cleavers, spoons, and forks as big as brooms, or almost. I'm in a kitchen, he realized. That's why it smells of fish. He listened again. The man was looking for him, not very hard, grumbling disbelief, rolling up the hose. The man wanted to get home. I wonder where the freezers are, Illis thought, one ear towards the grumbles. And the stoves. His legs felt cramped. He stood up to ease them. He heard the door open, and close. Wait'll I tell mother I got inside a kitchen!

He found the freezers. They had dials and signs all over them, and even if he'd wanted to look inside, the handle was too far away for him to swing on it. He pictured fish from the farms in there, all frozen and silvery, like pieces of ice with eyes. He found a huge bin of dried kelp. He found the giant broilers; four of them, protected by steel-mesh gates.

I could climb over *these*.

He measured the gates with his eyes. The broilers sat silent, empty, mouths shut, DANGER! WHEN LIGHT FLASHES RED, BROILER IS ON! There were no flashing red lights. The broilers were off. I could even open the door, he thought. Easily, quietly, he climbed the fence. The broilers looked even bigger from close up. The button marked "Open Door" was sitting only centimeters above his head.

It was a freak of time, incalculable and unforeseen, that his finger on the button opened the broiler door just as that broiler—preset—began a self-cleaning cycle.

A red light flashed.

As the door gaped wider, the broiler shut itself off, and the door stopped moving—but not in time.

Illis's clothes flamed.

They packed him round with ice before moving him to Medica.

"You're a mess," Lazlo, Senior Medic, told him. "Does it hurt?"

"No." Two amber eyes looked up at him. Christ! What am I going to do for him? Lazlo thought.

"Well, you have to stop climbing for a while," he said. "You got to stay in here and grow new skin." *Damned if I know where it's going to come from.* The boy had flung his left arm across his eyes. The skin round his eyes, his eyelids, his mouth and nose, a strip on his left cheek, and another strip on his left arm, remained untouched. Methodically he checked the IV tubing and the catheter. "Are you warm enough?" Already, under his light sterile gown, he was sweating.

"Yes." Something—laughter?—touched the boy's eyes. "That's funny," he murmured. Lazlo grinned at him with his eyes, over the top of his mask.

"Is it?" he said. "Good. You know how to call people if you want anything? Good. There'll be people in and out of here all the time, and anyone you want to see, you tell us. You get to float in here, we call it the G-room, for a bit. Tomorrow we'll take you to surgery and remove all the old burned skin that's still sticking to you. You'll be all peeled. After that we'll take skin from your arm and your cheek and start growing it all over you."

"Grafts," Illis said, knowledgeably. He must know that word from Janna, Lazlo thought, with all her years of working here.

"Exactly. What you have to do now is, you have to move, and you have to eat."

"It's real easy to move in here," Illis said, looking at the gold-painted walls, the white net bed holding him, and the piles of machines humming in the corners of the small room.

"That's why you're in here, and not in a regular bed, in a room with regular gravity. We can increase the gravity in here, slowly, so that your muscles don't get weak. And you have to eat. Lots. Whatever you like, you tell us. You can have anything, anytime. You *must* eat."

"I understand," whispered the boy, staring at his raw, scorched flesh, from which fluid was leaking.

"I'll be in to see you every day."

A set of sealed doors with a tiny supply room between them kept Illis in strict reverse isolation. It was called the Lock. Lazlo inventoried the supplies as he went through it: sterile cloths, gowns, masks, gloves, bottles of fluids. The blood was in its freezer. For the thousandth time he praised the foresight of the first City generation, who had guessed how badly the city would need medical supplies. The hum of the air purifier filled the tiny room. He couldn't put it off. He opened the outer door and stepped into the corridor. Janna was waiting for him there.

Bright polished tools swung from loops on her hips. Every City adult worked part of the year on Maintenance. The glare of the sun through the window gave her the cut-away carved look of a mahogany figurehead. She saw his face—"It's bad," she said, before he could say it. And glared at him as if he were an enemy. "I want to stay with him."

"No," he said. "You can visit him—"

"You're an arbitrary absolutist son-of-a-bitch!" she said furiously. "Why?"

"It will upset him," he said reasonably. "And it will break you. If he asks to see more of you, we'll get Maintenance to set up a direct com-screen link, your room to G-room."

"I want to be with him," she repeated.

"What does he like to eat? Get me a list. Your pain will only distract him from healing. He *has* to eat, or he won't live long enough to grow new skin."

"I want to take care of him—"

"The City will take care of Illis. You want to help him—make me a list."

"Damn you!" she cried at him. "No, don't touch me! I'll make you a list."

Janna was shaking by the time she reached her rooms. It was not *fair* to keep her from her son. Obsessively, she had pictured Illis dead a hundred times since his birth, from any one of a hundred birth defects—but never hurting, wasting and hurting! She paced and raged. *I taught Illis to climb.* She twisted in anger and guilt.

It was not *fair* . . .

His father had died of radiation poisoning. Had that been fair?

She had done it before. She knew the routine. She could sit with him, coax him to eat, change his dressings, regulate his fluids, . . . Maintenance would let her go. The beeper on her belt screeched at her. She fumed at it. Hadn't they heard, Illis was hurt? She was supposed to be in the soil lab, working on some defective wiring—but every adult in the City could use pliers! They could find someone to take her place.

You taught him to climb.

She had had six miscarriages before Illis. She was thirty-five, and likely not to have another child. If Illis died—the light on the com-screen was flashing. A neighbor, maybe, calling to console, to patter platitudes into her ears. I will have a seventh ghost face, she thought, to add to the six that anguish my dreams . . .

Don't give up hope—we will survive, Vancouver will survive—*I don't give a damn*, Janna thought. I don't care about the City—but my son is hurting—why? For what?

Floating in the isolation of his room, Illis slept and ate, slept and ate more, replenishing the nourishment leaking from his flesh. He developed pneumonia, and recovered from it. He exercised, painfully. But at the end of two months he weighed twenty-nine kilos.

"His body's rejecting the secondary grafts," Lazlo said, in staff conference. "We expected it. Skin from the freezer or from donors doesn't last very long. It's a temporary protection. But he seems to be rejecting it with uncommon swiftness—and there's too little of his own skin. It just isn't growing fast enough." Dressed in her Maintenance jumpsuit, jangling with tools, Janna sat at the table, making notes. Lazlo did not look at her as he talked.

"How about plastics?" someone asked.

Mitra, from Research, answered. "We've been using a laminated nylon dressing," she said. "And we are working now on an adaptive protein paint, to be used in all kinds of wound cases. But it's still experimental. Our supply of plastic is very limited, and anyway, the dressing lasts no longer than the secondary grafts. There's no substitute for skin."

Someone else asked: "What happens now?"

"We keep on," Lazlo said. "The boy's very tough. He may yet make it. We keep on."

After the others cleared out, Lazlo walked around to where Janna was sitting. "How are you?" he asked.

"I'm fine." She would not give an inch. *Illis' condition has become a battleground on which we maneuver,* he thought. "I am coming to work in the labs tomorrow," she said. "Perhaps they will find me something on which I can work off my obsession."

"Are you eating?" he persisted. "You look thinner."

"I!" She glared at him. Then she relented. Lazlo spent an hour every day in the G-room, talking with Illis, playing games to make him move, checking the too-few patches of new skin, changing the bio-adherent dressings. *Doing the things he will not let me do.* "I'm all right, Lazlo. Thank you." She touched his hand. Then her spine straightened. She picked up her notes. "Maybe I will see you tomorrow." she said to him. "Tell me when I may be permitted to spend more time with my son."

In the morning, Mitra took Janna to a table with a shelf and a bank of machines. The shelf had her name on it; as if, Janna thought, I had never been away. "You work here," Mitra said. She pointed at a stack of papers. "The problem's there. Read."

Janna ate dinner in the refectory in Medica that evening. Lazlo came to sit with her. "How're you doing?" he asked.

She grinned at him. "I'm eating."

It made him smile, and emboldened him. "I see you're

dressed in whites," he said. "What are you working on? Something good?"

Her eyes gleamed out of her dark face, a look fierce as a predator's. "Skin," she said. "I'm working on skin."

Somewhere amid the piles of the printouts on her shelf was a fact or formula that would help Illis.

Working with epithelial cells grown in culture media, she sorted through a dozen experiments designed to stimulate or regenerate damaged tissue. She haunted her desk late at night; she dreamed about the helical collagen molecule. She plunged into the library to scour the pre-Change records on immuno-suppressive nutrient solutions, a way to counteract the rejector mechanisms that kept Illis from using her skin, Lazlo's skin, anybody's skin. Mitra, at her desk nearby, was working on her own project, the all-purpose protein paint. She wanted a substance—like synthetic insulin—which the City's bioengineers could make. Janna listened to her grumbles, in between her own. *Skin. I'm working on skin.*

Lazlo came from a late visit to the wards, one night, and saw her in silhouette against a western window. Summer sunset had left streaks of red and lavender across the sky. He went to her. "It's getting late."

Her voice was heavy with fatigue. "Yes."

"Illis gained weight this week," he said.

She turned around. "How much?"

"Almost two kilos."

"That's good."

"Two grafts on his left arm seem to be taking."

"That's good."

"Have you stopped at all today?" he demanded. "You're punchy! Come on, you're getting out of here. I'll help you close up." He went around the lab for her, turning off the lights. She leaned on him as they left. "Fool woman!" he said. Her shoulder blades winged sharply under his fingers, and there were dark hollows under her eyes. "Don't you *dare* get sick! How would I tell Illis?"

He took her to the refectory. She ate in absent-minded gulps, not looking at the food, fork and fingers moving like the claw of an automaton.

"What keeps you up so late?" Lazlo asked.

"New skin for Illis."

"You're not going to get anywhere if you don't sleep at night."

She looked directly at him. "I used to have nightmares when I slept," she said. "I dreamed about Illis, a dark little ghost face crying, going away from me, going to join the others. I hated to sleep alone."

"You don't have to sleep alone," Lazlo said.

"I don't dream that anymore. I don't dream at all anymore. I am a dream, Laz, a dream that the City is dreaming."

"I think you need to go to bed," Lazlo said.

She let him take her there.

Janna woke in the night.

Her pillow smelled of Lazlo. The room smelled of sex and of growing things; some of her plants were blossoming. She had just dreamed, and the memory of pain had awakened her. She had dreamed that Illis had turned into a bright silver fish, and she had swallowed him. He swam into her womb, and all over again, she gave birth to him. She passed her hands across her belly. It was flat and muscular, smooth—of course.

What was the dream telling her?

Silver—her memory jumped to the lab, and Mitra holding up a test tube filled with silver liquid. "Promising," she had commented tersely. "Needs more tests." Janna stalked naked to the com-screen and punched out a number.

"Mitra? What were you playing around with this morning? A test substance for the paint? It was silver."

The screen said two short sibilant words, and then said something rude, and was silent.

Janna reached for clothes. The lab will be empty, she thought, seeing deserted City corridors, passengerless lifts, herself alone, private, unobserved in the vacant lab—doing what? I will know, when I get there, what needs doing. Detachedly she saw herself open the door, leave her room, walk quickly down the hall—I am a dream of the City, she thought. The City is dreaming me.

Illis woke when the light went bright.

His mother was bending over him.

His mouth filled with questions. She had not come to visit

him for ten days. "Hello," she said. Her voice was muffled in the fabric of the mask. He saw it stretch over her smile. "Hello, baby. You don't have to talk to me. Just lie back and watch."

He lay curious, feasting his eyes on her graceful movements, as she carried in a box through the door, and then knelt down by the other door of the Lock, hands busy, head bent secretively. She had made the room heavy again. Painfully he pulled himself up in the bed to watch her. She saw him, and came to sit on the chair beside the bed.

"Look!" she commanded, and she pushed up the sleeve on her left arm with her right hand. "Look at my arm."

The skin along her left forearm was thickened and scaly, and it *glittered*.

"What—" Where it touched the dark of her own skin, it thinned away. He reached with his left arm, the good one, and touched the silver. It was warm and dry.

"It's skin," she said.

"Is it real?"

"It's growing there."

"What's it made of?" He stroked it.

She chuckled, and watched his yearning face. "Fish scales. Mitra made it, in Research. It looks like paint, and it's made of protein, protein very like the components of your skin." She touched his left cheek with her gloved hand. "It's for you."

There was a loud click, and Lazlo's voice came into the room. "What's going on in there?"

Janna called out cheerfully, "I'm visiting my son!"

"At four in the morning?"

"Yes. And yes, I did jam the door. You aren't going to be able to get in here without screwing Illis's protective isolation all to hell." She walked over to the com-screen unit and did something to it. Then she came back to the bed. "That'll keep 'em busy," she said. "Hold still now. I want to look at you." She turned the light up, and pulled the netting away. The grafts looked better then they had ten days back—but there were still too few of them. Illis's bones poked up through the devastated body as if they were trying to climb out.

"I'm pretty ugly," Illis said.

"You're going to be pretty flashy soon," Janna answered. "I'm going to color you silver."

"Now?" Illis whispered.

"Now." She stepped to the box, and took from it an ordinary glass jar, filled with a thick silver liquid, and a prosaic brush. "I'm going to do one whole side of you," she said. "It'll be cold, at first, and then it will sink in. Which side shall I do?"

"My right one," Illis said.

Janna set her teeth, and began to slowly paint the iridescent fibrous material over the raw wounds on her son's body. He whimpered, but held still, as she dabbed his throat, chest, abdomen, and right side. She put down the brush and wiped her sweating forehead, and then continued, working down his groin and his right leg. "That's all," she said, as she brushed the paint over his heel, and she capped the jar with shaking hands.

"It is cold," he reported.

"It will pass."

"The cold is going away."

"Good." At last she was able to look at him. He looked like a starved harlequin. "It will itch," she warned him. "You'd better not scratch. Not even in your sleep!"

It took her a long time to unjam the door.

Lazlo was waiting on the other side. He grabbed her. "What did you do?"

"Go and look."

Careless of isolation procedure, he strode inside the room. Illis waved at him from the net bed. "What—what is it?"

She laughed, sagging against the wall, and held up her glittering arm. "It's the protein paint," she said. "I had a dream—and the dream told me something, Laz. I stole some. And then I burned myself, a third degree burn. I poured the paint on. It healed—like this, Lazlo. With no grafting, just like this!" She was crying. He grabbed her by the shoulders and shook her. One or two tears splashed his face.

From the bed, Illis watched with undiminished curiosity.

"You did this because of a *dream*! Blast you, Janna. How could you take such a risk!"

"For Illis," she said. And grinned. "Now I can stay with him."

"Ah, Christ!"

The whole City heard the news, and waited. Lazlo became an unwilling daily reporter. The paint remained unchanged on the emaciated boy for two weeks. Three weeks. After twenty-two days, it began to grow along the right arm, up the collarbone, to meet the healthy skin growing down the neck. They installed a mirror at the foot of Illis's bed, so that he could watch. "It's growing," he said with wonder, flexing the elbow of his right arm, touching his shoulder with his finger.

"Yes," said Lazlo. *"Don't scratch."*

With novel luxury, Illis wriggled in bed.

They patch-painted him all over. The new skin grew in faster each day. "Hey—will I be able to go home soon?" he asked his mother.

"Soon."

And Illis ate for three, watched the mirror, and wept when his new skin itched.

When she came to get him, to take him home, Illis was standing at the window, looking up at the sky. She went to stand beside him. So close, one could see their kinship in the shape of noses and ears, the way their mouths were set, their amber eyes—only Janna's skin was a warm, dark brown, and Illis's shone bright, scaly, hairless, and delicately mottled, like the integument of an eel.

"What are you doing?" she asked him.

"Dreaming." He turned to her, intrigue in his eyes, looking like a quicksilver monkey. "I'm going to go there, someday," he said.

It was the City's dream—the return. "Sure you are," she said gently.

He danced a little, phoenix-brilliant in the summer sunlight. Her heart clenched.

"Have you been there?"

"No."

"Why not?" he demanded.

"The radiation level's too high. The only people who can go are those who've had their children, or who are sterile."

"Is it green yet?"

"No." It was still too early for renaissance. Throughout the City, desire fleshed a vision of plowable soil, drinkable water, rivers brimming with fish instead of chemical death. But the City scavengers would find rocks and steel, lichens, moss, and insects. The insects had re-inherited the earth.

"I *will* go." Illis said. "I will swim there." He grinned. "I am a fish, now."

"You are an imp."

He looked up again. "I dream about them," he said. "In the sky, with the sun shining on their wings. Next time, Mama—make me feathers. I want to be a bird."

•The Island•

Shirley Jackson was one of the finest horror writers to ever pick up a pen. No one has surpassed her chilling, literate prose: she is the mistress of quiet horror. This story was written in tribute to her work. It does not imitate her style—that would be both rude and impossible—but it does, I think, I *hope*, catch something of her mood.

> *Cape Cod girls they have no combs*
> *Heave away, haul away,*
> *Comb their hair with codfish bones*
> *We are bound for Australia.*
> *Heave away my bully bully boys*
> *Heave away, haul away,*
> *Heave away and don't you make a noise*
> *We are bound for Australia. . . .*
>
> TRADITIONAL SEA CHANTY.

The island sat in a ring of stone and a nest of fog.

It was a flat and sandy land, treeless, silent, smooth and white. Its toothy wet escarpment looked like a good place to lay lobster pots, but the fishermen never did. The way to it was treacherous. Once there had been a bell-buoy marking where the secret rocks began their rise, but something had happened to it. Fog lingered round it. Its name on the sea charts was variously rendered as Seal Island or Silk Island. On some charts it was not named at all.

Douglas Murdoch saw it from the bedroom window.

He leaned out the window feeling the foggy wind on his cheeks, cool with the promise of winter. The Labor Day crowds were gone. The Turrets had hosted a few tourists, but most people didn't want to have to climb the paths from the ancient cupola'd guest house to the beach and the shops. Mrs. Alverson was negative about cars. There was no driveway up to The Turrets, just the rutted tracks laid down by Sally Ives' jeep. He heard from the kitchen below the sound of his seven-year-old daughter singing. It had been a good idea to stay here, he decided. They had almost stayed in a slick hotel in the village. But the peace and isolation felt good to him, and Janna seemed happy. They were going sailing today, the second time. He gazed north at the boulder-strewn coast.

And saw the island for the first time as it floated in the morning fog.

He went, slowly, down the steep old stairs.

Janna said, "Mrs. Alverson had to leave and she said for you to get your own breakfast. I had eggs."

He opened the capacious refrigerator. Eggs, bacon, milk, butter. Salt, pepper, garlic. Onions. He took the smallest cast-iron skillet from the wall.

"Did you fold the quilts?" she asked him.

"I forgot."

"I'll do it." She slid off her chair. He could not get it through her head that Mrs. Alverson would do that, or else she did not want to relinquish the habit that her mother had taught her... Laura. He pushed the weight and pain of memory away—the eggs. Look at the eggs, stir the eggs. They'll burn. I hate burned eggs.

In his head the voice was Laura's.

No, This would not be one of those days. Would *not* be. Would NOT.

Janna came down the stairs. "Da, where are we going today?"

"Sailing."

"*Where* sailing?"

Janna was important. Think of Janna. "I thought maybe north today."

"I want to see the windmill again."

On the first excursion they had gone south and seen an old

battered mill, vanes still turning, though three of them were splintered stubs. A relic. God that's an ugly word. That was Laura now, a relic.

The windmill, think about the windmill. He had asked Sally Ives about it.

("The old Bigelow mill. It's been empty for years. It never worked well, the vanes kept breaking. The wind's too strong.")

"Wouldn't you like to see a new thing?" he asked Janna.

"*What* new thing?"

"Um. I don't know . . . I saw a little island out in the fog, a little baby island, just right for two people to picnic on. We could go there." That was good, that was better. Janna nodded so hard that her black braids flew. He levered the eggs out of the pan and sat at the long wood kitchen table to eat. She brought him a napkin. "Thank you, lovey."

She leaned into him shyly. It hurt him that she was still so shy of him. You lay four months in a hospital ward bandaged like a mummy, and she got to see you twice a day for five minutes; how could she be anything but shy of you? "Let's go to the island," she whispered.

They climbed down the steep cliffside path to the village. Janna ran ahead. Douglas took his time. The accident had left him with shattered legs. The doctors had rebuilt them, but the left was an inch shorter than the right, and both were full of metal bits and pins that ached when it rained, like shrapnel. He had spent a month learning how to walk at the rehabilitation hospital in Boston. He had only been out three weeks.

He caught up with Janna. She was sitting on a rock singing with great energy: "Fifteen men on a dead man's chest, Yo-ho-ho and a bottle of rum!"

Sally grinned at them when they came into the store. "Where you goin' today?" she asked Janna. She was an immense woman, six feet tall, 180 pounds and none of it fat. She ran the Emporium, the grocery and goods store in the village of Kennequit. She was forty, unmarried; she lived with her seventy-year-old parents in a small old house on a cliff. Mrs. Alverson had told Douglas that, and more, when she had told him that Sally Ives could rent him a boat. ("She owns two of them. She'll rent them to you—*if* you can sail.")

"To an island," said Janna. "Can I have a jelly bean, Sally?"

There was a jar of jelly beans on the counter. Sally tipped it down. Janna hunted with concentration for a green one. She only liked the green ones.

"Which island?" Sally asked.

"I saw it from The Turrets' window," said Douglas. "North of here, small and round and very flat, almost like a Pacific island. You know the one I mean?"

"Seal Island. I wouldn't go there. It takes some pretty fancy sailing."

"I'm not a novice."

"I know. You're renting my boat. The channels to it aren't marked and there are a lot of rocks around it. The water's shallower there than you might think."

"All right."

Janna was listening. "We can't go?" she said.

"Sorry, lovey. Sally says we better not."

"Have you been there?" Janna asked Sally.

"No." The woman's voice was almost gruff.

"There'll be other islands, lovey," Douglas said.

Janna nodded. Another child might have argued or wheedled. Janna accepted, stoic.

So she had looked at him, expressionless, shoulders set, when he told her Laura was not getting better, was not coming home, was dead.

"Come on, lovey," he said to his strange girl, his bleak baby. "Let's go to the dock."

Kennequit harbor was famous. There were half a dozen picture postcards of it—at sunrise, at sunset, in fog—and one Early American painting which hung in a Boston museum. Sally's boats were named the *H2* and the *0*. The *0* was the small one. They raised the sails. Janna was serious and careful as she strapped herself into her lifevest. Douglas hated the bulky things.

He stowed his under the seat, close to hand. "Shall I untie the lines?" asked Janna. She loved nautical words and now called all ropes *lines*, even pieces of string that had never touched water. They maneuvered slowly out of the marina. The wind was just right. It belled the sail. When they were clear of the other boats, Douglas handed the tiller to Janna. She steered lightly and surely, she was a natural sailor, better than he would ever be. He wished that Laura could see her.

His nerves knotted. Janna was singing. "Cape Cod girls they have no combs, Heave away, haul away, Comb their hair with codfish bones..." Laura had taught her the song, sung it with her. The lonesome thin soprano rose again. "Cape Cod boys they have no sleds, Heave away, haul away..." They had told him at the hospital that he had to forget, that he would forget. How *could* he forget?

"Janna!" he said.

She stopped.

No, he thought, you mustn't stifle her. You came here to make barriers dissolve, not reinforce them. Praise her. Tightly he said, "Go ahead, Jan. I like it when you sing."

She shook her head. She was watching his face. Her eyes were blue, like her mother's, just like her mother's. She had seen his pain and was guarding her tongue.

"I remember when mother used to sing that with you," he said. "Other songs too. You remember the Greenland whale song?" He tried to sing. "Oh, Greenland is a dreadful place, it's a place that's never green. Where there's ice and there's snow and the whale fishes blow—"

"That's the end," Janna said.

"Sing it."

She shook her head again. "Can we go look at the island?" she asked.

"Yes. We'll do that."

They nosed up the coast.

For no good reason, it was hard to find. Finally Janna steered straight at a blowy patch of fog, and there it was. Douglas caught the tiller. They zigzagged around the island. It looked a perfect place to picnic. The fog stayed just offshore of it, and the bright autumn sun made the white beach glitter. There was an ethereal quality about the place. But except for the clinging fog there was nothing soft about it. It was white and sharp and as unshadowed as a piece of paper.

Then he saw her.

She was sitting on a rock, her feet in the spray. She wore a long thing like a caftan, and her hair fell around it, black and thick and long. She was not looking at him. He knew how her hair would feel...His breath clogged in his throat. *No.*

She stood up. He slammed his fist on the gunnel. She—!

She walked into the center of the island.

Her walk was a stranger's.

"Da!" said Janna.

Douglas wrenched his mind back to his daughter, the boat, the sea—they were too close. He tussled the boat away from the island. He kept wanting to look away, to look at the beach. The boat balked, it would not come.

"Let me," said Janna. She closed her hand round the stick. The boat turned like an obedient dog.

The fog blew in, hiding the island.

Douglas sweated. Laura was five and a half months dead; he had lain beneath a car a foot from her, helpless, trapped, and heard her die—but he had seen her, there! He hit the gunnel again to make it stop. So there was another woman in the world with hair like thick and inky rain . . . That someone, not Laura, was on the island. A local woman, with a knowledge of the rocks and tides.

"Let's go back now, lovey," he said to his daughter.

"Well," said Sally, "did you have fun?" She tipped the jelly bean jar for Janna.

"Where'd you go today?"

"To the island," said Janna.

Sally looked at Douglas. "We just sailed around it," he said hastily. "We didn't land. Janna really wanted to see it. There was someone on it."

"Oh?" She was annoyed.

"A woman. With black hair. Tall woman. Do you know who it might be?"

"Could be anyone. Some tourist."

She was not going to help him. He would have to ask Mrs. Alverson. He collected Janna. "Come on, Captain."

Sally relented as they neared the door. "You want to take the boat out tomorrow?"

"We'd like to," Douglas said.

"Not that many more days of good weather. You might as well take advantage of them while you're here."

"Thank you."

He had his hand on the door when she said, "What kind of a boat did she have?"

"Boat." He thought. "I didn't see it."

• • •

He was driving. His eyes felt like sand and his arms like lead. He had been driving for four hours. Laura sat beside him, frowning at the dark road, hands knotted in her lap. Her tension reproached and irked him. "Janna's all right," *he said. She glanced at him, eyes like blue ice. The babysitter had called. Janna was feverish. They had been out on Cape Cod for a rare three-day vacation, just the two of them—*

"All kids get fevers. Let's stay and call in the morning. It's a six-hour drive."

"No. I want to go home."

He argued.

"I want to go home."

The road was a monotonous strip of white, leading nowhere. Douglas rubbed his eyes.

The truck lurched out in front of them from the right. He had not seen the crossroads. The big sluggish station wagon squealed as he fought to turn the wheel. He smelled rubber. Laura screamed. Under his hands the wheel spun and the car seemed to leap at the wallowing whalelike tanker. They hit it . . .

"I want to go home," *she whispered to him. He could hear the drip, drip—reason and his senses told him it was the gasoline running from the car, not blood, not her blood. Her voice got fainter.* "I want to go home, Doug."

"Laura!"

He clawed out of the dream. "Laura," he said. She was not there to hear him. She would never hear him. The pills were in the dresser drawer; they would put him out. Sweat coated him. He made himself stop shaking. He felt his way through the dark round room to the dresser. From the dresser to the door, from the door to the hall, to the bathroom, pills in hand— he took two. He would never forget. The doctors in Boston were crazy to think that he ever would, or could.

His dreams would see to that.

He went back to bed. He didn't try to sleep. The pills would make him sleep. He lay beneath the quilt and listened to the sea sound, rhythmic as the susurrus of cars on a highway.

In the next bed, his daughter slept, her breath even and untroubled.

The next day Douglas took the tiller. "Da, where are we going?" Janna asked.

"Oh, around."

They went north.

Douglas had no trouble finding the island.

She was there. She sat in the same place, maybe on the same rock. The sea surged roughly up. She seemed oblivious of the chill spray on her long legs. Maybe she owned the island. She sat there as if she owned it. He waited for her to see the sails and the tossing boat, to see him. He waited to see her face. She bent her head so that her hair hid her features wholly. She combed her hair.

"Janna."

"Um?"

"Look."

"What?"

"Do you see her? The woman?"

"I don't see anybody," she said. "Where is she, is she swimming?"

"No—there. On the island."

"No." She shook her head.

"Janna, look!" He didn't want to point. He caught her thin shoulder with one hand. "Look, there she is. She's combing her hair."

"I don't see anybody. There isn't anybody." Janna looked from him to the island. "Da, I don't like this game."

"Janna, this isn't a game. There's a woman sitting on the rock—she looks like mother! Can't you see her?" He couldn't believe her look of fright, confusion, innocence. He wanted to shake her. The denial seemed pointless. Was it because the woman looked so like Laura?

He would be patient. "Janna, honey, look there. Look again." The hands still moved, softly stroking. "She has black hair, she's sitting on that rock—"

"No!" said Janna, and burst into wild tears.

He had to turn the boat in order to comfort her.

"All right. All right, lovey, never mind. Never mind."

The psychiatrists in Boston would have fancy names for what she was doing. He cuddled her. Suppression, repression, avoidance. "I want to go home," she said into his knees.

"All right, lovey, we'll go home," he said. "Listen, we won't tell Sally we were at the island again today, okay. It will be our special secret. When she asks where we went, let's just say 'North.' Okay?"

"Okay."

"Well," said Sally, "where'd you go today?"

Janna's eyes were red and her nose was swollen, but she answered calmly, "North. Can I have two jelly beans, Sally?"

"Just north?" said Sally. She tipped the jar and looked at Douglas. *Nosey*, he thought.

"Just north," he said.

After dinner he spoke with Mrs. Alverson. "I think we'll go back tomorrow," he said. "We'll take off around noon. Maybe we'll come back next year in the summer."

She was stirring batter. "You do that. It's been good having you here, not like some. I'm making brownies. You want some to take with you on the road?"

"Oh, no, that's—"

"I'm making them anyway," she said. "For my grandkids. The youngest of them, Arabella, is three tomorrow."

He imagined her surrounded by grandchildren. She was all angles and bones, like her tall gaunt house. "Do they live here? In Kennequit?"

"My family's been fishing the Maine coast for 150 years, Mr. Murdoch."

"Then you must know just about everybody."

"They call me the Recorder," she said and grinned slyly. "Like the Recording Angel, you know? They call me that in church."

"Who is there in Kennequit with long black hair? A woman, I mean."

She shook her head, stirring, stirring. "Nope. Nobody I can think of. We're mostly blonds here. Swedes and Danes and Celts settled this part of the coast. Lots of Scots folks. Even a few Murdochs. Got any cousins in Maine?"

"No," he said. "The island? Seal Island?"

"Silk Island, we call it," she said. "I know it."

"It looks like a good place to fish."

"It isn't," she said. "Don't go there."

"Do you know who owns it?"

"Nobody owns it, Mr. Murdoch. It isn't a safe place. Nobody owns it."

He woke at dawn.

The house stayed compliantly still and silent as he dressed and limped down the stairs. The fog was thick and cold along the coast. Somewhere out on the sea the sun was rising. He walked down to the docks. Fishermen on their boats handling their traps watched him as he freed the *0* from her moorings and coaxed her out into the icy bay. He didn't know any of them.

Janna was asleep. He would go and come back so quietly that no one would know he had been out... He had to do it.

The fog twitched aside for him like a velvet grey curtain. He saw the island plainly: a white and shadowless space, glittery with quartz sand. He sailed around it. There seemed to be no good place to land. There had to be. He went round once more, looking for it. The fog smelled of salt and rain.

He saw her.

She was combing her hair. Her robe was green, like the sea. She was looking straight at him at last—he strained to see her face. The rising sun beat in his eyes.

He urged the boat a little closer.

She was singing.

"Cape Cod girls they have no combs..." Clear and sweet and thin, it mingled with the ocean rush dinning at his ears. She stood up. "Comb their hair with codfish bones..." She saw him at last. She waved, a curl of her hand. "Doug!" she called.

"Laura?" he said. He pointed the prow of the boat forward into the sun. "Laura!" Under his hands, the tiller bucked, the boat seemed to leap at the island. He felt beneath his keel the scrape and tear of the rocks. She was smiling. Water surged through the planking. He was close enough to see her eyes.

They were green as the sea wrack, green as the beckoning sea.

At her feet lay the flotsam and jetsam driven up by the sea: wooden planks, a torn sail like feathers, rusty bolts, half hidden in the sand. A bleached shard of something that might once have been a shirt.

Why? he thought.
He tried to hold on to the rocks. Why did I do this?

The island sat in a ring of stone and a nest of fog.

It was a flat and sandy land, treeless, silent, smooth and white. Its toothy wet escarpment looked like a good place to lay lobster pots, but the fishermen never did. The way to it was treacherous. Once there had been a bell-buoy marking where the secret rocks began their rise, but something had happened to it. Fog lingered round it. Its name on the sea charts was variously rendered as Seal Island or Silk Island. On some charts it was not named at all.

•The Dragon That Lived in the Sea•

A number of my stories have the sea in them. I was brought up on the East Coast, near the Atlantic, and now live four miles from the Pacific Ocean. I have lived on two of the Great Lakes. I've never seen a sea serpent, though I've looked and looked. I've never seen a whale, either, except in captivity. But once, off San Francisco's Ocean Beach, I saw a dolphin. I was sitting on the cliff, watching the waves, when one flung itself from the sea, twice. Out of that intense, solitary, and joyful moment, I wrote this.

There once was, in a far country, a dragon that lived in the sea.

He was a splendid beast, scaled and shiny, red and blue and gold and silver. His eyes were bright ruby, as dragons' eyes often are. The fisherfolk would see him from their villages as he dashed through the waves, stretching his long neck like a monstrous arrow shot from a bow, racing the sea wind or the hurricane. On those days they stayed home. For the dragon, being a dragon, thought their fishing boats were toys for him to play with, mere chips of wood, and so he blew at them with his bright fiery breath, and watched them burn. He did not know that the boats carried people, and would not have cared had he known it.

The fisherfolk hated the dragon, but could do nothing against him, for none of them was a warrior nor a magician, and only warriors and great magicians can kill dragons. They fished warily, watching the sea always for a sight of that treacherous beautiful head looming above the waves. Their catches grew smaller daily, and they grew poorer and poorer, till they could not even buy rope to mend their nets, or iron fishhooks. Parents starved themselves to feed their children. Everyone was always a little hungry.

The young men and women said to the elders: "Why must we live this way?"

Glancing at the white curling waters, the elders replied, "It is the dragon!"

One afternoon a stranger came to one of the shore villages. She seemed a simple elderly woman, but she walked alone, with only the help of a tall ash staff, and she looked at everything she passed with grey quiet eyes. The villagers guessed her to be a witch. Filled with great hope, the elders of the village came trundling out to meet her, and invited her to stay for a meal. The village cooks racked their pantries to prepare a feast. They made the best of the poor things they had. She thanked them for it without irony. They asked: "Are you traveling far, Lady?"

"I am," she said, and the elders sighed. When magic folk are on a journey you cannot hope to make them stay.

"Tell me your need," she said.

And they told her about the dragon living in the sea.

She said, "Even were I free to stay I could not help you. My art is with plants, herbs, chants, and the songs of healing. I cannot help you."

The very oldest of them all, a woman whose name was Lara, looked up from her place closest to the fire. "I am older even than thee, Lady," she said. "I have forgotten much. But I know that there are spells to harm and spells to guard, spells to keep and spells to cast away, and who should know these but a magician? Is it right that dragons should rule over humankind? This dragon has been our overlord for all my life, and my mother's lifetime, and hers before her.

"Can you not give us some spell, some ruse, some power that we might employ to chase this beast from our shore?"

A bold young man whispered, "She will give us a magic weapon, a magic sword!"

The witch shook her head at him gently. "Would you wield even a magic sword against a dragon, fisherman's son?"

The youngster thought of the dragon's great towering head and ruby eyes, and of his burning breath, and shrank into silence.

Lara said, "Have we no hope, then, Lady?"

The witch frowned. The sea wind crept round the house and rattled mockingly at the eaves. "There is always hope," the witch said. "But your hope cannot be in might. All that comes to me is a rhyme on the wind, which says in our tongue: *Mischief will flee a child without fear*."

Lara said, "Then the dragon will never be gone. For humankind fears birth, and fears life, and fears death. This you know."

"Yes," said the witch sadly, "I know. Poor thanks have I given you for hospitality. And now I must leave. May a child without fear be born among you, soon!"

In the house where the feast had been set dwelt a woman named Tace. She was young, with soft red hair and green eyes, but her eyes were always sad now. Her man, Mor, had gone to fish in his boat one morning, and the dragon had sprung out from the ocean, and blown a fiery breath into the sails. The boat had burned, and Tace had watched helplessly from the shore as Mor leaped from fire to water to die. When she heard the witch's words something sparked in her eyes. She cleaned the house slowly, stopping often to rest, for she was carrying a child, and her belly was big. "I know what the witch meant. I know." And her eyes lost their sadness as she awaited eagerly the coming of the child.

Her child was born beneath an ash tree, and the midwives were amazed, for she slipped out easily from Tace's body as if she wanted to be born. "Most babes fight to stay within the womb," said one, "but this little one is fierce for life. She thinks she will like it here. Poor child!"

Tace caught the wrinkled red face close to her breasts. "She will like it here!" she said. And the babe opened huge green eyes at her, and gurgled. All the midwives clucked at this.

"How strong she is, how forward!" said the one who had spoken before. "What is her name?"

"Her name is Elkas," said Tace.

The day Elkas was two months old, Tace wrapped her in a warm cloak and brought her to Lara's house. The elder admired the baby: "How big she is, and how quick! Look how she holds my finger. She will be crawling and walking months sooner than her cousins."

"She is the child the witch meant," said Tace.

"What?"

"The midwives can tell you how she slipped without a wail into life, and came right to my arms. You see she is brave. She fears nothing—and there must be nothing ever for her to fear. Nothing must ever hurt her or shame her or frighten her. She will overcome the dragon. I know it."

Lara looked at Tace's sure, set face. "We will make it so," she answered.

So little Elkas grew and thrived. She became the happiest, strongest and most spoiled child that ever was. Anything she desired she was given. She was never hungry or cold or lonely or teased, nor afraid of even the least little thing. "It is good," Tace often remarked, "that she has never desired the moon, for how would we give it to her? That would make her miserable. Spoiled brat," she said lovingly to her daughter. Elkas laughed, tossing her red curls. She was not afraid of her mother. And since the world was so good to her, she was good to the world. She was never angry or cruel or mean. All things were her friends and playmates, from the green grass snakes to the seagulls to the whitecapped waves that played and sang outside the cottage door. When the ocean stormed she crowed at it. To her it was all a game.

She was not afraid of the dragon. And the villagers were careful to keep from her their own fear, for if she thought there was something that other people were afraid of, she might be afraid of it, too.

The day Elkas was seven years old, Tace said to her, "Today shall be a very special day for you."

"Because I am seven!"

"Because of another thing."

"What is it?" the child pressed. "Tell me *now!*"

"Surprises are fun too," said Tace. "I will tell you soon, my heart. Go and play with the wind."

Elkas pretended to pout. But when she saw her face in the shiny bottom of the big copper kettle, she burst out laughing. She ran naked outside to tell the wind and the sun that it was her birthday.

Tace went to Lara's house. "Today is the day," she said.

Lara was almost blind. But she did not need to see Tace. Determination and purpose sang out of her words. "Go then, child," said the old woman. "May *thy* child, who has been our hope, truly be our deliverance."

"She will!" Tace said. And she went out of Lara's house and down to the harbor where the fishing boats sat rocking. She said to the fishers: "Make ready the boats."

They answered her: "No! The dragon has been chasing whales off our shores all morning. We dare not go out."

They turned. The great red and blue bulk of his coils lifted and shone and shook the sea apart.

Tace's heart sang with hatred. My child will conquer you, she said silently at the dragon. My daughter Elkas will conquer you, killer. "Do as I say!" she told the fishers. Reluctantly the fishers made ready the boats. Tace ran to fetch Elkas from her play.

They sailed out into the deep ocean. Elkas stood on the prow of the first boat, held tight by her mother—a living figurehead. Out they sailed, toward the scaled and brilliant dragon. Elkas danced up and down with joy. She had never been so close to something so beautiful before. "He is made of rainbows!" she cried. "How beautiful he is. Come here and play with me, dragon!"

Lazy in the sun, the dragon heard her. Dragons have very keen ears. By now he knew that there were living things in those chips of carved wood. He knew that they feared him. Yet here was one of them calling to him! Curious, he swam very slowly toward the fleet and nosed his great snout between the boats. The villagers shuddered with terror as he touched the wood. Even Tace trembled as the ruby eyes stared down at her and at Elkas. Be not afraid, she begged her daughter silently. Be not afraid!

Elkas stretched out her small lovely arms to the dragon. "Come and play!" she repeated.

The dragon gazed down upon her laughing face. Surely the human things feared him, as did the dolphins and the whales and even the sharks who feared nothing else—and yet this human thing was not afraid. He could smell that she was not afraid, for the scent of fear is particular and peculiar and like nothing else. Elkas was not afraid.

Shamed in his deepest pride, the dragon laid his great head down and sank beneath the waves.

The villagers on the boats cheered and danced and chanted

their joy. Tace stood tall and triumphant as they sailed back to shore. Only Elkas did not rejoice. She stood silently at the prow. At last she turned to her mother. The first tears she had ever shed were falling from her eyes.

"Why wouldn't the dragon play with me?" she cried. "I want the dragon to come back and play with me; he is so beautiful!" She sobbed and sobbed and would not be comforted, for this was the first time she had not been given her want.

The dragon never reappeared. But upon that coast at dawn and dusk sometimes a fog rose from the water where fog had never come before. The fisherfolk said it was the dragon blowing his fiery breath through the chilly ocean. Elkas grew to tall and graceful womanhood. She never spoke of the dragon save to her youngest daughter, who she had named Lara. To Lara she said only, "He was made of rainbows." And her daughter, who was like all other children, trembled, and did not understand the look of wistful loss upon her mother's face.

•*Mindseye*•

This story first appeared in a corner of my mind around 1974. It went through several metamorphoses. For one thing, I could not decide which aspect of the story I wanted to concentrate on, the symbolic or the literal. It had started out as a fairly simple adventure story, but it rapidly transformed itself to a rather complicated story about madness and alienation—in short, it kept changing shape. I almost threw it out twice. Finally I changed the sex of the protagonist, Phil became Phillipa, and darkness light. The myth of the Ice Princess barreled out of my unconscious and took its place at the story's climax.

They hovered over the planet at the edge of light.

Sunlight and heat poured across one face of the world; the other was left to starlight and cold. Bands of red light flickered around the room, glowing a red warning. Phillipa reached out a hand to brush them away. She barked her knuckles on the wall. She stared out, down, transfixed above a world cut in two, one side light, one dark, one hot, one frozen. The light shields closed. She fumbled to strap in.

The ship, a silver graceful sliver, sliced out of space, through an obscuring sky, and down into dark.

Phillipa walked to the control room. Xavier sat at his desk console, staring at numbers on his comp-screen. "This place is a freak," he said.

Phillipa sat down in a chair. She touched the light switches for a moment, and tripped the light shields. They went up. Darkness crawled outside the window. A crowd of stars lit the planet with the force of a moon. The rocks reflected starlight. She touched the switch again. The shields went down; the lights came on in the cabin. "Has this place got a name?"

"No. Just a number. M427-something. Want to name it?"

"I'd like to go outside."

Xavier scowled. It was the scowl of a punchinello puppet, ferocious and red on the dark narrow face. Phillipa said, "The reports say it has a breathable atmosphere and a gravity just under 1G. There's no good reason why I can't take a walk, Zave. If my antibac shots don't hold up, I'll sue."

"If your antibac shots don't hold up you'll be dead," Xavier said gloomily.

"What's the matter with you?"

Xavier looked away from the hidden windows. "I don't like freaks. This planet ought to be a Janus world, one light side, one dark side, and no rotation. It's not. It has an atmosphere—an oxygen atmosphere, yet. It has plants. It's weird."

"Can we walk around without machinery?"

"I don't want to walk around at all," Xavier said. "I like things and places that are one thing or another, and I like knowing which they are."

"We're an X-Team, Zave," Phillipa said. "That's the thing we are."

"Go out if you want to," the captain said. "We'll sit for a few days. Lui's found a bug in the Drive that he wants to fix. Seth would like us to move to the day side. It has more vegetation."

"What's the day side look like?"

"Hot, marshy, slightly volcanic. Seth says it looks like a Cretaceous mangrove swamp. Hot. About 170 degrees Fahrenheit."

"I wish you wouldn't do that," Phillipa said. "What's that in Centigrade?"

Xavier scowled at the ceiling. "About 76 degrees."

Phillipa had a sudden vision of the other side. Clouds, steam, black sooty smoke, coiling in the grip of hot winds, plumed across the dim red sky. In space a sky. On the other side of the thick clouds, in space, a huge red sun pulsed like a flapping flag. Tough twisted vines clung strongly to the stones. Lizards hid in the vines, purple and orange. As the world rotated slowly, inch by tired inch passing from day to night, shadows fell across the rocks. The vines contracted tensely. Storms lashed the twilit plains. The lizards crawled for shelter into the cracks and holes in the cooling earth. They blinked their eyelids as the light faded and the night brought out the stars their eyes would never see.

"I asked him if he wanted to wear an HT suit while he gathered his specimens. At least on the dark side he can walk out without back-packing a heating system."

"How cold is it?"

"One degree below Centigrade zero, mean temperature."

"Break out the parkas."

"Think this planet has any people on it?" Xavier said.

Phillipa nodded once. *That* was what was worrying him. Not a place, but people who might be different or strange or even dangerous. Aliens. If they are here, I'll find them, she thought. But no Exploration Team has yet found aliens. Why should we? Just alien places. "Who'd colonize the place? We won't. The Verdians wouldn't. They couldn't live here either."

"I wasn't thinking of them." Verdians were aliens but they were familiar, known. It was they who had found Terra, anyway, falling out of the sky a hundred years ago. "But there could be something here, living in caves—"

"To coexist with the polar bears? Who've you been reading, Walt Disney?"

"Who?" said Xavier blankly.

Phillipa grinned. "A twentieth century artist. Never mind. Look, anything smarter than we are would have gotten off this planet long ago." Xavier was still scowling. She imitated him.

"You don't *feel* anything?"

"When I'm locked up in the ship with the rest of you bums," Phillipa said, "the only thing I can feel is you. To do my work I have to go outside."

"So go! I said you could go. Maybe I'll take a trek—stretch my legs a bit. Even if this place *is* creepy."

Phillipa said, "Creepy? That's not a very scientific term. You going to put that into your report, Zave? This place is creepy, folks."

But creepy was a good word. This place makes me feel like there's something creeping up on me.

She was sitting in a cul-de-sac of rock. Beyond the jagged brim above her head, the lights of the ship glimmered a false dawn. True dawn was long ago and far away. She had looked closely at the reports before leaving the ship. It took this planet nine standard years to go around the sun, and almost a thousand standard years to turn from dawn to dawn. A year was nine years long and a day was a millenium. Five hundred years of night.

It felt good to be away from the ship for a while. Phillipa relaxed and extended her mind. Nothing. Some animals, too dull to catch. This was their final stop; from here they were going home to Main Base on Nexus. One more long Jump through the Hype. She counted. They had stopped on four planets. Too many. Already the team was beginning to show signs of entropic disturbances. Xavier's xenophobia was not normal. And the Drive crew, Lui especially, had lapsed into near-autism. Too many jumps between spacetime normal and hyperspace would do that, would joggle the brain. She could feel their limits stretching, the shape of their sanities changing. And she, Phillipa, the telepath of a team—who would feel it when she broke? Who would heal the tear?

She shook herself mentally. There it was again, that creeping depression. Have to stop that.

The cold was getting at her hands and she tucked them under her armpits, into the warmth of the parka. The cold slapped her cheeks with hands of windblown ice. She reached up and pulled the drawstrings tighter, pulling the fur hood round her face. She tried to imagine herself home on Terra, standing in a field, with the bright yellow lights of houses shining across snow. The picture came strangely into her mind. Memory distortion, said a remembered voice, is an early clinical sign of entropic disorientation. Andresson, at the Institute. She had said that.

Phillipa stamped around on the rock. Time to be getting back. The ship's lights glared across the tundra as if it were facing an enemy. The ice-coated rocks glared back. Did animals truly live in this cold? This cold that never let up, that lasted a thousand years? She pictured little furry things, rats, owls with immense eyes, and scaly lizards that hid in the thickly matted vines. She tugged on a tendril of vine. It gave reluctantly. Water slicked her glove. The drops, tinged with orange, made her think of eyes.

She turned to leave the cul-de-sac.

Stopped.

There was a youth standing in the mouth of the cul-de-sac. White skin, white hair, white eyebrows—an albino, Phillipa thought. But, no, his eyes are black. Then she realized that those were the youth's pupils, round, huge, like cats' eyes, like an owl's eyes. He was about 1.7 meters tall. He was naked. He was human.

Phillipa felt her heartbeat race. Eyes, ears, nose, fingers and toes, bare toes on the ground, it made no sense! Amazed, she looked into the other's face.

A claw dug into her brain. She was a battered branch whipped by a tossing wind.

At Psi Center, where she had trained to work on an X-Team, the final examination had been a no-holds-barred attempt at telepathic takeover. It had not been gentle, it had left her shaking and sick, but whole. She had passed. This was like death.

She felt her body break, and fall.

She came out of the mind's darkness into more darkness. Above her there were stars. She was lying on something soft. She turned to look; it was the vines. They smelt metallic. She shifted, braced her hands against them, trying to sit up. She only achieved a deep trembling. She lay still.

Black eyes in a white face bent over her. She flinched.

"I am sorry," said a soft voice in her own language. "I did not mean to hurt you."

"I'm just weak," she said. She tried to sit up again. An arm came round her shoulders to help. Through the fabric and fur of her parka she felt it, like a cold bar against her flesh.

"You have been unconscious," said the alien.

"How long?"

"Three standard hours." All that is taken from my mind, Phillipa thought. She felt emptied. Check for the pattern. You are an X-Team telepath, that is your skill and your training and your job. All beings have patterns. Find out what kind of a being this is—touch its mind.

She could not. She was too weak.

"What is your name?" she asked.

"My name is Cold."

A tutelary spirit? This isn't real. I'm hallucinating. I must tell Zave. She closed her eyes, trying to will herself into the ship's infirmary, with its deep-sided bunks and shaded lights.

But when she opened her eyes it was all still there, vines, ice, Cold. She forced her numb hand towards her face, and touched the stud of her communicator.

"Phil!" Xavier's voice fell thudding into the small space. "Where the hell are you?"

"In a small dead-end canyon. I can see the lights of the ship."

"Are you hurt?"

"I'm not sure. I fell and blacked out." She looked at the alien. "Zave, listen. There are people on this planet. One, anyway. Humanoid, advanced, and not hostile. I'm serious."

"Sure, but are you sane? Don't switch off, you hear? We'll find you."

When Xavier and the others came, the alien had gone, and Phillipa had managed to stand up.

They put her in the Infirmary, and Mickey put her to sleep. When she woke, the ship's time was morning. Xavier was sitting by the bed. "Hi," she said.

"Hi. How you feeling?"

She stretched. She was weakened. Her mind felt bruised. "Tired."

"Mickey says there's nothing the matter with you that some rest won't fix. Out in the cold too long. What the hell happened to you?"

"Maybe I fell over a rock."

"Could be. And you had a dream about friendly humanoids?"

Phillipa said, "It wasn't a dream, Zave. He was there."

"Did you speak with him?"

"Yes."

"In what language?"

"In my own." She saw Zave's face twist skeptically. "He took it from my mind, Zave. He was a telepath."

"It sounds nuts," Xavier said. "Lab is testing the vines now for hallucinogens. You fell on a bed of them. But I think the Hype is getting to you, Phil. Lui says he's almost finished playing with the Drive. It's time we all got home."

Phillipa turned her face to the wall. Home. What was home? There was a crack in her mind, and the ice was coming through it. The cells in her brain had been pushed askew; she could almost feel them, like a break in a plate. "You don't understand," she said wearily. "He *was* there."

She woke again. Ship's time said late afternoon. Some measure of balance had returned to her. Maybe Xavier's right, she thought. Of course he's right! You noticed the early signs yourself, the depression, the memory distortion. Time for us all to be home. Back to Psi Center. But that thought brought back, with jolting force, the spongy sensation of vines beneath her back, a cold arm holding her, and a canopy of sky like a black blanket with stars poking through it like knives.

"Hey, Mickey."

The medic turned around. "You awake again? How do you feel?"

"Better." Phillipa sat up. "Can I get out of here, or do I have to stay in bed?"

"You're not confined," Mickey said. She pushed the buttons that released the sides of the bed. "Just take it easy. Your clothes are in that panel. If you begin to feel disoriented, come back here and go to sleep some more."

"All right."

She went to the Drive Core to watch the engineers. At Psi Center they had trained for a while on a simulated ship. Phillipa knew enough to keep out of the way. The Verdians had discovered the principles of hyperdrive but had been unable to do more. Ilse Perse on Old Terra had created the Drive and seen the first starship Jump out into the Hype.

Warp space, hyperspace, the Hype—there were no stars in it, just clouds of congealing dust. Entropy was different within hyperspace. It was partially congruent to spacetime normal. The routes it provided through the galaxy could be mapped— were being mapped. Unmanned ships with sensors did the mappings, and peopled ships followed them, Jumping through the Hype to one and then another place within spacetime normal.

The first men and women to go into warp space had come back insane, when they came back at all.

That discovery had resulted in the word hyperspace being shortened to the bitter exclamation: *The Hype.* Phillipa had seen—not met, you could not call it a meeting—some of these returnees; people of immense courage and hope, shut in a box bounded by the bone of their skulls, locked into an internal reality so cohesive and demanding that the most skilled therapists, the most powerful telepaths, and all the drugs in the world could not touch them. The Hype had done that to them. The Hype could do that to me. It would be like climbing endlessly within a mountain range of ice; clear, smooth, reflecting ice, ice like a mirror, so that wherever you went you saw only, in a hundred thousand different distortions, your own face.

Stop that!

"Hey." Xavier bobbed up in front of her, his clown's face a mask of concern. "What're you doing, just sitting here? Come and eat dinner."

Phillipa looked around. The Core was empty; the engineers had gone. "Now why the hell didn't they tell me?" she grumbled. But she knew why; they most likely hadn't seen her. Creeping autism, she thought. I'm not real to them anymore, none of us are. Only machines are real. They forgot that I might want to eat. The Drive doesn't.

"You're looking better."

"Maybe hallucinating is good for me."

"Doubt it," grunted Xavier.

"I gather nobody else has seen a thing."

"Nothing but rocks and ice and snow and those damn vines. But if anybody has a similar vision I'll let you know."

"If they start seeing naked albinos creeping around—"

"I'll apologize."

Xavier was afraid. She could feel his fear. He was afraid of what was happening to her, to him, to them all. "We're all right, Zave," she said gently. "We're all right and we're going to get home safe. What's there to stop us?"

"Imaginary albino telepaths," Zave said. "I don't mind you hallucinating aliens, Phil, but naked humans, in a place where no human would ever survive naked—why human?"

"I guess it means I want to go home, Zave."

After dinner she went to her cubicle and lay down. She thought about home, Terra, Earth they called it once. Now there were colonies on many planets. She made a litany of their names and sang it: New Terra, New Terrain, Nexus Compcenter, Ley, Pellin, Azure, Ambience, Altair, Enchanter, Skell—all with bright suns and flowers and years made of days, not days made of years. It was hard to concentrate: her thoughts kept sliding into the ice and darkness outside the walls. Go to the Infirmary. Get Mickey to take a look at you. What for? It's my mind. Nobody can heal my mind, except another telepath. She started to walk to the Infirmary anyway, tripping all the light shields as she passed them, because it was important that as little of the darkness as possible get into the ship. She could see it, in her mind's eye, pressing on the windows, trying to creep in.

Takeo and Zave and Seth were standing in the hall. "I'm going to take a walk," Takeo said. "How much time have I got?"

"About an hour," said the captain.

"I won't stay out that long, it's cold out there, man!"

"I'll come with you," Seth said. "I want to hack off a few more plant samples." Cold out there. Was Cold trying to get into the ship, with the dark? She didn't want him. She would tell him that, she would go to him and tell him to stay out of the ship, stay away, stay out of my mind. She was a telepath, he was a telepath, she could talk to him.

She crept down the corridor after Takeo.

The wind on the tundra numbed cheeks and fingers and toes. Takeo and Seth had put on their LT suits, and they trundled along like obscene mummified snowmen, Phillipa, walking unseen in the shadows, felt winged in comparison. She let them get ahead of her, and then turned. What would the animals in the crevices of the rocks think of the strange beings stomping at them? She laughed. They would barely notice her. She had been there before—she was not a stranger anymore.

The darkness seemed pleasant now, natural, not threatening at all. The ice rustled and chattered around her as she walked into a maze of tall crags. Soon she could not see the ship's lights. She walked through darkness until a white hand came out of the night and led her into a cave. There was a fire leaping within a rocky niche. It lit the interior with a sullen glow. "Am I dreaming you?" Phillipa said to the alien. "Are you only something in my mind?"

"I am real," said the soft voice.

Phillipa said, "Why do you look human? Why are you naked?"

"I am *Myrkt*."

A name? Yes, but not a personal name, a racial name. "I don't understand," Phillipa said. Even here, by the fire, the cold numbed her mind.

"We are—chameleon? Yes. That word. To you I am human. To a Verdian I will be a Verdian. To a fish, a fish. To the rock-lizards I am a scaly god."

"Are there more of you?"

"I am alone here."

"Are there any more like you? Where is your home-world, your home?"

"Home? What is home? I live here. One lives there." The white arm flung out, pointing at the stars. "One lives there. One lives there. That is all. There are no more."

Not human. "How long have you been here?"

"A day and a night, of this world."

A day and a night of this world was a thousand years.

"Phillipa!" a voice boomed at her. "Phil, turn on your communicator. Phil!" Silence, and then it began again. "Phil!"

What could you do for a thousand years? The alien touched her, drew her deeper into the cave. Eyes sparkled at her, scores of them, unblinking, unmoving. Animals, birds, fish, people, great sculptures made of ice. There was a bird with outflung wings, and a woman bending her body into a hoop to the ground, and a giant beetle with outjutting claws. A voice still called her name. The fire in the niche leaped higher, and the ice sculptures shone. The Myrkt's skin glittered like the things he had made.

"What is human?" said the Myrkt.

Human is..."There are patterns," Phillipa said. For a moment she thought of tall blond Andresson. Andresson, that is human. How did you get in here, Kirsten? "There are twenty-two, no, twenty-five patterns. Twelve Verdian patterns. That is human, those mental patterns."

"What is alien? Am I? I look like you."

"You can look like anything, you told me."

"Did I?" A woman's voice. A woman in white stood by her, with frosty hair. Phillipa knew her. Named her.

"The Ice Princess."

"What is that?" The black eyes were rapacious. "Tell me."

"The Ice Princess lives on top of a mountain of ice. She is very beautiful, but she has no heart. Men climb the ice mountain for love of her beauty, and perish in the cold and the dark. The mountain is covered with bodies, frozen bodies of men, dogs, birds, fishes, beetles..." That's not how it goes! She couldn't remember. The ice in the cave glittered terribly.

"Was she human?"

"I don't know," Phillipa said. "She could have been, but she had no heart."

"What is that—heart? Heart is like a pattern? How may I get it?" A white face stooped to hers. It was a burning cinder, a cold star. Palms touched her face.

Cold—cold as death, cold as cold metal burning against bare skin. Illusion swirled and changed and died. Inside her mind something spoke to her, telling of loss, of loneliness, of desperate greed. Then the pictures shattered.

They found her at last after a four-hour search, crouching in a corner of rock and ice, in a cave, unseeing and silent as the ice. She was alive, that was all. Mickey felt her all over. "Nothing broken. Phillipa? Phil?" They could not rouse her. At last they made a cradle and carried her between them, limp, out of the grotesquely embellished cave. And Xavier, using his heavy metal searchlight as a club, hammered at as many of the statues as he could reach until a rubble of broken ice littered the frozen lightless ground.

•*The Man Who Was Pregnant*•

Riding on a San Francisco bus one afternoon, I saw a stranger, a man, wearing a bright orange caftan. He looked pregnant. From that glimpse came this story. It was remarkably easy to write and now, when people come to me and say, "But what's it about?" I grumble and mutter and change the subject.

He was an unlikely looking man to be a mother: tall, with a bushy brown beard and long hair, stolidly and solidly male. He was hairy and not very strong. As a child he had been fat. He liked loose clothes; tunics, dashikis. The first thing he did when he realized he was pregnant was buy a bright orange caftan and hang it away in his closet. Sometimes he would touch it, the coarse sturdy cotton like the kind bedspreads are made from, and picture himself inside it, swelling it out like a tent. Both his sisters had worn maternity clothes during their respective pregnancies and would have been glad to lend him shirts and tunics, but he preferred the somewhat asexual look of the caftan. It lent dignity to an otherwise puzzling and slightly ridiculous event.

He was unsure how he could be pregnant. He had had all the usual childhood diseases and examinations. In 1969 during his Army physical (he had been rejected for active duty for a heart murmur about which he had never known and which never gave him any trouble) doctors had probed and palpated and x-rayed (it seemed) every inch of him and had found no anomalies, nothing out of place, no extra organs. He went to the main library and looked for other cases like his own. The librarian directed him to the references on sympathetic pregnancies. He read them dutifully but they told him nothing. There was no such thing, after all, as a sympathetic rabbit test. He *was* pregnant.

It was even more of a puzzle to him how he could have gotten pregnant. His sex life was healthy. He was between attachments but had two steady liaisons going, one with Louise who worked in a bookstore, the other with Sandy who waited tables in a men's bar. Louise could clearly have had nothing to do with the event, and therefore Sandy must have—but the logistics seemed shaky. His sisters made rude and ribald comments about virgin births.

The doctors at first simply refused to believe that he was pregnant, despite all their test results. They decided that he was crazy, or hoaxing them, or that he had a "mass" or lesion or a hernia or anything but a baby growing inside him. The woman doctor who examined him was just as intransigent as the men. They wanted to keep him in the hospital, they told him. He realized that they wanted to keep him the full nine months. He decided that this was an unnatural situation in which to have a baby and signed out AMA, which meant against medical advice.

His sisters, Ruth and Nancy, swung between sisterly concern and incredulity. It did not help that they were both older than he. When he started getting morning sickness in his third month they told him to cut out all the coffee before lunch. It worked. They could both sew, he had never learned; he brought his pants to them to open the waistbands and seams.

He started "showing" at the fourth month. By the fifth he was able to take the caftan from its hanger and slip it on. He wore T-shirts under the caftan. One morning he left off the T-shirt. The coarse fabric rubbed his nipples pleasantly. He stopped wearing T-shirts altogether. He liked sunlight. The window of his studio faced south; he moved his bed into the area of sun. During the day he lay naked on the bed, drenched in sun, touching himself—his nipples, his cock, and the swelling flesh between. He masturbated. It was dizzying to feel his cock stiffen in one palm, and pass his other palm over the soft stretched skin of his belly.

One afternoon as he caressed himself the baby moved, kicked. He cried out. The baby was there, alive, there.

He was a printer, but he had been unemployed for nearly a year and had gotten used to daytime solitude. Every once in a while he missed the companionship of the shop. But he had always preferred having lovers to having friends. He visited

Louise at the bookstore. She liked to chat with him, she even set aside baby books for him to look at, but she would not visit his apartment. He was too shy to go into the men's bars; his relationship with Sandy came to an abrupt but natural end.

He spent a lot of time with his sisters and their friends. At night he read or watched television. His downstairs neighbors, a couple with a two-year-old son, invited him to dinner. He went. They were vegetarians. After dinner they passed a joint. Sara remarked that she had smoked dope all through her pregnancy and that Jorma (named after Jorma Kaukonen of Jefferson Airplane) didn't seem the worse for it. Tony said that he had read that it was okay after the fifth month. Jorma fell asleep on the floor.

In the seventh month he got tremendously depressed. The abnormality of his state began to terrify him. There was no one like him in the world, no one to reassure him or tell him what to do. How could he have a baby? Where would it come out? He read in his books about ectopic pregnancies. He contemplated going back to the hospital but could not see how that would help. The doctors knew less than he. He stopped going out, except to buy food at a corner store. He watched a lot of television, even daytime television, although the game shows repelled him. He sat in his window and watched the traffic pass on the street below. His back hurt.

In the eighth month his breasts began to grow and ache and his cock to shrink. He understood: his body was making a pathway for the baby. His depression vanished. He went back to the bookstore and bought books on natural childbirth. Sara and Tony helped him do the exercises and learn the breathing techniques. His sisters had a fight over whether or not he should go to the hospital. Nancy stopped speaking to him or to Ruth. But one day she called him, crying, to tell him she loved him and that he should do whatever he wanted to do, that he would always be her baby brother.

He went into labor one night at home. Sara called a woman she knew from a midwife collective to help. Tony counted and rubbed his back and yelled at him to breathe. The labor went on for a long time; he fell asleep in the middle of it (not a real sleep, just a drowse) until the contractions woke him up. The baby was born in the afternoon, in the sun, and named Kris. It was his mother's name. Sara pointed out it was short for

Krishna. He could not remember when Ruth and Nancy had arrived, but they were there. The midwife praised them all for their spirit, and gave them the name of a pediatrician. It did not seem to him that it could be over. He rubbed his nipple against the baby's tiny lips.

When the doctors finally came around to check on him, he pretended to be his own (nonexistent) brother. He told them that he had moved away. They seemed relieved to hear that. They shook his hand. The woman doctor smiled at Kris.

After that nobody came to ask questions. He lost all the weight that he had gained during the pregnancy. His cock regained its normal size. Except for the stretch marks and the darkened wide aureoles of his breasts there was nothing to show that he had been pregnant. Under Jorma's tutelage, Kris began to call him Da and not Ma.

The orange caftan hung shapeless and unused in the closet. He took it out one day, meaning to give it to Ruth to make into a shirt. The smell of it was familiar and interesting. He put it on, and wore it like regalia around the studio, till one of his sisters commented unmaliciously that it made him look swish. The word offended. He took it off again, and when he went to look for it some months later it had disappeared.

•Obsessions•

I have a bad habit of straddling categories. (Or, in some cases, of abandoning them altogether.) This story, however, appeared in an anthology which itself straddled categories: *Dark Sins, Dark Dreams*, a science fiction/crime anthology, the creation of Bill Pronzini and Barry Malzberg. At the time I wrote it there had been a lot of arson in San Francisco. Much of it was (much of it *is*) professionally devised, arranged by the owners of the decaying property for the insurance money. Often the buildings are still being lived in.

Barry and Bill, with my permission, changed the title of the story to "The Fire Man." I have changed it back. The story troubles me; I've reworked it over and over, and can't help feeling that there's something missing in it. It's the only one of my stories with which I am strongly dissatisfied.

Tony Dellara knew that he was being watched.

In the middle of a torching, nothing disturbed him. He went about his work with a specialist's precision. Firemen in their asbestos rigs, sweating in the sun, were a familiar annoyance; the presence of a stranger in civvies an ignorable one—but sharper. He distrusted observers in suits.

He poured a gasoline trail down the Victorian hallway, and sight-checked the windows. No glass. Once they had stopped him halfway through because some marshal had missed a stained-glass window. This was the last house—the trigger house. Soon the block would erupt, a small nova, to flare inward and burn to ash. Up on Parnassus Heights, the poured-concrete buildings of the hospital leered at him. We're safe, they said. We're not wood. Lording it over a valley of wreckage. Devastation Row.

One of us will get you, he thought. Wind, water, fire, or the earthquake. You won't stand.

He tucked an end of soft rope into a crack of the wooden oil-soaked floor, and began to back up, unrolling it. His arms and legs were aching with tension, and the gasoline smell was making his throat catch. With painful self-discipline Dellara forced himself to slow down, to pace the yards out. If they would only let him work at night—the sight, the sound of flames against the night sky!

Far enough. He took a box of kitchen matches from his pocket, and fumbled one out. The sizzle and flare as it caught calmed him rock-steady. He touched the flame to the end of the cord, and watched it travel across the bare earth up to the door of the house. Kneeling, he laid his head on his knees, cloth rough on his face, and rocked, back, forth, back, forth . . .

It caught. Air bellowed as it rushed into the house, drawn through window and door frames by the sucking fire. The firemen moved back a little. The visitor went with them. Tony Dellara knelt, watching the conflagration.

When he was sure that no power short of the hand of God could put the fire out, he stood up. Home now, to an old rooming house on Buena Vista, a firebug's gingerbread dream. From its windows he could see the rubbish that was downtown San Francisco. The quake had ripped the city like rotten cloth, toppling its towers: Coit Tower, Transamerica, the Hilton, and leaving the wreck of the Bay Bridge scattered over Treasure Island like the bones of a beached whale. The Golden Gate still stood; the city's symbol. No one used it now. Its approaches were down.

It gleamed orange in the sunlight, like his fire.

Now there was time to check out the stranger. The man's head was cocked back; he was watching the fire. Tony strolled over to Lee Harris, the chief marshal. Mostly the firemen ignored him: some of them, Tony guessed, feared or despised or envied him. Lee Harris, for reasons he never needed to voice, hated the arsonist's guts. "Nice day," he said. "No wind." Lee nodded. "Department being investigated?"

"Not that I know of. Why?"

"The dude in a suit. He's been watching pretty close."

Lee grinned tightly. "He's watching *you*, Dellara. He's some big shot from Recon, name of Susman. Think they're going to take you off the job?"

"Maybe," Tony said softly. You'd like that, wouldn't you, you bastard. He repeated to himself, as he walked away: "Susman. From Recon."

Jake Susman walked into Marta Riordan's office.

"Claudia, is she in?" he demanded.

The secretary looked at him coldly. She did not like him. She knew he wanted Marta's job. "She's in, Mr. Susman. She wanted an hour free to get some work done, and she's getting it."

Jake sighed. "Please call me when the hour's up." He went back to his desk. He shuffled papers, emptied the overflowing ash tray, put a file away. He read the top paper on the pile on his desk, buried it under six reports, and then fished it out again. He could take it to Marta. "We, the undersigned, respectfully petition the Department of Urban Reconstruction to exempt from its program blah-blah, blah-blah." A house on Duboce, near Noe, built in 1886, still standing. He knew what she would say. No.

When Claudia called him, he walked in holding the petition before him like a shield. "What d'ya think?"

Marta took it, looked at it, and laid it down on the desk. "Why waste my time with this crap?" she said.

"I know the area—I live there. It's right near Franklin Hospital. That block's in pretty good shape."

"You want me to approve it? Okay, Jake. Now—what do you really want to talk about?"

She had short black hair and classic Irish skin, like cream. The jade pendant the office staff had given her for her thirtieth birthday matched the green of her eyes.

"Come to dinner with me tonight?"

"No, Jake."

"You'll have to say yes sometime."

She shrugged. He gave it up, slapped his pockets for his cigarettes, and then ostentatiously folded his hands on his lap. "It's about your pyrotechnics experiment—Tony Dellara." She raised her eyebrows. "I watched him Friday morning." He wished Marta allowed smoking in her office. He suddenly needed something to do with his hands.

"Odd occupation for a day off."

"He burned a block of the old Haight. Just like that—gone."

"That's his job."

"I thought we were hired to build the city up, not burn it down," he said.

Marta tapped a pencil on the desk. "Burning takes less time than the bulldozers, cranes, and trucks, and uses less gasoline than they do. Those old blocks are mostly deathtraps. You know that. We can build over them after we clear them out."

"Burning's dangerous."

"So far there hasn't been an accident."

"It doesn't employ as many people as the bulldozers."

"It frees them to work on the building projects."

"It pollutes the air."

"True."

She did not want to fight with him. "And Dellara?" he said. "What made you pick him for the job?"

"He applied for it. And I knew him casually, ten years ago in New York. He was a fire insurance investigator for twelve years. He knows his work."

"You ought to see his face, when he lights that fuse," Jake said. "It's just not normal, Marta. Have you thought—he's got to be obsessive?"

"You're not a psychiatrist. Have you talked with him, Jake? He's a sensitive man."

"I looked up his file. I was curious. Did you know he was twice questioned in cases of suspected arson?"

"Along with every volunteer fireman in the Bronx!" she said. "He told me about it when I interviewed him."

Jake's fingers itched for a cigarette. "What he does is essentially destructive."

"At the moment it's helping us rebuild San Francisco. What's eating you, Jake? Show me something wrong. Show me where Dellara's made a mistake—I'll drop the experiment like that!" Her palm cracked the desk. "But till the experiment proves valueless, your suspicions sound as irrational to me as those of a businessman who won't hire kikes."

Jake flushed. "Okay," he capitulated. "Let's drop it." He grinned. "It isn't that important. Are you sure you can't make dinner tonight?"

"Goodby, Jake," she said.

He went back to his cubicle, and reached for his smokes, savoring the harsh taste. What the hell does she care about Tony Dellara? he wondered. He saw in his mind the figure kneeling—like a goddamn sun-worshiper—in the dust. I'll go again. Today's Tuesday. Friday—I'll go again.

Friday Jake followed Tony Dellara home.

I don't understand what makes a man like that tick. He doesn't look crazy—but neither do men who molest little girls . . . Nice place he lives. I wonder what we're paying him. I think Marta liked him. Cool, so cool, green eyes, jade eyes— she doesn't go out at all. Executive women . . . Do his neighbors know? Hello Mr. Jones, I'm your next door neighbor, I'm a pyromaniac . . . Slander, that's slander, I'm only guessing— maybe I'm wrong and Marta's right . . .

He stopped by the mailbox to light a cigarette, careful to keep his face turned away from the windows of the house.

Tony Dellara watched Susman strike the match.

Did he think I wouldn't notice someone following me home? Shucks his suit for a denim jacket and he thinks it's a disguise. He wanted to go down and grab Susman by his clean, pressed collar, shake him, scream at him. Why are you following me? Recklessly he went down the street. Susman was still there, smoking. Tony tapped him on the shoulder. "Got a spare?" he said. Susman slapped his pocket for his pack, and shook out a cigarette. "Thanks." Tony pulled out his matches and lit it. The flame burned between them. "You live around here?"

"Uh—no," Susman said. "See you around."

Dellara waited until he turned the corner of Roosevelt, heading down. Then, slowly, he started to walk in the same direction.

From the pay phone at the corner of Henry Street, he made his call, grinning at the thought of Susman. Wouldn't you like to know . . . "May I tell her who's calling?" the secretary said.

"Tell her it's Tony Dellara."

In a moment he heard her voice. "Tony? You *swore* you wouldn't call me here."

"It's important. About a guy who works for you. Name of Susman."

"Jake? What—"

"He watched me last Friday. And this morning. He even followed me home. It's getting me nervous. Pull him off, Marta. You're his boss."

"Friday's his day off, Tony; he can go where he likes."

"I don't like being watched."

"Yes," she said, "I remember." He saw her for a moment as he had first seen her, back in the Bronx, ten years ago: thin white face, black curls, green eyes, trembling against the brick wall in the light of the flames. He recalled his own unholy burst of fear and rage.

"He doesn't know, does he?"

"No. Nobody knows."

But me. "Tell him to lay off," he said again, trying to be gentle. "Suggest it to him, Marta. It's bad luck to rattle a torch."

"Tony!"

He hung up. Then he stood with his forehead pressed to the cold plastic of the phone booth, forcing himself under control. *Get cool. Get cool.*

Jake Susman stood at the window of his house.

Bitch. Charlie had gotten the blanket spread out under the tree, and the girl was making him wait. Jake sympathized. There she was. Nice. She came quickly across the yard and into the shadows, screened by the tall grass. Almost immediately they were in each other's arms, clothes off and pushed to one side. Jake could feel himself getting hot.

He left the window. *What are you, a voyeur? Getting into teen-agers?* The air in the cottage smelled suddenly stale, poisoned with the reek of a thousand dead cigarettes. *Marta's right, I should stop smoking.*

He was sure, positive, that Marta Riordan had once had something going with Dellara. She jumped so quickly to his defense..."He's a sensitive man." He went to the window again, and opened it. They were still at it.

It was not enough to tell himself that there were a lot of other women, that all cats were gray in the dark, and that if he waited long enough, asked often enough, she would say yes, or he would lose interest.

Monday, he thought. *Monday I'll get in there again, talk to her about Dellara. Suggest that she have an impartial ob-*

server evaluate the success of the burning program. The Army? She's so damn sure of herself, always. I need to shake her up a little.

Despite himself, he looked out the window. Charlie and the girl were still joined, but clearly finished. The tension in his own groin was turning into an ache. Ah, damn. He went to the bed. Marta, he thought. So cool—so beautiful and so cool— bitch...

Tony Dellara went prowling on Henry St. Monday night. There were lights on in the second floor apartment of the Victorian. He eased open the basement door. The passageway to the yard was cluttered with garbage cans. He went through. A dark shape in the back of the yard, the cottage seemed very small. Nice yard; well kept. A lemon tree. A concrete barbecue pit. He went to look at it. Perfect.

It was stuffed with papers and old rags. He dropped the laundry bag he was carrying to the ground. In it were more rags, stained with paint and turpentine. A coil of dirty clothesline, a can of paint thinner. A half-used, untraceable book of matches.

Party noise blared from the house in front. Tony took a pair of cheap gardener's gloves from the bag and stooped to rub them in the dirt. Then he put them on and unrolled the clothesline. He uncapped the paint thinner and began to dip the line in the can at random. When it was spotted completely with liquid, he laid one end of it in the barbecue pit and snaked it through the yard to the steps of the cottage, letting it fall in haphazard circles. He peered in curiously through the front window, but could see nothing except the shadowy fronds of a hanging fern.

Get moving. There are people in that front house. He went back to the barbecue pit and stuffed the rags he had brought on top of the debris already there. Then he poured some paint thinner around, not very much, and lodged the partially full can in the pit.

You can't stay and watch this one. You'll have to imagine it. The adrenaline rush was beginning to race his heartbeat. He took out a cigarette and lit it, savoring the blue flare of the little flame in the darkness. He took a few puffs. Then he stuck the cigarette against the inside of the matchbook, almost touching the cardboard but not quite. He folded the flap over, compressing the cigarette a little, and tucked the end in.

He cleared a space in the pit and laid the matchbook in it. Then he picked up the laundry bag, and, with one quick backward longing look, left.

He threw the laundry bag into an alley a block away, after scuffing his feet on it a few times. He threw the gloves over a fence. Then he went to the pay phone.

She answered at once, as if she'd been expecting it. It's been a long time. "A gift for you," he said. "The one hundred block of Henry Street."

She said nothing. He hung up. He began to run slowly, a man out jogging on a summer's night.

Jake Susman saw the fire trucks halfway down the street. Hell. Hope it's not too close. A few steps more he realized how close it was, and ran.

They had snaked a hose through the basement steps of the Victorian. A fireman blocked his way. "Can't get in there, buddy."

"But that's my house back there!" They had another hose going up the front steps. Charlie was standing on the sidewalk. "Charlie, what happened?"

"Dunno, man. We were partying, and all of a sudden— whoosh! Fire. These folks sure messing up our house."

"How bad—"

"Couldn't see. Looked like it started in the yard, but it spread fast." He spoke with unconscious relish. "You got insurance?"

"Are you kidding?" Jake grabbed at one of the firemen. There seemed to be fifty of them around the house. "Can I go in there—" he pointed to the first floor of the Victorian. "All I want to do is look. That's my cottage back there."

"Yeah, okay." Jake ran down the hall, jumping over the hose. Obscenely stiff with water, it went through the hall, into the kitchen, and out the back door into the yard. A fireman grabbed him before he got to the kitchen.

"But that's my *house!*" said. He looked over the man's shoulder. All he could see was flame.

"We've got to wet this place down; get outside! There's enough alcohol upstairs to fly a plane. You want the rest of the block to go, too? Get out of here!"

He went back into the street. A crowd had gathered. They always do at fires. Goddam ghouls. Disaster's a spectator sport. Smoke stung his eyes. A red glow came through the windows of the Victorian. The firemen were still inside. They came out, running, dragging the hose, and began to back into the street, playing a stream of water on the front of the house. "Back, get back." The police were there. Helplessly, Jake moved back. This isn't real, he thought. It's a movie by Sam Peckinpah.

Fire shot out the second-floor window of the Victorian.

Jake suddenly saw Marta.

She was backed against the street light, her eyes on the firemen—no, on the flames. He shoved his way over to her. "Marta!" he yelled. "What are you doing here?"

For an instant he thought she had not heard him, and he took a breath to yell again. Then she turned to stare at him. She seemed to be looking at him from very far away.

She nodded, once, and then, as if pulled by a magnet, she turned back to the flames. Christ. Oh, Christ. His mouth was suddenly dry. He wet his lips to talk to her. Another tongue of flame shot out the window of the house. Her whole body shook.

He understood, then. But there was nothing he could say to her that she would hear. Dellara, he thought. But it barely seemed important.

He slumped against the street light pole. "Ahh," said the crowd, moving restlessly. The fire made a hungry sound. Then it began to eat out the front of the house.

•The Woman in the Phone Booth•

This story is a piece of fluff. Once every year I write something like this, just for fun. It will usually end up in the garbage. But this one seemed more coherent than the others, so I sent it out, and people seemed willing to give me real money for it! That's more than I would have done.

I am riding the bus, coming home from work on the 22 line like I always do, when I see this woman sitting in a phone booth.

She isn't making a call. She isn't waiting for one either; people are impatient when they do that, and they keep looking at the phone. She's just sitting on the floor of the booth, knees flexed, hands clasped around her knees, real relaxed.

I'm pretty close to my stop. So I get off and walk back up the hill to the corner. I do things like that. I want to know how come this lady is sitting in a phone booth.

I got nothing much against phone booths; sometimes they have great graffiti. They are plastic and too small and the phones rarely work. Clark Kent liked to change clothes in them, which maybe explains why he never made it with Lois Lane. I mean, who wants to go out with a guy who takes off his clothes in transparent boxes? But I never thought of them as being restful.

So I walk up to her, lean against the door, and say: "How come you're sitting in a phone booth?"

She doesn't tell me to flake off. She just looks up and says, "I'm waiting for a friend. But I'm early."

She's nice-looking. She has brown skin and brown eyes and long brown hair all pulled back and tied up on her head in some complicated way which I admire. Her eyes slant, which makes me wonder where she comes from, or her parents, or whoever. So I ask her. I'm not shy.

She tells me. It's a place I never heard of. "Where's that?" She points. Up.

"About fourteen light years away."

Now, I am not as dumb as some people think. She's telling me she comes from another planet. I don't believe it—I mean, suppose somebody tells you she comes from another planet, you expect her to look weird, or smell weird, or something. Well, this woman has five fingers on each hand, and two eyes, and one nose, and she smells of toothpaste. So I know she is putting me on.

But I get off on other people's fantasies, too. "Then how come you're sitting in this phone booth?" I ask her. "Shouldn't you be in Washington, saying, *Take me to your leader?*"

"Him?" She laughs. "Who wants to talk to him?"

I happen to agree with her, no argument there. I laugh, too.

"Phone booths are very useful," she says. "Anyone can use one. They're practically free. They appear in every city and town in most civilized countries. They're light, easily movable, and no one is surprised to see one—or to see one gone. This one"—she pats the plastic—"has been traveling with me for almost five months."

Wha—wait a minute. Flying phone booths? Is this the answer to the UFO racket? But she looks so serious that I get kind of edgy. Mostly just for something to do, I lean in to look at the phone. "Oh, it doesn't work," she says. "We disconnected it. We got it in Chicago."

I look at the dial. The area code is 312, and the prefix is one I've never seen before.

I decide to humor her. "Why," I ask, "are you, an alien from another planet, traveling around in a phone booth? It's not very, um, elegant. If you want to communicate with our government, or take us over, or something, why don't you land in your spaceship?"

"Why would we want to do that?" she says.

"Then what are you doing here?"

"Studying," she says, kind of primly.

"Oh, a government survey." I can't help my tone. I know about those things. My brother works for some regional office that's always doing them, and he makes $17,000 a year for stamping forms with a red stamp and putting them on someone else's desk.

"Oh, no." She shakes her head. A bus goes by, going the other way, and she stops talking to look at it. "Just a school. Comparative galactic cultures 437."

"Graduate school?" I guess. A friend of mine who went to graduate school told me about spending six months in Nepal.

"Like that. I didn't have the money but my mother lent it to me for an early graduation present."

"When do you graduate?"

"In ¢%#¢@$." I don't know what she said. It makes me nervous again. I don't believe, really, that this woman is an alien. I'm not sure how she gimmicked the phone booth, but you never know about the phone company, maybe they borrowed a booth from Illinois Bell and haven't gotten around to changing the number and hooking up the line. Maybe it is hooked up. I only have her screwy word for that.

I pick up the receiver, take out a dime, drop it in the slot, and dial a number. The door closes, pushing me inside the booth. I reach one hand to open it. It's stuck.

"I told you it didn't work!" She takes the phone from my hand and sets it back on the cradle. Now she's standing up. I can see why she sits on the floor in phone booths. She's way over six feet. Her head bumps the top of the booth and she has to kind of hunch down. It's pretty cramped. "Now you've called the ship!"

"What ship?"

"They come whenever anybody starts to use the phone. The door locks automatically. I was going to wait here for them but I'm early, and they'll think you're a specimen." She glares at me. "I can't take you. I talked to you. Go away. Now. Go!" She does something brusque. The door snaps open.

I go. I scramble the hell away from that thing as if it were radioactive. I scoot across the street, and the kids who're playing on the sidewalk stare at me. Maybe I look funny. I sit down on a stoop to catch my breath. Then I watch, real quietly.

And what I see is—nothing. Whatever comes down out of the sky is invisible, but it isn't transparent. It's, whadayacallit, opaque. I see a blank, moving across a backdrop of old painted houses and dirty street. It's dizzying. I can't look at it. So I look at the phone booth.

She's inside it standing up with the door closed, and, I guess, locked. I bet she's making up some kind of story to tell. *Someone left a dime in the phone, and I was just playing around...*

I see the ship come down. I see that nothingness, that hole, engulf the phone booth from top to bottom, as if a door opened in the bottom of the ship and swallowed the booth up. Then it lifts. I see the street reappear. The ship goes up very fast, and then it's gone.

And that's all.

I've never seen her again. I've seen people who look like her, but hell, she looked so normal! If I ask some tall guy, "Hey, are you an alien?" I'll probably get punched in the nose. And I haven't written any letters to the papers, no. They'll all think what you're thinking, that I'm some kind of a nut. I did think of checking up on missing persons. But I don't know how to do it; I don't have the chutzpah to ask grieving relatives: "Was he maybe just going out to make a phone call?"

I didn't get a chance to ask her: *Do you put them back?*

If I could think of something to do, I'd do it. Can you? See, I told you.

Just be real careful where you use the telephone.

•Don't Look At Me•

This, like many of my stories (and books) straddles
categories. It is a science fiction story, a crime story,
a love story, a mystery, a chess story (sort of), a story
about sleight of hand, a story about telepathy. Mostly,
it is a story about what it feels like to be different. It
was written for Cedric Clute, who edited the magical/
mystery anthology *Sleight Of Crime*. It was to go in the
second volume. That volume never materialized, and
Cedric gave me permission to offer it elsewhere. Roy
Torgeson bought it for *Chrysalis 2*.

The magician's hands say: *Look at this!*

His feet and legs crossed yogi-fashion in the seat of the
armchair in the lounge, Mischa Dramov is playing with the
cards. He cuts, shuffles, makes the picked card disappear,
plucks it out of the air again. A crowd gathers to watch the
impromptu performance. He speaks no patter; he mimes. They
murmur applause.

"Misdirection," he says to them. "Illusion."

("Mama, why is he so small? I'm bigger than he is!"—
"He's a dwarf, that's why."—"Is he sick?"—"No. It's a thing
you're born with, honey, like the color of your hair.")

ALL PASSENGERS DISEMBARKING ON ZOLL RE-
PORT WITH HAND LUGGAGE TO THE LOUNGE.

The metallic voice repeats the command twice, in six lan-
guages. The magician stacks his cards and folds his hands atop
them. All but one of the spectators drift away: to the bar, to
their staterooms, or closer to the giant observation window
across the huge lounge through which they can watch the stars.
She stays. She had been sitting way in the back during the
show the night before. It helps to have a face to play to; hers

had stood out, pale skin and tight pale curls singular in a mass of dark faces, dark hair. He had played to her. She says: "That was fascinating."

"Thank you."

"I loved the show last night."

"Most of it was improvised. Our big pieces of equipment are crated."

"When your partner did the trick with the linking rings I tried to watch her hands but I couldn't. She's dazzling, with that height, and the silver skin and hair!"

"That's the effect we work for," he answers, pleased. Proud.

"Is it a wig?" she asks.

"Chaka's hair? No, it's real."

She nods. It's the first gesture he has seen from her. She sits with straight back, very controlled, hands still, not moving, except for her eyes. Her eyes are light turquoise, and very wide. Cosmetic lenses? He wonders.

She says, "My name is Elsen Zakar."

He inclines—a bow. "Mischa Dramov."

"Where are you from?"

"From Earth—Terra."

"Are you? Maybe I will go there one day. What is it like?"

"I never think about the places I have left," says the magician, "only about the place I am going."

"Where are you going?"

"To Zoll."

"So am I," she says softly.

To vacation, he thinks, to lie in the sun, to be entertained, to watch the show. Ah, well. Mischa, she is making polite conversation with you, the funny little magician, that's all. "I'm told it's one of the most beautiful planets in the Living Worlds," he says politely.

"It's a paradise."

"You've been there before?"

"I was born there. It's warm, gently warm, all over. If you like cold, there's cold at the poles, and snow in the mountains. You can float a glider off a snow-covered peak and ride the currents down into the valley...I've done that. The oceans, too, are warm. But now," she says, "I live on Gilbert's World."

He cannot remember what it is he knows about Gilbert's

World. It is famous for something. As Zoll is famous for its beauty and because it is a world of telepaths. Mischa thinks, I have never met a telepath before. Automatically he begins to shuffle the cards. Misdirection. Illusion. "We will be working at a hotel in Rigga—the Embassy Hotel."

"I'm staying in Rigga. At the Embassy Hotel."

ALL PASSENGERS DISEMBARKING ON ZOLL PLEASE ASSEMBLE WITH HAND LUGGAGE IN THE LOUNGE.

Space between the chairs begins to fill. The ship will be landing soon on Zoll's larger moon. People press towards the window. Mischa says, "You don't want to watch the landing?"

"I've seen it before. Many times. You?"

"I can't. My eyes are on a level with most people's waists. Chaka rubbernecks for both of us."

"Yes. I can see her there." She is watching the crowd. Five people float out of it to hang, legs decorously crossed, above everybody's head, even Chaka's. Large brown ghosts in sports clothes. One of them is holding a tennis racket. She waves to them. The one with the tennis racket waves back.

("Mama, look, they're flying!"—"No, they're teleports from Gilbert's World. It's a thing they can do, like you can read music, and Uncle Henry can dance.")

Mischa watches her, half-expecting her to float up and join them. But no, her feet remain firm against the metal floor of the ship. "You have family on Zoll?" he asks.

"My father is Elk Zekar, the chess player. You've heard of him?"

"No."

"I visit him every year."

Then why is she staying at the Embassy Hotel he wonders, if she has family to stay with? and then feels a fool. He fumbles with the cards. Drops one.

"What is it?" she asks.

"I'm sorry. I've never met a telepath before."

"You haven't now. I am not a telepath. And you won't on Zoll. The Zollians never go to the Embassy Hotel, or anywhere else the tourists go, and the tourists may only go to certain places on Zoll. Non-telepaths are too coarse, too insensitive and raw for Zollian telepaths to be near."

"But you—"

"I stay at the hotel when I come to Zoll, or I would destroy my father's peace, his harmony. Peace and harmony are very important to good chess, you know. I visit him for a few hours. That is all of me he can stand—and I of him." Her mouth twists.

"I understand."

"Do you?" She looks at him. He almost puts his hands up to hide his eyes. "Yes, you do." Her voice softens. "You know what it feels like to be a freak, to be gawked at and then shoved out of sight, to be teased and scolded for something you can't hide and can't change."

"Yes."

"You don't want to meet a telepath, magician, take my word for it." She leaves him.

Chaka strides up and sinks into the vacated chair. "What's her name?"

"Elsen Zekar," he says.

"Those people in the air are blocking my view," Chaka says, bemused. She stretches her long legs out into the aisle, and kicks someone in the ankle. "Sorry." She curls her legs with a grimace—"Fooey! Everything on this ship is so damn small!"

Mischa Dramov, who stands four feet three inches tall with shoes on, and for whom everything everywhere is so damn tall, smiles.

Yoshio Atawak is the owner of the Embassy Hotel. He is a mammoth of a man.

"Come in, come in! Sit down! They call me the Ambassador. Want some lunch?" Two platters piled with food take up the entire top of his six-foot desk. "No? Not even a snack?" He leans forward—the chair groans—to offer Chaka a can of what could be salted nuts or sautéed bacon bits or tempuraed grass-hoppers. "No? How about some beer? *Beer!*" he roars. His secretary staggers in with a pitcher of dark foamy beer and three huge steins. "Glad to have you with us. *Contracts!* Your shows will be a welcome change from the usual entertain-ment—bad bands and worse dancers and rotten comics. You thought this was a classy joint, right? Nobody intelligent comes to Zoll. If I didn't own the hotel I wouldn't be here either. *Sign here.* The Zollians are a pack of standoffish wet fish, and the tourists are rich bums. Rich and drunken bums."

Chaka asks, "What do they come here to do?"

"Swim, sun, climb mountains, ski, sail, play tennis, fly gliders, and talk to each other about it. They won't appreciate you. But I will."

"What do you do?" asks Mischa, liking him.

"Eat. And play chess with Vadek. You have heard of Vadek Amrill. He is chess champion of the Living Worlds, here to play a match. He is staying at the hotel, and every morning I play chess with him, over breakfast. I am *his* breakfast. You must meet him; he is intelligent, he'll like you."

As they cross the lobby, Mischa sees a familiar face. Hair like pale wire. Turquoise eyes.

A woman with a surfboard nearly knocks him down. "Watchwhereyuhgoing!" she snarls. "Creep!"

He ignores her—he maneuvers across the room. "Elsen."

Turquoise eyes like beams of coherent light. She looks at him. *She looks at him.* "Mischa," she says. "Hello."

"May I take you to lunch?"

Chaka says, "Mischa, we're doing a show tonight!"

"A short lunch?"

"Well—I'm due this afternoon at my father's house. Lunch—I would like lunch. Maybe I'll wait till tomorrow to see my father. He won't care. I would like to see your first show on Zoll."

"Mischa!"

Lunch. Dinner. They meet and touch in a dark room. "How old are you?"

"How old are you?"

"Are you happy, Elsen?"

"Happy . . ." Her hands are small in the darkness.

"May I stay with you tonight?"

"Yes," she says, "stay. Stay."

In the morning she says, "I cannot see my father today, I am too content."

"I am glad."

"I will go tomorrow, I must."

"I will stay with you until you leave the hotel."

"You will not!" She turns on him. "No one sees me then. Anger is ugly."

"You hate him so much?"

"Wouldn't you hate someone who never saw what you were, only what you were not, and despised you for what you couldn't be or do, and claimed nevertheless to love you?"

"People cannot always see the thing they love clearly."

"Zollians know nothing of love. They suppress and fear it, like all emotion. Love, hate, pain, joy, you never let go, you are never free to feel—" She is crying. "Leave me, Mischa. Please go."

"No," he says, touching her back.

She trembles in the bed, and then turns to him again.

He meets Vadek Amrill in the hotel lobby. He is small, for a non-dwarf. On sight, Mischa likes him. He is thin and tense and powerful.

"I liked your show last night," he says.

"Thank you."

"Have breakfast with me?"

"I don't play chess," says Mischa.

"I cannot palm cards."

They sit and talk about nothing. Vadek sets up a practice game. Almost under the table, the magician's hands play with his cards, turn them, stroke them, ace of spades, ace of clubs, ace of diamonds, ace of hearts, jack of diamonds, *look at this, look at this!*

Vadek Amrill says, "You do not have to do that with me, you know."

Startled, Mischa stops.

A commotion at the lobby door heralds the emergence of Yoshio Atawak from his office. "Good morning, Vadek! Ready to beat me?"

"Certainly." Vadek clears the board of his practice game and together they set the pieces up. They make an odd trio; the huge hotelier, the thin chess champion, (eyes of dark grey, like stone) and the beardless dwarf. "But you shouldn't be so certain of your loss, Ambassador. You're improving."

"*Beer!* Vadek, you flatter me ridiculously. You played better chess when you were nine than I do now. *And sandwiches!*"

They bring an extra chair to hold the platter of food.

Vadek says to Mischa, "It's too bad you don't play chess."

Mischa picks up a black pawn and makes it disappear. "Check." Vadek laughs. Mischa brings the pawn back. "I can't sit for hours with my legs dangling."

"If you played chess you could."

Yoshio Atawak says, "Only if you are a monomaniac. Vadek, you'd sell your soul to the devil for the chance to beat him at chess. When is your match with Elk Zekar?"

"Yoshio, I thought you knew everything."

"I do not. Almost everything. Is it tonight?"

"No—a few days."

"His daughter is staying in the hotel, you know, Elsen Zekar." Yoshio is looking at Mischa. Under the table Mischa's hands are moving: look at this look at *this!*

Vadek says, "Is she?" He examines the chess board, unconcerned. But after a moment he says gently, "Mischa, stop that."

Mischa stops.

Yoshio Atawak looks at them both, and then shrugs.

Mischa asks, "What is Elk Zekar like?"

"I like him," Vadek says. "I like the way he plays chess."

Atawak says, "I admire you. I would not agree to contest a telepath at tying shoelaces."

"Can you still tie your own shoes?" says Vadek. He moves a pawn.

"Of course. No matter that it takes me an hour to bend down." Atawak moves a pawn. Vadek moves a bishop. "Now why the hell did you do that?"

Mischa asks, "Will you win this time, too?"

"I think so."

"Are you still happy, Elsen?"

"Happy . . . Yes."

"Don't go tomorrow. Stay another day in the hotel with me. One more day."

"Another day . . . But then I must go."

"Why if it makes you so unhappy? Why must you see him at all?"

She will not answer him.

• • •

Yoshio Atawak sticks his head into the closet dressing room. It is all that he can get inside the door. "Message for you from Vadek," he says. "He will not be at the show tonight, because he is playing that chess game, but he sends his regards."

Mischa nods. He has become used to the champion's presence during the shows, just as he has become used to Elsen's warmth in the dark night . . . "I wish him well."

"I saw him off. He seemed confident. Chess games take hours sometimes. I don't think he ate enough dinner, either—"

"By whose standards, Yoshio?"

"Oh, not you too, Mischa!"

Mischa escapes to the stage. He misses Vadek—but Elsen is there, pale skin, pale hair, eyes like gems. She is going to see her father in the morning, he has not been able to talk her out of it. What is a telepath in a bad mood like? he wonders. Do Zollians let themselves have bad moods? Will her father be in a bad mood if Vadek beats him at chess?

Almost, he wishes that Vadek would lose.

He looks for Elsen after, but she is gone, and he guesses that she is hiding from him. ("Anger is ugly, Mischa. Go away, don't look at me!")

"Mischa, Mischa." Chaka's voice. Reluctantly he comes awake in a bed that is too big for him. Chaka is leaning above him. "Mischa, please wake up. Vadek's in jail!"

"Jail?" A nightmare—he is not awake.

"Wake up! They say he murdered that Zekar person."

Mischa comes awake. "Atawak."

"He isn't here, he's at the jail. He called from there. It's morning. He asks us to come there, Mischa. Vadek asked for you."

"For me?"

They meet Yoshio Atawak at the jail. His face is blotchy. His secretary is with him. "I spoke with Dov Dolk, the prosecutor. It seems that Vadek went in to play the match with Zekar—and walked out of the room a few moments later, dazed, with a bloody letter opener in his hand. Zekar was dead on the floor. They let me see Vadek a moment, only a moment. He asked for you. Then he kept saying my name over and over, as if it were a rock he could hold on to." The secretary holds out a sandwich. Atawak takes it and stares at it in loathing. "I don't want it. Take it away."

"But you haven't eaten!"

"Take it *away!*"

The room in the jail is bare, white, dreadful, and Vadek sits in its center and shivers, as if cold. "I can't remember," he says. Panic nibbles the edges of his voice. "I went to the study—the pieces were all set up; it's a beautiful set, blue and white on a crystal board—Zekar came round the desk to meet me. He was smiling. I *think* he was smiling. I felt warmth, and then a wave of fear, anger, hatred and rage, like an electric shock. It was horrible. I don't know what happened then. I was holding the letter opener and Zekar was bleeding on the floor." He shakes. "They took away my chess set, the little peg one. It was in my pocket. I wish I had it."

The prosecutor deigns to speak with them, her distaste for non-telepaths plain in her thinned lips, her shuttered eyes. "We have ascertained that there were no other visitors to Elk Zekar's house. Vadek Amrill was alone with Elk Zekar. The story he tells, the hatred he says he felt, were his own. Zollians do not hate, we are disciplined."

"Vadek—Vadek's not like that," Mischa says. Dov Dolk looks down at him and does not answer. "What will you do to him?"

"We have doctors for such people. We will fix him."

"Change him?"

"For the better, I assure you. It does not hurt."

Vadek says, "What do they say, Mischa?" Mischa tells him. Atawak is roaring protest in the halls. "Change me? What am I, an animal? A freak? What will they turn me into? They cannot make me a telepath. What will they take from my mind?"

"Don't, Vadek."

"Will they take my *chess?*"

Mischa walks out into the hall. Atawak is raging; Dov Dolk is icy cold. Mischa holds his cards, shuffles, palms. Misdirection. Illusion. Atawak is purple and his voice is shaking the walls. *In another minute they will throw us out.* Dov Dolk is holding her head in pain.

"Yoshio. Yoshio!"

"What!"

"Shut up." Yoshio shuts up. Mischa says to the prosecutor, "Please listen to me. For just a little while."

They have drugged her and blindfolded her. "Elsen?" he says.

"*You* told them."

"Yes."

"Why did you tell them?"

"For Vadek—and all of us."

"How did you know? I handed *him* the letter opener."

"You used my techniques. Misdirection. Illusion. You gave the Zollians Vadek, knowing their dislike and contempt for non-telepaths would blind them. But I know Vadek. The hatred was not his, it was yours, funnelled through your dying father's mind. Your fear, your anger, your rage. It dazed Vadek as you knew it would."

"It did. Why didn't it blind you, too?"

"I looked at you, and remembered where you live, where you chose to live. On Gilbert's World. A planet of teleports."

"You looked at me. Mime, magician, freak, why did you look, why did you speak? It was easy; it was so easy. You gave me the courage to do it, Mischa. I loved you a little. Trapped—you trapped me. Tell me, will Chaka be your lover, freak? Will Vadek? Will anyone again? Who would want you, with your little boy's body, but a freak and a fool? We all make a magic, magician; the illusion is the loving. I am a freak, she is a freak, he is a freak, you are a freak—ugly little man—I hate you, Mischa Dramov! I hate you."

Ace of spades, jack of diamonds, queen of hearts, joker. Play, hands, play with the cards.

ALL PASSENGERS DISEMBARKING ON LYR RE-PORT WITH HAND LUGGAGE TO THE LOUNGE.

("Hey, Mama, look at that funny little man!"—"Ssh! It's rude to point. Remember him—that's the magician!")

Don't look at me, say Mischa Dramov's hands, don't look at me, look at the cards, look at *this,* don't look at *me.* DON'T LOOK AT ME!

•Jubilee's Story•

The original title of this story was "Gimme Shelter." Virginia Kidd, when she bought the story for *Millennial Women*, asked if she might change it, saying she felt it was somewhat obscure. I agreed. Upon reflection, I think she was probably right. But I wanted you, the readers, to know about it, because I wanted you—those of you who can—to remember what the Stones were singing about in that song, to remember what it felt like to exist so consciously at the moment of change. Remember the lyrics: "It's just a shot away . . . it's just a kiss away." There are moments in our lives when we can feel the universe pivot. I tried to show one of those moments, which are always personal and often quite small, through the mind of Jubilee.

Jubilee, Apprentice Historian, to Dorian, Historian of the White River Pack: Greetings.

I wanted to make this History very orderly, very formal, as you taught me. But it's hard to do that, sitting here in a strange room, trying to write, trying to remember. Memories aren't orderly. Hannako, the Historian here at Ephesus, says that confusion always happens when one is newly come to the page. She says I should write the story any way I want to. So I will just set it down as I would tell it pretending that I am home, talking to my little sister. Today is Tuesday, June eleventh. We entered the territory of Upper Misery Friday evening.

Elspeth was going to Ephesus to live with Josepha for a while. Josepha was going to have her fourth baby. I was going with Elspeth because I wanted to see Josepha, too, and because I love going to new places. Ruth came with me so that we could be together. And Corinna traveled with us to take care of us, because not all of the territory between White River and Ephesus is safe. Corinna is an amazon.

The territorial markers for Upper Misery were very odd. They were only pieces of old wood, with scribbled chalk words across them, as if a child or someone very feeble had put them up. I asked Elspeth, when we first saw them, "Why would anyone choose to name a place Upper Misery?"

She shrugged. "Overweening pessimism."

It was very quiet. Birds screamed sunset challenges at us from all the trees. Corinna went on ahead of us. She came back to tell us, "There's no town." There was just a jumble of ramshackle buildings surrounded by scored farmland. I think the road had once been paved, but now it was all chopped up with holes, and covered with dust and brush. It looked rarely used. No one had tried to repair it.

We went past the buildings. There was one well-kept house. "I wonder where the people are," Ruth muttered. "It's weird."

"In that house," Corinna said. I thought I saw a face look through a window at us. But no one came out.

We found an abandoned barn to sleep in. "Maybe they think we're devils," Corinna said. "Gah, this place stinks of horse dung!"

"They can't be that ignorant," Elspeth said. "Though we are surely dangerous to them, if they follow the old customs. Free women!"

We all smiled. Ruth stretched, showing off her muscles. Ruth is very strong, and very beautiful. "Even living in this pigsty, they must believe they're free," she commented. "What is the opposite of us?"

Elspeth was suddenly somber. "Slaves."

The visitor came while we were eating breakfast. "Well?" Elspeth said.

He flushed under his red beard. They are not used to women talking to them like that. Then he said: "My wife—Kathy— she's going to have a baby. Maybe today. She's thin, very small, maybe too small to bear a child—" He stopped in mid-spate. "We are all alone here," he said.

Just looking at her face, I knew what Elspeth would do.

"How old is Kathy?" she asked him.

"Seventeen," he said. Elspeth looked at me. That is only two years older than I am.

"I will come," she said.

Ruth said, "You will go into his house?"

Elspeth said, "What do you think, Corinna?" We all turned to her. She is tiny, like a fist, or an arrowhead. She seems lazy, until you see her move, and then she's fast as a thrown knife. I would not like to get in Corinna's way.

"What about Josepha?" she said.

"Josepha is not alone," Elspeth said.

"I think it will be all right," Corinna said.

"Thank you," the boy stammered. I could see that behind the beard he was probably not much older than seventeen himself.

We went with him into the travesty of a town, to that one unbroken house. As we entered the hallway, a man with a big gray-and-red beard came out of a door. "Jonathan—I told you I didn't want them," he said angrily.

Jonathan said, "Kathleen is *my* wife."

The older man scowled and then seemed to change his mind. He said, "Since you've done it, it's done." And went back into the room he'd come out of. On its door was a piece of board with a word chalked on it, like the markers. It said: *Library*.

"He is my father," Jonathan said. "He is sick, and tired. Mostly he sleeps and reads. But he likes to think that he is still master of the house, and we let him think so."

Corinna asked, "Who else lives here?"

"Me," said Jonathan, "and Kathy. And my brother Simon."

We heard, then, from back inside the house, a wailing call, a woman's voice. Jonathan tensed. "That's Kathy," he said.

"Take us there," said Elspeth.

They had her trussed up in the old way, lying flat on the bed, with sheet strips hanging limp and ready for her to pull upon. She was breathing in raggedy chops. When we came in, she scrabbled for a sheet to cover herself, as if there were something to be ashamed of in being ready to give birth! It made me angry, but I pushed the anger out. It is not a useful tool to deal with fear. She was looking at us with wild eyes, as if her fear and Jonathan's fear for her had driven her a little mad.

I sat down on the chair by the bed. "Hello," I said. I took her hand. It was cold, despite the heat of the room. She gripped my fingers as if she would tear them off.

"Can you help me?"

"We came to help you," I said. "Jonathan brought us. My name is Jubilee. That is Elspeth. The tall woman is Ruth, and the short one is Corinna."

"She is small, too," said Kathy.

"Yes," said Elspeth, over my shoulder, "and so am I small, but I have three children." I tried to get up to give Elspeth my seat, but Kathleen kept hold of my fingers so tightly— "You sit, Jubilee," Elspeth said. "You are doing fine." I was pleased. I have seen births before, of course, even difficult ones. But this was different. Elspeth was really saying to me: *I trust you not to make a mistake.* That is a real compliment from one's mother.

Just then Kathleen gripped my hand so painfully that I wanted to yell, too. Her fingers were thin as twigs—but strong! "It hurts!" she cried.

"Let me see," Elspeth said. I moved my chair. She drew the covering away, and put her head between Kathy's drawn-up legs. Then she straightened up and laid a hand gently on the woman's belly. Kathleen moaned—from fear, I think, not because it hurt. Why should it? "Your pains just started, right?"

"Yes," said Kathleen.

"Are they close together?"

"N-no."

"Good," said Elspeth. "Very good. I don't think this is going to be as hard as you think."

Jonathan came up to the bed. "You hear that, Kathy?" he said.

I let Jonathan have my seat (and Kathy's hand). Her contractions were coming about every ten minutes, but I knew they could go on for hours like that. She didn't know how to breathe; she was breathing with her neck and shoulders rigid and her belly tense. And she kept looking at Jonathan with this loving-guilty glance, as if she was ashamed of what was happening to her.

There was a sudden noise outside the door of the room, and it opened, hard, banging back against the wall. Kathleen shrank into the bed. A man walked in. Like Jonathan, he had red hair;

it was the thing I noticed about him first of all. He looked at Kathy, and then at us, and then at Jonathan, who stood up.

"Hello, Simon," he said.

"Who let *them* in here?"

"Papa said they could come," said Jonathan.

The other man made a brushing motion with one hand. "Papa can barely see to piss," he said. "You brought them."

"Yes."

Simon clenched a fist and stepped forward. Jonathan didn't even put up his hands. The blow caught him on the side of the face and sent him back against the wall.

I saw Corinna move close to Elspeth.

"You ask *me*," said Simon. He turned toward the bed. I could smell his sweat. "Kathleen," he said. "You want them here?"

"Yes, Simon. Please." He stared at her. Her hands were twisting the sheet. Her breasts were bare. She didn't cover them up.

"They can stay," he said. "For the baby—they can stay."

"Thank you," she said.

Jonathan waited until Simon left before he moved. Then he came and sat in the chair by the bed and reached for Kathleen's hand. "We shall have to go away," he said. "When the baby is born, Kathy, we'll go away."

Kathleen tensed, and then cried out softly, as a contraction came and went. "Not now," she said. "Not now."

Jonathan was little help, but we couldn't tell him to get out. Elspeth let me sit with Kathleen, talk to her, rub her back, and show her a little about breathing. Her water broke, and it made her feel better. The contractions began to come faster, and that made her feel better, too. "I just don't want it to last too long," she said. She tried to breathe like I told her, what we call sea breathing, long and steady, rising with the contraction. "Hours and hours, they say. I can stand anything as long as it doesn't last too long." Every once in a while Elspeth came to look at her and reassure her. "Please," Kathy said to her, "keep him out."

"Who?" Elspeth asked.

"Simon. Keep him out."

Jonathan looked hard at her. Then he looked away, at the floor.

She was in labor for about twenty-four hours. We stayed, of course. She gripped my hand, and talked to me. "We're all alone. The old man's crazy, writing his words all over the walls. No one comes here anymore...Jonathan visited Ephesus. I've never been there. We farm. There's no one here to talk to. Who will the baby play with here? All alone..." Jonathan sat in the room and grew paler and paler. Every so often Elspeth sent him out to get himself or one of us water or food.

Around four in the morning, I went out for a breath of air. Simon was there. He saw me and came over to me. "She's all right." It was not a question but a demand. "And the baby?"

"Still coming. Everything seems fine." I tried to sound sure, as Elsepth always sounds sure, even when she is saying "I don't know."

"It's too long."

"Not for a first labor."

"Is my brother in there now?"

"I don't know," I said.

He turned and made for the house. I followed him.

He went right into Kathy's room. She was wet with sweat and some tears, but she had learned that it made it worse to fight the pain and was trying to ride it out. Jonathan was not there. Simon bent over her. She put up a hand to thrust him off. "Get out of here!" she said with lovely fierceness. "I don't need you now."

"Bitch," he said to her, "the baby's mine. You can say it now. He's mine."

She slowly shook her head from side to side. "No," she said. "It's Jonathan's."

"Jonathan was away in September," he said. "All month."

"It's early," she said. "Eight months. Happens all the time."

"You can't know that," he said angrily. "You're just saying it."

"I'll say it," she said. "And say it and say it and say it." A contraction came. She breathed it down. They were coming every three minutes now. "Get out."

I thought he would hit her. But then he whirled and left the room, nearly knocking Elspeth down. Jonathan was just outside the doorway and moved aside to give him room.

At last the baby began to move fast. I always imagine it as

a little worm, pushing and shoving down the birth canal, even though I know that's not what happens at all. As the head crowned, Kathy screamed, a wide open-throated yell of triumph. The baby slid into Elspeth's hands. I was ready with the bath. In the warm water Elspeth stroked him, and he smiled, and we brought him to Kathy so she could see that luminous ecstatic smile of the newborn. Jonathan, who had been almost fainting, pulled himself together and came to look. "A boy," he said. "I must tell Papa."

Kathy said, "I want to wash." We brought her a towel and a clean sheet. She wiped the sweat from her face and neck and breasts, and held out her arms for her son—and Simon came in.

"Let me see him."

Jonathan stood in his way. "Simon," he said, "go away. Leave us with our son."

Simon laughed at him. "*Your* son," he said, with contempt. "Mine, Jonny. Who do you think kept Kathy sheltered from the cold, September, while you were away buying supplies in Ephesus? Papa?"

Jonathan's face worked like a child's. "It doesn't matter," he said finally. "Kathy's *my* wife."

Simon stepped up to him and pushed him. "*You* go," he said. "Go keep Papa company, him and his books. He'll be all that's left, when winter comes. Kathy and I'll be gone."

Jonathan flailed at him like a windmill, all arms.

Kathy grabbed for the baby as Simon fell across the bed. Simon sprang up again and lunged for Jonathan. The baby started to howl. The two men struggled, panting, Simon cursing. Jonathan had his hands around Simon's throat. Simon seized the oil lamp from the table and struck at Jonathan, once, twice—and the third time Corinna caught his arm and twisted the weapon away, very calmly, just as if it were practice.

Jonathan's cheek was bleeding. Oil slithered across his throat and his shirt. He lurched and fell down suddenly, and just lay there. I could see a crease across his skull, where the metal base of the lamp had hit him.

Simon looked down at him. He looked young, and afraid, and dreadfully like Jonathan.

The door opened. The old man stood there. "Jonathan," he

said. He looked at Simon. His voice was very hard. "Go away," he said.

Simon said hoarsely, "I'm going nowhere."

The old man took a step. "You will go. This is my house. I built it, with my two hands. Now it is stained—" His voice fumbled with that word, then picked up cadence again. "You *will* go." He pulled the door open with one hand. "Leave now."

Simon might have fought or defied another man. But with all of us looking on, and the force suddenly back in his father's voice, as it had not been for a long time, maybe, and his brother dead by his hand, he couldn't. He walked through the door, and we heard him go down the hall.

The father knelt. He tried to turn the body. Blood and oil smeared his hands. He looked up at us, and then spoke directly to Ruth. "Excuse me, sir," he said, "would you help me bury my son?"

They dug a grave for him, back of the house. We waited. Later Ruth told me about it, crying a little in the circle of my arms. "He talked to me about the farm, and how much work needed to be done on it before the winter, and how hard it would be, now that he was alone. He didn't mention Simon's or Jonathan's name, once."

After they finished the burial, the old man disappeared for a while. I heard hammering. I went toward it. It was him—he was hammering a piece of wood onto the door of Kathy's room, an old piece of wood chalked with a word.

The word was *Whore*.

Kathy would not open her door to us. Ruth raged at Elspeth for leaving. "How can you leave her there? With a newborn baby, and that hideous old man?"

Elspeth would only say, "She has to make her own choices."

We passed the old barn. For a moment I thought I saw someone standing in its doorway. We passed the last of the markers and went round a bend in the road—and Kathy was standing there, with the baby in her arms.

"Here!" she said. "Take him!"

Automatically Elspeth's arms went out. I grabbed the corked jug just as Kathy let that go. It dropped into my hands.

"Ephesus will be better for him than Upper Misery," she said. She pointed to the jug. "That's milk."

"Come with us," urged Ruth. "You don't have to stay."

"Simon's in the barn," Kathy said. "Skulking there. The old man will forget his strength soon. Simon will come back. I used to be Jonathan's wife—I'm still Simon's whore."

We took him with us, of course. We named him Nathan: it means "gift." He is going to live with Josepha—she says she always has enough milk for two. Did I say that he had red hair?

But Ruth and I keep thinking about Kathy, alone in that house, with Simon and that old man. We have talked about it. Ruth has decided: She wants to be an amazon. So we will be able to travel anywhere, just the two of us by ourselves.

One day, after winter is over, we will take that road again, to come home.

Kathy had said to me: "I can stand anything, as long as it doesn't last too long."

She will come. I am sure of it. She will come.

•*The Circus That Disappeared*•

Theodore Sturgeon once said, in my hearing, "Everyone has a circus story." I figured he ought to know. But *I* didn't—until I saw a squib in the newspaper which informed me that a circus in Britain (not a large country, after all) had been missing, lock, stock, and elephant, for three days. My imagination started to churn. Later I read that they found it, but by then I didn't want to know. After the story was published I got a letter from someone who had worked in a circus, praising me for having conveyed the authentic carnival flavor. I was very pleased, because I hadn't been in or near a circus for 20 years. But I didn't have the heart to tell her the truth.

Once again I have restored the title, from "Circus" to the original. Roy Torgeson, when he changed it, said that "Circus" was more succinct, but I think "The Circus That Disappeared" simply took up too much space on the page...

Evening was dark and warm beneath a sky spangled with stars and laden with the scent of elephant. Angelo sat on the top stair of the trailer. He was mending his leopard skin, which had ripped last week during his wrestling match with Lila, the lioness. Lynellen danced in the dusk a few feet away. Dressed in tights and one of his shirts, she was practicing her belly dancing. She looked sixteen, which was not the case. Bells tinkled on her wrists and ankles.

She sang, incongruously, *"Chicago, Chicago, that wonderful town!"*

"Can't you sing something else?"

"You're jealous," she said, "because you're not going home."

Angelo grinned. He recalled his home town, a half-assed, tired hick town in Marion county, Florida, with neither enthusiasm nor nostalgia. He had ridden a flatcar out of it when he turned fourteen. He'd never much wanted to go back. But he'd never liked Chicago, either, with its crammed streets and smelly imitation beaches. "I'm jealous you're singing a song to a goddam city and not to me."

She rippled her stomach muscles at him and went gliding away to the second trailer. The doors were shut, but Angelo could hear through the metal walls the raucous clatter of the rock music that Ricky loved, and played incessantly. In the three months they'd been on the road together he'd never heard the radio click off. The announcers' accents changed as they traveled, but the music stayed the same. Lynellen knocked on the door. As Millicent opened it the music yelled, sounding like a soul escaping into the night. Lila roared in her cage. She sounded lonely. Angelo rose.

You can put a circus anywhere. Everyone loves the circus. All you need is enough space and willing people to erect the tents, clean the grounds, water and feed the animals, and answer the telephone. *Marvel the Magician's Miniature Carnival* needed little space: a park, an old baseball diamond, any place with running water and a space to stick a gate. There are always people to help when the circus comes to town. Kids watching the highway see the trucks pull into town and drag their parents (whose memories of earlier circuses lie soft in their bellies) to look. They gape when Jugger and Angelo, the elephant and the animal trainer (also lion tamer, strong man, and catcher for the trapeze act) lug the big canvas tent out onto the grounds. Angelo and Jugger had played the same scene over four states. They would play once more tonight in this Indiana town. Ricky and Millicent in their clown makeup, Lynellen in her sequins, Tony in his tights, and Marvel the Magician in his ringmaster's get-up strolled into the crowd, saying, "Help put up the circus! Come on!"

And the kids, fresh out of high school and still on the farm, followed the giant black ringmaster or the dwarf clowns or the dancing acrobats to the pile of canvas, where Angelo told them: *"Here, hold this and grab those stakes, the frame's aluminum but the name of the game's the same, the tent goes up by sundown . . ."* pushing them with patter and jokes into a clumsy crew that, by god, got the tent up by sundown. It always worked. At sundown, when the tall lights flicked on, they hauled their friends to the tent. *"See this? I put this stake in, with Angelo, the strong man. Hey, Angelo!"* Angelo waved to them all, making up names—*"Hey, Curly, hey, Lefty, how ya doing?"*—to see them swell and grin.

Sometimes Ricky grumbled, "Is this the way to run a circus?"

Millicent always answered him. "Damn right." They all knew it was. The circus was more than a profession. It was a passion, it was their life, it was the only game in town. Each of them, Angelo and Lynellen and Ricky and Millicent and Tony, even Lila and Jugger (short for Juggernaut) was a Barnum bust, an act tossed out of other circuses for being too bad, too good, too simple, too subtle, too lazy, or too late. Lynellen had been a stripper, Tony had been tricking in Dallas, Angelo had been bumming, pitch to pitch, when Marvel picked him up. Each would give his skin to keep *Marvel the Magician's Miniature Carnival* in business.

Angelo heard Lila pacing. "Hey baby." She swung her great head toward him but refused to stop. He sat and talked to her. At last her pacing slowed. She stood against the bars, and when he put his hand through, licked it raspingly, a gesture of trust and affection. She had never, except in fear, hurt him. Tony joked, *"Her mother was an alley cat."* She was the tamest lioness Angelo had ever seen.

He said good-bye to her and went on to the other cage, where Jugger slept, standing immobile as a gray rock. Tony was filling her water tub. His shadowy form bent over it. Water splashed from the hose. He was talking. "You wanna go to Chicago, big mamma? I bet you don't. What d'you say we take a run. I open the cage, jump on your back. You run like hell. Think we can find you a bull elephant, maybe in some cornfield away from Chicago?"

Angelo said, "Jugger wouldn't know what to do with a bull even if you found her one."

Tony started. "Hey. You move like that damn cat," he said. "You could say hello."

"Sorry," said Angelo. He sat on a nearby crate. "Animals okay?"

"Restless," Tony said. "They donwanna go to no city."

Angelo nodded. Lila rumbled from her cage.

"Why are we going to Chicago, anyway?" said Tony. "The big shows go to Chicago. Shriner's. Ringling's. They don-wanna see us.

"I don't know," said Angelo. This had bothered him, too.

Tony shrugged with his palms. "I guess Marvel knows what he's doin'."

"I guess."

"You wanna go?"

Angelo dug a heel into the soft damp dirt. "Not much," he said.

"Why not?"

"I don't like cities. Too cold and hard. Buildings like metal and concrete boxes, and no trees."

"Um. I like cities sometimes." Tony spoke wistfully. "There's more people like me in 'em. I miss the bars."

"You could find a city gig," said Angelo.

Tony turned the hose so that it sprayed a dark puddle on the dusty ground. He shut it off. "City circuses got all the pretty boys they want, man." He spoke without bitterness, and with just a tinge of regret. "I'm getting too old for it. I'll stick with Marvel. He's a good manager. It's a good gig, getting the kids to roustabout, sticking to the small towns. He knows what he's doing." He pulled out a cigarette. "You thinkin' of leaving?"

"No," Angelo said. "I just don't want to go to Chicago."

"Yeah." Tony's cigarette glowed.

"You shouldn't smoke, it'll cut your wind."

The acrobat chuckled. "I'm thirty-five, my wind's shot anyway. I'm a has-been. We're all has-beens."

"Give me one," said the strong man. Tony passed him the pack. They sat in companionable silence while the music from the clowns' trailer leaked over the fairground, distant as if it came from another galaxy.

The next night the tent filled until it almost burst its seams. The kids played usher for their own neighbors, ran errands for Lynellen, and gingerly, under Angelo's direction, set up the movable lion's cage in the center of the ring. Two of them, with Ricky's rough and expert help, put on ruffs and whiteface and went to cartwheel and pratfall like professionals in front of Marvel as he strode to the ring, his whip snaking and snapping inches above their heads.

Angelo waited behind curtain for his cue. Marvel was a masterful showman. His deep voice resonated to every seat in the bleachers, making the tent expand until its one small ring seemed like three, or ten. Tony juggled. Lynellen danced. Then Marvel said, "In THIS corner, ladies and gentlemen, we present the most SPECTACULAR lion act you've ever witnessed, or ever will witness: Angelo the Animal Man, and LILA!" The audience applauded happily. They were ripe for it. Angelo gripped the loose skin at Lila's neck and took a long deep breath. The big cat gathered herself together. Tony drew back the curtain. They walked out.

The noise continued for a moment, and then stopped. They paced across the tent floor, the man in his leopard skin and the lioness, tawny fur gleaming under the lights, walking silent and controlled and loose at his side. This was Angelo's act, the act that Ringling and Shriner's would not take because it was too small, too dangerous, and because no audience (they said) would believe that a man could control a lion with his hands.

They stalked to the cage. Angelo opened the door. Lila went in. He followed her, and closed it behind him.

Out of deference to whatever T.V. circuses the crowd might have seen, Angelo put Lila through a balancing act (without chair or whip), jumping, walking the beam, and so on. The audience oohed and aahed and asked for more. Marvel looked at Angelo. Angelo nodded. He sat Lila down like a sphinx on the floor. Marvel played with words. Angelo no longer heard them, but he heard the tune they made. When it was time he held up his empty hands and walked towards Lila. Like the lioness she was, she crouched, growling with delight. He looked into her eyes and gestured. She rolled on her back, hind legs poised to rip him open, claws carefully gentled for her favorite game.

He lunged on top of her, hands against her neck. The audience shrieked. Angelo crooned at Lila and counted seconds. At the count of thirty he rubbed her throat and she went limp. He stood up and put his foot on her belly, clasping his hands above his head like a winning boxer. The people screamed and cheered and stamped on the benches. He lifted his foot. Lila rolled upright. He caught her ruff and with stately grace they retraced the walk to the curtained exit. Lila jumped into her home cage, curling up in a corner like the mythical alley cat. Jugger set her broad brow against the bars, and pushed the cage back to its place.

Angelo went to the trailer to change for the strong man's act. Lynellen was in it putting the finishing touches on her makeup. She wore sequins again. "Sounded good," she said.

He kissed her. "You smell good."

"I smell sweaty."

"That's what I mean." He tried to hug her but she slipped from his hands and ran toward the tent. Someday, he thought, we'll go somewhere alone, without Marvel, a faggot, two dwarves, a lion, and a goddamn elephant!

He pulled on the strong man's costume. It was made of scratchy gold net. Under the lights it glittered like golden chains. He found the ice bucket and took a handful of ice. He rubbed it down his sides and chest. It cooled him. He walked slowly back to the tent. From the tone of the laughter he could tell that Lynellen and Jugger were almost through with their part of the act.

"Angelo?" It was a whisper. He turned to meet it. She was scrawny and young, with feathery brown hair and stick-thin wrists. She held out a hand to him. "Can I talk to you, please?"

He thought, *Another one lovestruck.* But she didn't have that dreamy-eyed look. "What's up, kiddo?" he said lightly.

"Could—could I join your circus?"

He smiled at her. "Beautiful, you don't want to join the circus. The circus for you is one or two or three nights. But for us it's forever. You don't want that. Hell, you're in the circus now. Didn't I see you running around ushering?"

She nodded eagerly. "Yes. But I do want it forever. I can learn to dance, and to do the elephant act. See what I can do already!" Like a swift wheel she did an acrobat's flip. "Please, say that I can join."

"You don't have to join the circus just to get out of town," Angelo said gently. "Move to Chicago. Be a secretary."

"Secretary!" She infused terrible scorn into the word. "Would you be a—a bus driver when you could be a strong man? I *won't* be a secretary. Please. I'm old enough."

From the way she said it, Angelo knew she was not. "Sweetheart, it isn't my circus," he said. "This is *Marvel the Magician's Miniature Carnival*, and Marvel is the man who calls the shots. I work for him. I don't tell him what to do. You have to ask him."

"I have to ask him." She sighed, and walked away, head sagging. They never did, the glitter-struck kids. Marvel was unapproachable.

A hard fist struck Angelo's thigh. He looked down. "Get out there, you big hulk," said Ricky. "You're late."

So he went out there, and lifted weights. Ricky and Millicent came in and tumbled and played and teased the crowd, until Lynellen and Angelo and Tony could sweep back in, wearing black and silver and red, and climb to the trapeze. Ricky sat at the bass drum and went boom with each somersault. It was their tightest act, and they made it good, swooping and flying, until Marvel brought them down. They bowed the carnival to a close. Marvel raised his whip in crackling gratitude to the people of the town, "whose love of carnival makes it happen. But there's one more night of carnival, ladies and gentlemen," Marvel sang, "so don't despair, but be there!"

After the show they turned all but the trailer lights off, and sat in the great vacant tent. It cooled down. Ricky and Millicent sat together. Lynellen, in jeans and work shirt, prowled the tent with a plastic bag, picking up beer cans. Tony smoked a cigarette. Only Marvel did not share in this ritual. He was in his trailer. They talked a little of the show, of other shows. Tony's cigarette was almost spent when a slim figure in a silver leotard and blue tights danced into the tent. It was the girl with the feathery hair. She ran up to them. "He said *Yes!*" She turned a back flip for joy. "I asked him and he said *Yes!*"

"What the hell?" demanded Ricky.

"I asked Marvel if I could join the circus and he said I could!" She turned as Lynellen came up to her. "Can I wear this? He said I could ride the elephant, like you. My name's Susie Green. I don't—I don't have makeup. Can I borrow yours?"

"I—sure," said Lynellen.

"Oh, thank you. Thank you, Angelo. I'll see you all tomorrow." She waved and ran off. Lynellen turned to Angelo.

"Do you know that girl?"

"She came to ask me if she could join the circus, earlier tonight," he said. "I told her what we always tell them, to ask Marvel. They never do. You know they never do."

"Well, this one did," said Lynellen, hands on her hips. "Marvel must be crazy! She's a child, she can't be more than sixteen. You have to talk to him. We'll get arrested, or lynched!"

"Don't be silly," said Angelo uneasily. "He didn't mean it."

Tony said, from the darkness, "She thinks he does."

"You're the one said he knows what he's doing!" Angelo said. Tony shrugged.

"I want you to talk to him," said Lynellen.

"Jesus, I don't want to talk to him. Why should I? It's his business!" But Lynellen just looked at him. So did Ricky and Millicent. "All right. All right." Angelo got up. "Don't wait around for me, huh?" he said roughly. "I'll talk to him." He stomped away from them, annoyed that they all had been so quick to get him to speak to Marvel; why, if she wanted to say something to Marvel couldn't Lynellen have done it herself . . . ?

He went to the lion's tent. After a while four shadows came out of the big top, and drifted to the trailers. He heard the click of the doors. He did not want to talk to Marvel until Lynellen was in bed.

He knocked on the owner's trailer door. After a moment it swung open. Marvel stood just inside the doorway. "Angelo."

"Something on my mind," Angelo said.

"Come in." The ringmaster stepped back to give the strong man room. Angelo mounted the steps. The trailer was small; they crowded it. As always when they stood at arm's length from each other, Angelo felt dwarfed by Marvel's size. Though he was a big man, Marvel topped him, standing six-foot-eight, ebony black, supple, snaky smooth, big without bulk. It let him know how Ricky and Millicent felt. His trailer was bare, with a bed and shelves and a file cabinet. On the cabinet sat the phone and a huge fancy radio which was never played. "What is it?" The blacksnake whip stood in a corner casting a shadow across the floor.

"It's that girl," said Angelo.

"Yes." The syllable meant nothing. The ringmaster's face

was unreadable, barely visible in the dim light.

"She thinks you're going to let her join the carny, come with us to Chicago."

"Maybe I am," said the ringmaster.

"She's very young. We could get into trouble."

"My business, Angelo."

"I think it's our business."

"My business," said the black magician inexorably. "The door's behind you."

"Goddamn it, Marvel—" Angelo began. He reached for Marvel's shoulder, to shake him. "Listen—" He said the next word to the floorboards.

He didn't know how he'd got there. He could not remember being hit, but the taste of blood swelled under his tongue. He put his palms to the floor and started to rise. His muscles shook. There was no strength in them. He lay with his cheek to the floor, looking up. Marvel towered over him, whip in hand. Angelo had seen it cut. He shut his eyes.

"Poor Angelo." The words were a resonant croon. The hand descended. The whip snake, deliberately slow, cool, light, across his back and spine. The caress turned his belly to ground-glass knots. He couldn't move. The dark figure stepped over him, and was gone.

It seemed a long time before his body obeyed him again. He stumbled from the trailer and found his way to the animal cage. He felt violated. He knelt in the grass and was sick, rasping and retching. Then he wiped his mouth, stuck his head under the cold-water hose for a moment, and dragged himself to bed.

The next day he stayed out of Marvel's way.

"What did he say?" demanded Lynellen in the morning.

"He said it was none of my business."

"Is that all?"

"Yes. I don't want to talk about it, Lyn."

"All right," she said. "What's the matter, are you sick?"

"I don't know," he said.

"You're never sick." But she made him a cup of tea on the hot plate in the trailer, and sat with him while he drank it. It made him feel better.

When they went on that night, Sunday night, it was Susie

who rode Jugger around the ring. The audience roared its pleasure at this treat. She held the clubs for Tony when he did his juggling act, and after the weight lifting, she and Tony did some acrobatics, which consisted mainly of her posing from the security of Tony's shoulders. After the trapeze act she joined Angelo and Tony and Lynellen behind the curtain. She was bubbling. "Was I good? Was I all right?"

Lynellen said dryly, "Marvelous."

"Ssh!" said Angelo, waiting for his signal. Marvel stood in center ring. He gestured. This was the finale, his specialty. He did it only once in every town. Angelo dimmed the lights. The crowd quieted.

One red spot shone on the tall magician. Millicent, at the calliope, coaxed from it an eerie inhuman wail. Marvel extended the blacksnake whip, drawing slow hypnotic circles with it in the dust of the ring. (Angelo fought a sudden sickness.) As if pulled by a magnet, the dust rose and wreathed the magician, obscuring him within a lurid cloud. The music stopped. And the cloud began to shape itself. It shifted and writhed. A great coiling illusion of a snake reared its hooded head to the top of the tent. Its gaze transfixed the audience. A dark tongue flickered at them. A tail like a scorpion's arched over their heads. The snake hissed. Angelo trembled, chilled to his bones.

Then the illusion dissolved into swirling red smoke, revealing the magician standing alone in the ring. A hush measured the crowd's awe. Then the applause began. With a slashing beckon of his whip, Marvel brought his performers into the ring.

"Ladies, gentlemen, children, roustabouts," he bowed to the bench where the high school kids were sitting, "my deepest thanks to you all. *Marvel the Magician's Miniature Carnival*, the finest circus of its size you'll ever see, must leave you now. When you awake in the morning, we will be gone, a dream of straw and sawdust. But remember, as you dream tonight of the big top, that our carnival is a fleeting thing, but that all over the world, all over the universe, the Circus lives forever!"

The people roared love at them, heating the tiny tent until Angelo, holding Lynellen on one shoulder and Susie on the other, could hardly stand it. "Down, ladies," he muttered. Lynellen leaped down. Angelo looked up, to urge Susie to jump. The tent top had ripped somehow. He could see the stars through it. He started to speak, to say, "Look—" and a wave of heat, a dragon's exhalation, blazed at him, followed by a freezing, bone-snapping chill. The tent was transparent. He looked at stars; they were all around him, and it was cold. Then there was nothing at all.

He awoke in a little room, a bare-walled, metal room. He was naked. He was warm. The room had no door, no windows, just a cot without blankets for him to lie on. It looked and felt like a cage. He sat up on the cot.

As if it had been activated by his shifting weight, an opening appeared in the wall. He looked through it without moving from the cot. It led into a long metal corridor. He stood up and sat down again, wondering if he could make the door close. It didn't. Finally, he went into the corridor. The door closed behind him. He walked. The walls were cold. He was a bug scuttling inside a shiny metal box. When he got to the end of it, a second door appeared in front of him. Through it was a space, with chairs. On one of them, curled like a baby with her knees flexed, lay Lynellen. She was naked. He walked to her. Her eyes opened. She considered him.

"Angelo?"

"Yes."

She sat up, cross-legged. Finally she reached out a hand and drew him down to sit beside her. "Did you wake up in a little room?"

"Yes. Then a door opened and I came here."

"Me, too. I wonder if the others are here. I wonder where *here* is." He tried to put an arm around her. "No. Don't." So he didn't. They sat. A different piece of the wall opened, like a mouth, and Tony came in. He, too, was naked.

"Anybody know what the fuck is going on?" he said, with a stunning faggot swagger.

"No," said Angelo, but it made him smile. Lynellen smiled, too.

"Honey, it ain't Chicago," she said. Then she began to cry. Her whole body shook. "I don't like it," she sobbed. "I want to go home!" She stopped crying abruptly when Susie came into the room, crying even harder. She ran to the girl. "Hey, it's okay," she said. "Look, we're together. Ricky and Milly will be here, they'll show up any minute, you'll see. Nothing can be so bad if we're all together." Angelo felt a spasm of jealousy as she hugged and patted the frightened kid.

"If I don't get some attention," he said. "Tony and I will start holding each other."

"She needs it more than you do!" snapped Lynellen.

Angelo saw the look in Tony's eye, and was sorry. When Millicent and Ricky did walk in, he turned to them. Ricky was subdued. Milly wouldn't look at them. She curled on a chair, just like Lynellen had been when Angelo found her.

"What's the matter with her?" Angelo asked Ricky.

Ricky said, "She's naked."

"We're all naked."

"Yeah. But she's a naked dwarf. That's ugly. I don't care, but she does."

The door opened again.

What came in was—nothing. Before the door closed Angelo glimpsed a scattering of ice-white stars in a black sky. But there was something strange in the room now. It showed as a blurring of light and a twisting of dimension, a discontinuity that crawled up the wall and halfway over the ceiling. You couldn't look at it, but you couldn't see through it. Angelo tried and his eyes filled with tears. Lynellen, scared and angry, said, "Damn you, be one thing or another!"

A familiar deep voice said, "What I really am you would not want to see."

Ricky jumped. "Marvel?"

Silence. Within the blur of light Angelo saw a dark shadow thicken, until the ringmaster stood before them, uncertain like a picture out of focus, carrying the blacksnake whip, dressed in his tails and top hat. Lynellen said. "What—who are you? Where are we?"

"You are on—*gabble*." The word came out nonsense to their ears. "I am the ringmaster."

"What have you done with Lila and Jugger?" Angelo demanded. "What happened to the circus, the tent, the people—"

The form within the blur faced him. "They did not come with us," Marvel said. The whip in his hand undulated rhythmically, like some monstrous tail. "We left them."

Lynellen's voice rose, "Where are we?"

One whole side of a wall, like a picture screen rolling up

after a movie, slid out of sight. Behind it, going on and on into infinity, were only stars. Even Milly lifted her head and uncurled her stumpy body to look. Susie giggled. The sound was shocking in the alien place. "He turned the tent into a spaceship and poof!" she said, and shook, weeping without sound, her fists like claw on the smooth, cool fabric of the chair.

Angelo said, "You're a thing from the stars. From another planet? You brought us here. Why? For what?" He had a horrifying vision of them all captive in their little boxes, being observed through cosmic keyholes. Or were they just going to be strapped to tables and dissected?

The Marvel-form dissolved into a shimmer of light, as if the being had become tired or bored with maintaining it. "You will be in the circus," it said. The wall of stars vanished.

They looked through a window at a strange and yet familiar place. There was a suggestion of a tent. Within it, inside a hundred rings, creatures of all sizes and shapes and colors cavorted. There was music, and the sound of hissing in the wind. The scene was bright and far away, like a painting come to life.

Millicent said, "I see people in there."

"Where?"

The scene swooped at them. They hovered like birds over one ring. In it were six people, three men, three women, doing a high-wire act in silver spangles and long rainbow plumes. They were good.

"But where's the audience?" Ricky said. They looked at the shimmer in the air.

"Maybe they're invisible, like him," said Millicent. Angelo didn't think he was invisible. Behind the shapeless glow he sensed a truer shape, coiling and uncoiling against the metal wall.

"You brought us here to be in a circus?" he asked.

"Yes."

"A circus in the stars. We're not that good. You know that. Why didn't you steal the Flying Wallendas?"

"You are a much more interesting act," Marvel said, "by *our* standards."

Tony stood up, hands on hips. "Man, you are crazy," he said. "I don't perform for some gook I can't even *see*. You just pick us up and take us home." Lynellen nodded.

Behind the shimmer a body thickened, congealing slowly out of air. A snake's head and body reared above them, immense tail poised, tongue flickering in the giant fanged mouth, ruby eyes sentient and cold and patient as the dark between stars. "You will sssstay." it said. Susie hid her face on the chair.

"For how long?" whispered Lynellen.

The snake said nothing.

Angelo felt a wrenching sickness in his belly. "We have to stay," he said. "But you can't make us work. You'll take us home when you get tired of feeding us."

The fanged mouth opened wide. "What makessss you think you will be fed?"

The act unrolls against the spiral patterns of the stars. Ricky beats the bass drum as Tony and Lynellen and Angelo and Susie fly beneath the barest hint of a tent. An audience claps. Marvel stands in the ring. "Aren't they GREAT, ladies and gentlemen," his deep voice cries. But that is an illusion, made for their mind. If they look they can see the great hooded serpent head and the scorpion tail. They do not look too closely at him or at the audience.

After their act they walk home across a park to their trailers. The noises of the circus come to their ears on the wind. But there is no wind. Orion, striding across the night sky, is also an illusion. He never moves. Their nights are always moonless. The aliens have never bothered to make them a moon.

"Next week," Lynellen says, "we're playing in Cleveland." Or Des Moines, or Toledo. She never says Chicago. Angelo agrees. Time passes. They eat and drink, sleep and make love, fight and make up.

But there is no time in the Circus. Months have passed, or is it years? "I'm asking Marvel for a raise," Lynellen quips.

Sometimes, under the vast illusion of the big top, they think they see human beings. Ricky swears to have seen clowns. But they have never met the other beings in the ring. Other acts never look their way. Angelo wonders about the blue lizard people that he thinks he sees sometimes in a ring close to their own. But they know only each other, and the great snake-thing they still call Marvel. The universe has got very small. Was there, really, a place called Chicago, a planet named Earth, a gentle lioness named Lila? Angelo is no longer sure. He dreams of them, but they may be only dreams. The stars loom above them like rubious eyes, watching. The hiss on the wind may be laughter, or contempt, or applause. They do not know. There is only the Circus, after all. The Circus goes on forever.

•The White King's Dream•

This is another one of my category-straddling stories. Although it was published in *Shadows 2*, I don't think it's really a horror story. It came out of five years of working in and around hospitals. The title comes from Lewis Carroll's *Through The Looking Glass*, in which the Red King lies dreaming the world. Why, you ask, is my dreamer the White King?

Figure it out.

The straps across her shoulders were cutting through the thin cloth gown. I'm cold, she thought. "Okay, Louise, time to wake up now," said a voice warm as honey—but I am awake, Luisa thought, and wondered why she could not see the light that she could feel falling on her eyes.

"Baby, I'll move you into the sun while I change those dirty sheets. You messed the bed again, Louise. I know you can't help it but I sure wish you wouldn't do it." At least I can hear, Luisa thought. She heard the voice, and a crying sound, quite close. The sheets were clammy under her. She smelled a stale and sour smell. The straps fell away. Something lifted her.

She was afraid.

She was set in a hard chair. The straps came back. The chair was metal and cold. Now she was sitting in the sunlight. She wanted to say *thank you* but her mouth would not move. The close crying sound increased. It was herself; she was crying. The stale sour scent was her own. Helen. Day shift. Every day began like this, except the days when it rained. Helen still came, then, to change her bedclothes, wash her, feed her, shove pills down her shriveled throat; but there was no sunlight to sit in when it rained, and they would never open the windows so that she could smell the rain. All she smelled was her own melting flesh. In Lord Byron there was a fat man crying to get out, and in me there is a skeleton wailing for release.

"Baby, why you screwing up your face like that? Are you too hot?" No, Luisa wanted to scream, no, but Helen's inexorable hands pulled her out of the warmth and dumped her into her cold barren bed. "Breakfast in a while, Louise. You just put your head back into the pillow and dream, now."

Even dreams are dreams, Luisa thought. *Y los sueños sueños son.* Dreams no longer meant sleep, and what good was sleep when she had to wake from it again? Sleep just meant the Night shift, and then the Day shift, the sun looking through the windows, *busy old fool, unruly sun.* Breakfast, she thought with loathing. They fed her with a tube down her throat. Sometimes they put a tube like an arm into her and pumped air through her, making her breathe. She hated tubes. Is that Freudian, she wondered, to hate tubes? She wanted to be back in the sunlight, in the warm. She began to cry again, a cat-mewl of sound. Helen might hear it; Helen listened, sometimes, and might understand; and might put her back into the sun.

"They just like babies," Helen said. "They're over ninety, most of them, and they can't hardly talk, but they can cry. If you watch their eyes you can figure out what it is they want— I can, anyways. You'll get the hang of it."

I don't give a damn, thought Mark Wald. But he nodded. The odors of feces and ammonia fought in the halls. He hated the geriatrics homes, but it was the only place he could get work anymore; the hospitals wouldn't hire him. The best thing about this place is that the lockers are in the basement and I can go down there to do my drinking in private, the way a man should drink. Unhurried snorts. He would read—he had the latest paperback thriller in his locker now—and drink, slowly, decently. No one would notice on the graveyard shift. During the day there were five aides, three orderlies, two R.N.s on duty. Graveyard shift there were two orderlies, two aides, one R.N., no baths to give or beds to make or people to feed. Stay up all night riding herd on a bunch of whimpering zombies— then go home and sleep till way past noon. Helen was still talking about the patients as if it mattered what they had once done or been. They were zombies now. This one had been a doctor. This one a lawyer. He pretended to listen as she stuck her head into every room.

"Honey, what is it?"

The old lady in the bed had a blind wrinkled face like a sun-struck turtle. She whimpered. "You wet? No, you not wet. Straps too tight?" She loosened the posey straps that held the thin gawk of a woman in bed. "This is Louise; she was a teacher in a college." The sounds went on. Helen laid a broad black hand on the woman's forehead and reached for her pulse with the other. "Your pulse's okay. You cold? I could put you back in the sun."

The crying stopped.

"That's it, right? Okay, baby, we'll put you in the chair. This is Mark, here, he's a new night shift worker." She was taking off the cloth restraints as she talked. Mark pulled the wheelchair over to the bed. Together they let down the high sides of the bed, helped Luisa to a sitting position, picked her up, and put her in the chair. Her long fingernails scratched lightly against Mark's neck. He shuddered.

I won't get old, he thought. Blind, half dead, a piece of meat in a bed for others to haul around. I'll die decently. Pills, or gas, or maybe I'll jump off the bridge. The alcohol will do it for me. He saw himself in an alcoholic stupor, staggering along the road . . . getting hit by a car, and dying, instantly, no pain, no bedpans, or tubes up his arms and in his ass and down his throat.

It was an old vision. Usually it waited till he was decently asleep. It was always night or early morning in the dream, and the car was always a red car. "Excuse me," he said to Helen. He ran downstairs. Let her think he had to piss. He twirled the dial of the combination lock on his locker, got it wrong, did it again, got it right, uncapped the bottle, and took a swallow. The bourbon eased down warmly—that was better. Sometimes he felt it was the only warm thing in the world. He screwed the cap on the bottle, locked it up, and sauntered up the stairs. They would know, of course. That Helen would smell it on him. What the hell, they wouldn't fire him unless he made a mistake. He wouldn't make a mistake.

Helen was waiting for him at the nursing station. "Let's

hope he doesn't end up like Harold," he heard her say. Who the hell was Harold? The nurse at the desk was old and stringy, on her way to looking like that senile crock down the hall.

"Hi," he said, smiling. "I'm Mark Wald, the new night shift orderly."

Graveyard shift was a breeze. The old crocks wheezed and cried and slept. The aides took turns sleeping in the bed in the back room. Mark read paperbacks and sucked on his bottle of bourbon. The other night orderly was an old fag named Morton. He liked playing cards. Mark preferred to read. Morton sulked and played solitaire at the nursing station desk.

"Who was Harold?"

Morton looked up from putting a red queen on a black king. "Oh, it's you."

"Who the hell else would it be?"

"Harold was the dude before you. Black and built. Younger than you."

"He was a fag, too?"

"The word is faggot, sweetie. No. Straight as they come, if you'll excuse the phrase."

"What happened to him—he get tired of this dump?"

Morton looked up again. "No, sweetie. He ripped off dope from the narcotics box and O.D.'d on it. Morphine, I think."

Now why should that Helen even think he would be like some blood who needled himself to death? He hated drugs.

"Su-i-cide, they called it," said Morton.

"Huh."

"They come and go. I've been working here five years, you know that? Only Helen's been here longer than I have." His hands kept placing the cards. He had soft, pudgy hands.

"Helen said this place is a rich people's dump."

"It is. Look at the equipment we got! Monitors, crash carts. Those things are for hospitals. The nurses all have standing orders, so that if someone goes Code Red they can give the drugs without calling the doctor on the phone. Ever try to find a doctor at dinnertime? Forget it. All these old bags have money, and their sons and daughters have guilt complexes waiting for them to die."

"It's still a dump," Mark said. His knee brushed the table

and all the cards slewed sideways off their piles. "Sorry."

Morton bent down. "Sure you are, sweetie," he said. "Sure you are."

Mark went down to his locker again. He sat with the bottle in his hand. The basement walls were dirty gray and nubby, like the stubble of old men's beards. He checked his watch. Near 4 A.M., time for somebody to die. It was true they often died at 4 A.M. They had had one respiratory failure that night already, the old lady in 209. Maybe she would die.

As if his thought had done it, a blinker over the basement door started flashing frantic red. Code Red, cardiac arrest. He stuck the bottle in the locker hastily and went up the stairs.

When he got to the room they were all in there. The EKG was jumping like a scalded mouse and the nurse was using the defibrillator. They all stood clear of the metal bedframe. The body on the bed jerked. Damn, Mark thought, in a nursing home they were supposed to let you die in peace.

"Call St. Francis' admitting," the R.N. said. "This one has to be in CCU."

Morton went to do that. Waste of time and money, Mark thought. Why can't they just let the bastards die?

It is a sophism to imagine that there is any strict dividing line between the waking world and the world of dreams. PROSPERO'S CELL, by Lawrence Durrell, Luisa thought. Today she was feeling strong, almost strong enough to tongue the respirator tube out of her throat. They would never let her do that. She had been to Greece, though not to Durrell's Corcyra. *Somewhere between Calabria and Corfu the blue really begins.* That was the book's first line. She tried to remember the blue and white, all the colors, the scent of lemon trees...."Hi, baby. They told us at report you had a bad night! What'd you want to stop breathing for, huh? You know they won't let you do that around here." Helen was moving closer to the bed. "It was busy here last night. That Friedman in 211, he arrested last night. They took him to St. Francis."

Yes, Luisa thought, *oh yes?*

Helen's voice was gentle as a kiss. "They called this morning to say he passed, baby." She went on. "Your son's coming in to see you today, baby; won't that be nice? He called to say he be in after lunch."

Johnny—she recalled a little boy named Johnny, who did not at all go with the man-sized voice that sometimes came and talked over her. Be nice, Johnny. She had often had to tell him that, a cranky little boy who liked to fuss...What could she tell him today? That they fed her through a tube and that she could no longer breathe through her own power? That food has no taste when it goes through a tube? That the sea around Greece is blue? How had she borne such an unimaginative child! He had sent her a postcard from Europe, where he had dutifully gone to honeymoon: a picture of the Paris Metro, a giant pneumatic tube. Tubes. Could she tell him she was sick of tubes?

Helen was talking to her. "Baby? Louise? Oh, damn." She half-felt hands on her. I can hear you perfectly, Luisa wanted to say. But Helen was muttering off to the nursing station. Luisa was walking the line between wakefulness and dreams, that was all. She imagined it as a thin line cut in concrete, like the lines in the sidewalks she had skipped over as a child, chanting, "Step on a crack, break your mother's back." If only they would stop pulling her back into life. Even Helen, who understood, who always told her when one of them had gone, even Helen held her to life. One day through the tubes they would feed her arsenic, and then it would be all over.

Fantasy. She built against the dark of her closed eyes the trembling blues of Corfu.

At six o'clock Mark made his final rounds. The fluorescent lights were watery in the dawn. Out of the beds the old people stared, sleepy, flat-eyed, blind-eyed. He was alone. Morton was in the hospital, St. Francis, cut up by a mugger, rolled on his way to work, left to bleed to death in an alley. What had he gone into an alley for? *Su-i-cide;* he could hear Morton saying it in that fag drawl.

Someone was moaning. He walked into 209. The old lady was shifting and turning her head. The tape that held the respirator tube was loose. She was supposed to be comatose, or semi-comatose. He watched her for a while. The movement looked purposeful. He reached out and patted the tape down again. She moaned. Her eyes were cloudy, and he remembered that she was blind. How did it feel to have hands come out of the night at you like that? Like the hands with the knife that had cut Morton. "Listen, sweetie," he said, "you want me to take that tape off? That tube out? If I do that you'll die, you know, poof, out like a damned light. You know that?" Her body was still, frozen, stiff as a board. He put his hand on the tape again to tease her. Comatose, semicomatose, what did doctors know? he thought. She'd heard him. I'd be scared; Christ, I'd be petrified. "I won't do it," he told her. "I could lose my job."

He drowsed through the report that ritualized the shift change, and then went downstairs to collect his book and his bottle. He leaned against the dirty gray wall and took a long drink. Warmer than any woman. One for the road. And one for Morton. He wondered how bad Morton was. He capped the bottle and tucked it, brownbagged, decently clad, under his arm. He wondered what Morton had left uncollected in his locker. A pack of cards?

The wind was bitter. He held tightly to the bottle, glad that his was only a short walk home. It came to him suddenly that he was drinking himself to death. The thought was mildly entertaining. It could be worse. On the ice patches he staggered, and it became a game to see if this one or the next one would trip him. He beat them all. He decided to shortcut through the tunnel under the freeway. There would be few cars through it on a Sunday morning, 7 A.M. on an icy day. The tunnel walls were gray and smooth. He found himself thinking back to 209. He had almost done it to the old lady. Christ. That would have been a mistake.

The car came diving into the neck of the tunnel, a bullet-shaped red toy. Mark watched at it slipped on the street ice. The driver took the skids, slid, and then pulled out, nonchalant as if it were a game for kids. Smooth, he thought.

The car grew suddenly very large and very red.

The dream, he thought, it's the car of the dream. The tunnel wall was flat and cold at his back. He was pressed down and there was nowhere he could go. The bright fender grazed him, and like a bull, the car was gone. The driver honked back at him. Bastard, you missed me, he thought, you missed me! Torn between rage and joy, he threw the bottle into the air. It went up like a rocket. His feet slipped out from under him. "Hey!" He was falling. You bastard, he thought in wonderment as the bottle shattered all around him, you bastard.

• • •

"Morning, baby. You doing any better today? It's raining. Gray outside. I almost didn't want to come to work this morning, it's so ugly. But then I thought, what would Louise think if I weren't there? She'd worry. Honey, you remember that night orderly Mark?" Helen's voice dropped. "You know, they found him under the freeway this morning with his neck broke, and all cut up and covered with whiskey. An accident. Isn't that something? He was young, too. But Morton, you remember Morton, he's okay and coming back to work tonight, so there'll be someone on duty to look after you. Imagine, he just slipped on the ice! Cruel way to die."

Luisa dreamed. Cruel. That was cruel. *April is the cruelest month, breeding lilacs out of the dead earth*...Lord, must these bones live? The tube in her chest pumped. Her mouth hurt, her back hurt. Mark, she thought, remembering his voice and the thick alcoholic breath of him and the feel of his hand on her cheek. It was cruel of him to tease me. Out like a light, he had said. *Out, out, brief candle*. The light in Greece stains the air like yellow wine. Why would they not let her go? Arsenic through the tube would be easy. That would be murder, they would never do that. She lay and dreamed of all the ways there were to die. Arsenic, gas, ropes and cliffs, *the white cliffs of Dover*, steely razor blades with blue edges, blue water to drown in, and cars, bright red lethal cars. So many ways to die, she thought, but not here, and her heart clenched in a sudden fury. Again, she urged it, again, again. They do it for each other, but not for us, the bastards, never for us.

•*The Woman Who Loved The Moon*•

When Jessica Amanda Salmonson asked me, three years ago, to contribute to her anthology *Amazons!*, I said yes although I had no idea what I would write. Aside from "Wizard's Domain," which was still unsold, I had written no heroic fantasy. Nevertheless I wanted to be a part of this project, and I was sure the story would come—I could feel it in my psyche. When I finally sat down at the typewriter to do the story, the setting emerged first, and I recognized the landscapes of my first invented country, Ryoka.

As it unwound in my head I saw that the story was a myth. When it was done I reworked it twice and sent it to Jessica. And that, I thought, is that—except that the culture and history of the story have taken root, as it were, in my mind. Someday there will be a book whose hero is Kai Talvela's great-great-great-many more greats-granddaughter.

They tell this story in the Middle Counties of Ryoka, and especially in the county of Issho, the home of the Talvela family. In Issho they know that the name of the woman who loved the Moon was Kai Talvela, one of the three warrior sisters of Issho. Though the trees round the Talvela house grow taller now than they did in Kai Talvela's time, her people have not forgotten her. But outside of Issho and in the cities they know her only as the Mirror Ghost.

Kai Talvela was the daughter of Roko Talvela, at a time when the domain of the Talvelai was smaller than it is now. Certainly it was smaller than Roko Talvela liked. He rode out often to skirmish at the borders of his land, and the men of the Talvelai went with him. The hills of Issho county resounded to their shouts. While he was gone the folk of the household went about their business, for the Talvela lands were famous then as they are now for their fine orchards and the fine dappled horses they breed. They were well protected, despite the dearth of soldiery, for Lia Talvela was a sorcerer, and Kai and her sisters Tei and Alin guarded the house. The sisters were a formidable enemy, for they had learned to ride and to fight. The Talvela armorer had fashioned for them fine light mail that glittered as if carved from gems. At dawn and dusk the three sisters rode across the estate. Alin wore a blue-dyed plume on her peaked helmet, and Tei wore a gold one on hers. Kai wore a feather dyed red as blood. In the dusk their armor gleamed, and when it caught the starlight it glittered like the rising Moon.

Kai was the oldest of the sisters; Alin the youngest. In looks and in affection the three were very close. They were—as Talvela women are even in our day—tall and slim, with coal-black hair. Tei was the proudest of the three, and Alin was the most laughing and gay. Kai, the oldest, was quietest, and while Tei frowned often and Alin laughed, Kai's look was grave, direct, and serene. They were all of an age to be wed, and Roko Talvela had tried to find husbands for them. But Kai, Tei, and Alin had agreed that they would take no lover and wed no man who could not match their skills in combat. Few men wished to meet the warrior sisters. Even the bravest found themselves oddly unnerved when they faced Tei's long barbed spear and grim smile, or Alin's laughing eyes as she spun her oaken horn-tipped cudgel. It whirled like a live thing in her palms. And none desired to meet Kai's great curved blade. It sang when she swung it, a thin clear sound, purer than the note of the winter thrush. Because of that sound Kai named her blade *Song*. She kept it sharp, sharp as a shadow in the full Moon's light. She had a jeweled scabbard made to hold it, and to honor it, she caused a great ruby to be fixed in the hilt of the sword.

One day in the late afternoon the sisters rode, as was their custom, to inspect the fences and guardposts of the estate, making sure that the men Roko Talvela had left under their command were vigilant in their job. Their page went with them. He was a boy from Nakasé county, and like many of the folk of Nakasé he was a musician. He carried a horn which, when sounded, would summon the small company of guards, and his stringed lute from Ujo. He also carried a long-necked pipe, which he was just learning how to play. It was autumn. The leaves were rusty on the trees. In the dry sad air they rattled in the breeze as if they had been made of brass. A red sun sat on the horizon, and overhead swung the great silver face of the full Moon.

The page had been playing a children's song on the pipe. He took his lips from it and spoke. The storytellers of Ujo, in Nakasé county, when they tell this tale, insist that he was in love with one of the sisters, or perhaps with all three. There is no way to know, of course, if that is true. Certainly they had all, even proud Tei, been very kind to him. But he gazed upon the sisters in the rising moonlight, and his eyes worshipped. Stammering, he said, "O my ladies, each of you is beautiful, and together you rival even the Moon!"

Alin laughed, and swung her hair. Like water against diamond it brushed her armor. Even Tei smiled. But Kai was troubled, "Don't say that," she said gently. "It's not lucky, and it isn't true."

"But everyone says it, Lady," said the page.

Suddenly Tei exclaimed. "Look!" Kai and Alin wheeled their horses. A warrior was riding slowly toward them, across the blue hills. His steed was black, black as obsidian, black as a starless night, and the feather on his helmet was blacker than a raven's wing. His bridle and saddle and reins and his armor were silver as the mail of the Talvela women. He bore across his lap a blackthorn cudgel, tipped with ivory, and beside it lay a great barbed spear. At his side bobbed a black sheath and the protruding hilt of a silver sword. Silently he rode up the hill, and the darkness thickened at his back. The hooves of the black horse made no sound on the pebbly road.

As the rider came closer, he lifted his head and gazed at the Talvelai, and they could all see that the person they had thought a man was in fact a woman. Her hair was white as snow, and her eyes gray as ash. The page lifted the horn to his lips to sound a warning. But Alin caught his wrist with her warm strong fingers. "Wait," she said. "I think she is alone, let us see what she wants." Behind the oncoming rider darkness thickened. A night bird called *Whooo?*

Tei said, "I did not know there was another woman warrior in the Middle Counties."

The warrior halted below the summit of the hill. Her voice was clear and cold as the winter wind blowing off the northern moors. "It is as they sing; you are indeed fair. Yet not so fair, I think as the shining Moon."

Uneasily the women of Issho gazed at this enigmatic stranger. Finally Kai said, "you seem to know who we are. But we do not know you. Who are you, and from where do you come? Your armor bears no device. Are you from the Middle Counties?"

"No," said the stranger, "my home is far away." A smile like light flickered on her lips. "My name is—Sedi."

Kai's dark brows drew together, and Tei frowned, for Sedi's armor was unmarred by dirt or stain, and her horse looked fresh and unwearied. Kai thought, what if she is an illusion, sent by Roko Talvela's enemies? She said, "You are chary of your answers."

But Alin laughed. "O my sister, you are too suspicious," she said. She pointed to the staff across the stranger's knees. "Can you use that pretty stick?"

"In my land," Sedi said, "I am matchless." She ran her hand down the black cudgel's grain.

"Then I challenge you!" said Alin promptly. She smiled at her sisters. "Do not look so sour. It has been so long since there has been anyone who could fight with me!" Faced with her teasing smile, even Tei smiled in return, for neither of the two older sisters could refuse Alin anything.

"I accept," said Sedi sweetly. Kai thought, *An illusion can not fight. Surely this woman is real.* Alin and Sedi dismounted their steeds. Sedi wore silks with silver and black markings beneath her shining mail. Kai looked at them and thought, I have seen those marks before. Yet as she stared at them she saw no discernible pattern. Under her armor Alin wore blue silk. She had woven it herself, and it was the color of a summer sky at dawn when the crickets are singing. She took her white cudgel in her hands, and made it spin in two great circles, so swiftly that it blurred in the air. Then she walked to the top of the hill, where the red sunlight and the pale moonlight lingered.

"Let us begin," she said.

Sedi moved opposite her. Her boots were black kid, and they made no sound as she stepped through the stubby grass. Kai felt a flower of fear wake in her heart. She almost turned to tell the page to wind his horn. But Alin set her staff to whirling, and it was too late. It spun and then with dizzying speed thrust toward Sedi's belly. Sedi parried the thrust, moving with flowing grace. Back and forth they struck and circled on the rise. Alin was laughing.

"This one is indeed a master, O my sisters," she called. "I have not been so tested in months!"

Suddenly the hard horn tip of Sedi's staff thrust toward Alin's face. She lifted her staff to deflect the blow. Quick as light, the black staff struck at her belly. Kai cried out. The head blow had been a feint. Alin gasped and fell, her arms folding over her stomach. Her lovely face was twisted with pain and white as moonlight on a lake. Blood bubbled from the corner of her mouth. Daintily, Sedi stepped away from her. Kai and Tei leaped from their horses. Kai unlaced her breastplate and lifted her helmet from her face.

"Oh," said Alin softly. "It hurts."

Tei whirled, reaching for her spear.

But Alin caught her arm with surprising strength. "No!" she said. "It was a fair fight, and I am fairly beaten."

Lightly Sedi mounted her horse. "Thy beauty is less than it was, women of Issho," she said. Noiselessly she guided her steed into the white mist coiling up the hill, and disappeared in its thick folds.

"Ride to the house," Kai said to the frightened page. "Bring aid and a litter. Hurry." She laid a palm on Alin's cheek. It was icy. Gently she began to chafe her sister's hands. The page raced away. Soon the men came from the house. They carried Alin Talvela to her bed, where her mother the sorcerer and healer waited to tend her.

But despite her mother's skills, Alin grew slowly more weak and wan. Lia Talvela said, "She bleeds within. I cannot stanch the wound." As Kai and Tei sat by the bed, Alin sank into a chill silence from which nothing, not even their loving touch, roused her. She died with the dawn. The folk of the household covered her with azure silk and laid her oaken staff at her hand. They coaxed Kai and Tei to their beds and gave them each a poppy potion, that they might sleep a dreamless sleep, undisturbed even by grief.

Word went to Roko Talvela to tell him of his daughter's death. Calling truce to his wars, he returned at once to Issho. All Issho county, and lords from the neighboring counties of

Chuyo, Ippa, and Nakasé, came to the funeral. Kai and Tei Talvela rode at the head of the sad procession that brought the body of their sister to burial. The folk who lined the road pointed them out to each other, marveling at their beauty. But the more discerning saw that their faces were cold as if they had been frost-touched, like flowers in spring caught by a sudden wayward chill.

Autumn passed to winter. Snow fell, covering the hills and valleys of Issho. Issho households put away their silks and linens and wrapped themselves in wool. Fires blazed in the manor of the Talvelai. The warrior sisters of Issho put aside their armor and busied themselves in women's work. And it seemed to all who knew them that Kai had grown more silent and serious, and that proud Tei had grown more grim. The page tried to cheer them with his music. He played war songs, and drinking songs, and bawdy songs. But none of these tunes pleased the sisters. One day in desperation he said, "O my ladies, what would you hear?"

Frowning, Tei shook her head. "Nothing," she said.

But Kai said, "Do you know 'The Riddle Song?'" naming a children's tune. The page nodded. "Play it." He played it. After it he played "Dancing Bear" and "The Happy Hunter" and all the songs of childhood he could think of. And it seemed to him that Tei's hard mouth softened as she listened.

In spring Roko Talvela returned to his wars. Kai and Tei re-donned their armor. At dawn and at dusk they rode the perimeter of the domain, keeping up their custom, accompanied by the page. Spring gave way to summer, and summer to autumn. The farmers burned leaves in the dusk, covering the hills with a blue haze.

And one soft afternoon a figure in silver on a coal-black horse came out of the haze.

The pale face of the full Moon gleamed at her back. "It's she!" cried the page. He reached for his horn.

Tei said, "Wait." Her voice was harsh with pain. She touched the long spear across her knees, and her eyes glittered.

"O my sister, let us not wait," said Kai softly. But Tei seemed not to hear. Sedi approached in silence. Kai lifted her voice. "Stay, traveler. There is no welcome for you in Issho."

The white-haired woman smiled a crooked smile. "I did not come for welcome, O daughters of the Talvelai."

"What brought you here, then?" said Kai.

The warrior woman made no answer. But her gray eyes beneath her pale brows looked at Kai with startling eloquence. They seemed to say, patience. You will see.

Tei said, "She comes to gloat. O my sister, that we are two, and lonely, who once were three."

"I do not think—" Kai began.

Tei interrupted her. "Evil woman," she said, with passion. "Alin was all that is trusting and fair, and you struck her without warning." Dismounting from her dappled mare, she took in hand her long barbed spear. "Come, Sedi. Come and fight *me*."

"As you will," said Sedi. She leaped from her horse, spear in hand, and strode to the spot where Tei waited for her, spear ready. They fought. They thrust and parried and lunged. Slowly the autumn chill settled over the countryside. The spears flashed in the moonlight. Kai sat her horse, fingering the worked setting of the ruby on her sword. Sometimes it seemed to her that Sedi was stronger than Tei, and at other times Tei seemed stronger than Sedi. The polish on their silver armor shone like flame in the darkness.

At last Tei tired. She breathed heavily, and her feet slipped in the nubby grass.

Kei had been waiting for this moment. She drew *Song* from the sheath and made ready to step between them. "Cease this!" she called. Sedi glanced at her.

"No!" cried Tei. She lunged. The tip of her spear sliced Sedi's arm. "I shall win!" she said.

Sedi grimaced. A cloud passed across the Moon. In the dimness, Sedi lunged forward. Her thrust slid under Tei's guard. The black-haired woman crumpled into the grass. Kai sprang to her sister's side. Blood poured from Tei's breast. "Tei!" Kai cried. Tei's eyes closed. Kai groaned. She knew death when she saw it. Raging, she called to the page, "Sound the horn!"

The sweet sound echoed over the valley. In the distance came the answering calls from the Talvela men. Kai looked at Sedi, seated on her black steed. "Do you hear those horns, O murderous stranger? The Talvela soldiers come. You will not escape."

Sedi smiled. "I am not caught so easily," she said. At that moment Tei shook in Kai's arms, and life passed from her.

The ground thrummed with the passage of horses. "Do you wish me caught, you must come seek me, Kai Talvela." Light flashed on her armor. Then the night rang with voices shouting.

The captain of the guard bent over Kai. "O my lady, who has done this thing?"

Kai started to point to the white-haired warrior. But among the dappled horses there was no black steed, and no sign of Sedi.

In vain the men of the Talvelai searched for her. In great sadness they brought the body of Tei Talvela home, and readied her for burial. Once more a procession rode the highway to the burial ground of the Talvelai. All Issho mourned.

But Kai Talvela did not weep. After the burial she went to her mother's chambers, and knelt at the sorcerer's knee. "O my mother, listen to me." And she told her mother everything she could remember of her sisters' meetings with the warrior who called herself Sedi.

Lia Talvela stroked her daughter's fine black hair. She listened, and her face grew pale. At last Kai ended. She waited for her mother to speak. "O my daughter," Lia Talvela said sadly, "I wish you had come to me when this Sedi first appeared. I could have told you then that she was no ordinary warrior. *Sedi* in the enchanter's tongue means Moon, and the woman you describe is one of the shades of that Lady. Her armor is impervious as the moonlight, and her steed is not a horse at all but Night itself taking animal shape. I fear that she heard the songs men sang praising the beauty of the women warriors of the Talvelai, and they made her angry. She came to earth to punish you."

"It was cruel," said Kai. "Are we responsible for what fools say and sing?"

"The elementals are often cruel," said Lia Talvela.

That night, Kai Talvela lay in her bed, unable to rest. Her bed seemed cold and strange to her. She reached to the left and then to the right, feeling the depressions in the great quilts where Alin and Tei had been used to sleep. She pictured herself growing older and older until she was old, the warrior woman of Issho, alone and lonely until the day she died and they buried her beside her sisters. The Talvelai are a long-lived folk. And it seemed to her that she would have preferred her sisters' fate.

• • •

The following spring travelers on the highways of Ryoka were treated to a strange apparition—a black-haired woman on a dappled horse riding slowly east.

She wore silver armor and carried a great curved sword, fashioned in the manner of the smiths of the Middle Counties. She moved from town to town. At the inns she would ask, "Where is the home of the nearest witch or wizard?" And when shown the way to the appropriate cottage or house or hollow or cave, she would go that way.

Of the wisefolk she asked always the same thing: "I look for the Lady who is sometimes known as Sedi." And the great among them gravely shook their heads, while the small grew frightened, and shrank away without response. Courteously she thanked them and returned to the road. When she came to the border of the Middle Counties, she did not hesitate, but continued into the Eastern Counties, where folk carry straight, double-edged blades, and the language they speak is strange.

At last she came to the hills that rise on the eastern edge of Ryoka. She was very weary. Her armor was encrusted with the grime of her journey. She drew her horse up the slope of a hill. It was twilight. The darkness out of the east seemed to sap the dappled stallion's strength, so that it plodded like a plowhorse. She was discouraged as well as weary, for in all her months of traveling she had heard no word of Sedi. I shall go home, she thought, and live in the Talvela manor, and wither. She gained the summit of the hill. There she halted. She looked down across the land, bones and heart aching. Beyond the dark shadows lay a line of silver like a silken ribbon in the dusk. And she knew that she could go no further. That silver line marked the edge of the world. She lifted her head and smelled the heavy salt scent of the open sea.

The silver sea grew brighter. Kai Talvela watched. Slowly the full Moon rose dripping out of the water.

So this is where the Moon lives, thought the woman warrior. She leaned on her horse. She was no fish, to chase the Moon into the ocean. But the thought of returning to Issho made her shiver. She raised her arms to the violet night. "O Moon, see me," she cried. "My armor is filth covered. My horse is worn to a skeleton. I am no longer beautiful. O jealous one, cease your anger. Out of your pity, let me join my sisters. Release me!"

She waited for an answer. None came. Suddenly she grew very sleepy. She turned the horse about and led it back down the slope to a hollow where she had seen the feathery shape of a willow silhouetted against the dusk, and heard the music of a stream. Taking off her armor, she wrapped herself in her red woolen cloak. Then she curled into the long soft grass and fell instantly asleep.

She woke to warmth and the smell of food. Rubbing her eyes, she lifted on an elbow. It was dawn. White-haired, cloaked in black, Sedi knelt beside a fire, turning a spit on which broiled three small fish. She looked across the wispy flames and smiled, eyes gray as ash. Her voice was clear and soft as the summer wind. "Come and eat."

It was chilly by the sea. Kai stretched her hands to the fire, rubbing her fingers. Sedi gave her the spit. She nibbled the fish. They were real, no shadow or illusion. Little bones crunched beneath her teeth. She sat up and ate all three fish. Sedi watched her and did not speak.

When she had done, Kai Talvela laid the spit in the fire. Kneeling by the stream, she drank and washed her face. She returned to the place where she had slept, and lifted from the sheath her great curved blade. She saluted Sedi. "O Moon," she said, "or shade of the Moon, or whatever you may be, long have I searched for you, by whose hand perished the two people most dear to me. Without them I no longer wish to live. Yet I am a daughter of the Talvelai, and a warrior, and I would die in battle. O Sedi, will you fight?"

"I will," said the white-haired woman. She drew her own sword from its sheath.

They circled and cut and parried and cut again, while light deepened in the eastern sky. Neither was wearing armor, and so each stroke was double-deadly. Sedi's face was serene as the lambent Moon as she cut and thrust, weaving the tip of her blade in a deadly tapestry. I have only to drop my guard, Kai Talvela thought, and she will kill me. Yet something held her back. Sweat rolled down her sides. The blood pounded in her temples. The salty wind kissed her cheeks. In the swaying willow a bird was singing. She heard the song over the clash of the meeting blades. It came to her that life was sweet. I do not want to die, she thought. I am Kai Talvela, the warrior woman of Issho. I am strong. I will live.

Aloud she panted, "Sedi, I will kill you." The white-haired woman's face did not change, but the speed of her attack increased. She is strong, Kai Talvela thought, but I am stronger. Her palms grew slippery with sweat. Her lungs ached. Still she did not weaken. It was Sedi who slowed, tiring. Kai Talvela shouted with triumph. She swept Sedi's blade to one side and thrust in.

Song's sharp tip came to rest a finger's breadth from Sedi's naked throat. Kai Talvela said, "Now, sister-killer, I have you."

Across the shining sword, Sedi smiled. Kai waited for her to beg for life. She said nothing, only smiled like flickering moonlight. Her hair shone like pearl, and her eyes seemed depthless as the sea. Kai's hands trembled. She let her sword fall. "You are too beautiful, O Sedi."

With cool, white fingers Sedi took *Song* from Kai's hands. She brought her to the fire, and gave her water to drink in her cupped palms. She stroked Kai's black hair and laid her cool lips on Kai's flushed cheek. Then she took Kai's hand in her own, and pointed at the hillside. The skin of the earth shivered, like a horse shaking off a fly. A great rent appeared in the hill. Straight as a shaft of moonlight, a path cut through earth to the water's smooth edge. Sedi said, "Come with me."

And so Kai Talvela followed the Moon to her cave beneath the ocean. Time is different there than it is beneath the light of the sun, and it seemed to her that no time passed at all. She slept by day, and rose at night to ride with the Moon across the dark sky's face, to race the wolves across the plains and watch the dolphins playing in the burnished sea. She drank cool water from beneath the earth. She did not seem to need to eat. Whenever she grew sad or thoughtful Sedi would laugh and shake her long bright hair, and say, "O my love, why so somber?" And the touch of her fingers drove all complaint from Kai's mind and lips.

But one sleep she dreamed of an old woman standing by a window, calling her name. There was something familiar and beloved in the crone's wrinkled face. Three times she dreamed that dream. The old voice woke in her a longing to see sunlight and shadow, green grass and the flowers on the trees. The longing grew strong. She thought, Something has happened to me.

Returning to the cave at dawn, she said to Sedi, "O my

friend and lover, let us sit awhile on land. I would watch the sunrise." Sedi consented. They sat at the foot of an immense willow beside a broad stream. A bird sang in the willow. Kai watched the grass color with the sunrise, turning from gray to rose, and from rose to green. And her memories awoke.

She said, "O my love, dear to me is the time I have spent with you beneath the sea. Yet I yearn for the country of my birth, for the sound of familiar voices, for the taste of wine and the smell of bread and meat. Sedi, let me go to my place."

Sedi rose from the grass. She stretched out both hands. "Truly, do you wish to leave me?" she said. There were tears in her gray eyes. Kai trembled. She almost stepped forward to take the white-haired woman in her arms and kiss the tears away.

"I do."

The form of Sedi shuddered, and changed. It grew until it towered in silver majesty above Kai's head, terrible, draped in light, eyes dark as night, a blazing giantess. Soft and awful as death, the Moon said, "Dare you say so, child of earth?"

Kai swallowed. Her voice remained steady. "I do."

The giantess dissolved into the form of Sedi. She regarded Kai. Her eyes were both sad and amused. "I cannot keep you. For in compelling you to love me I have learned to love you. I can no more coerce you than I can myself. But you must know, Kai Talvela, that much human time has passed since you entered the cave of the Moon. Roko Talvela is dead. Your cousin, Edan, is chief of the Talvelai. Your mother is alive but very old. The very steed that brought you here has long since turned to dust."

"I will walk home," said Kai. And she knew that the old woman of her dream had been her mother, the sorcerer Lia.

Sedi sighed. "You do not have to do that. I love you so well that I will even help you leave me. Clothes I will give you, and armor, and a sword." She gestured. Silk and steel rose up from the earth and wrapped themselves about Kai's waist. The weight of a sword dragged at her belt. A horse trotted to her. It was black, and its eyes were pale. "This steed will bring you to Issho in less than a day."

Kai fingered the hilt of the sword, feeling there the faceted lump of a gem. She pulled it upward to look at it and saw a ruby embedded within it. She lifted off her helmet. A red plume nodded in the wind. She lifted her hands to the smooth skin of her face.

"You have not aged," said Sedi. "Do you wish to see?" A silver mirror appeared in her hands. Kai stared at the image of the warrior woman. She looked the same as the day she left Issho.

She looked at the Moon, feeling within her heart for the compulsion that had made her follow Sedi under the sea. She could not feel it. She held out her hands. "Sedi, I love you," she said. They embraced. Kai felt the Moon's cold tears on her cheek.

Sedi pressed the mirror into Kai's hands. "Take this. And on the nights when the Moon is full, do this." She whispered in Kai's ears.

Kai put the mirror between her breasts and mounted the black horse. "Farewell," she called. Sedi waved. The black horse bugled, and shook its ebony mane, and leaped. When Kai looked back she could not see the willow. She bowed her head. Her hair whipped her face. Beneath the silent hooves of Night the earth unrolled like a great brown mat. Kai sighed, remembering the laughter and the loving, and the nightly rides. Never would she race the wolves across the plains, or watch the dolphins playing in the moonlit sea.

The black horse traveled so fast that Kai had no chance to observe the ways in which the world beneath her had changed. But when it halted she stared in puzzlement at the place it had brought her. Surely this was not her home. The trees were different. The house was too big. Yet the token of the Talvelai family gleamed on the tall front gate.

Seeing this lone warrior, the Talvelai guards came from the gatehouse. "Who are you?" they demanded. "What is your business here?"

"I am Kai Talvela," she said.

They scowled at her. "That is impossible. Kai Talvela disappeared fifty years ago!" And they barred her way to the house.

But she laughed at them; she who had fought and loved the Moon. She ripped her sword from its sheath, and it sang in the air with a deadly note. "I am Kai Talvela, and I want to see my mother. I would not suggest that any of you try to stop me." She dismounted. Patting the horse, she said, "Thank you,

O swift one. Now return to Sedi." The horse blew in her ear and vanished like smoke. The soldiers of the Talvelai froze in fear.

Kai Talvela found her mother in her bedroom, sitting by the window. She was ancient, tiny, a white-haired wrinkled woman dressed in lavender silk. Kai crossed the room and knelt by her mother's chair. "Mother," she said.

An elderly man, standing at the foot of the bed, opened his mouth to gape. He held a polished wooden flute. "Lady!"

Lia Talvela caressed her daughter's unaged cheek. "I have missed you," she said. "I called and called. Strong was the spell that held you. Where have you been?"

"In the cave of the Moon," Kai Talvela said. She put off her helmet, sword, and mail. Curled like a child against her mother's knee, she told the sorcerer everything. The old flute player started to leave the room. A gesture of Lia Talvela's stopped him. When she finished, Kai Talvela lifted her mother's hands to her lips. "I will never leave Issho again," she said.

Lia Talvela stroked her child's hair and said no more. Her hands stilled. When Kai looked up, her mother's eyes had closed. She was dead.

It took a long time before the Talvelai believed that this strange woman was truly Kai Talvela, returned from her journey, no older than the day she left Issho. Edan Talvela was especially loath to believe it. Truthfully, he was somewhat nervous of this fierce young woman. He could not understand why she would not tell them all where she had been for fifty years. "Who is to say she is not enchanted?" he said. But the flute master, who had been the sisters' page, recognized her, and said so steadfastly. Edan Talvela grew less nervous when Kai told him that she had no quarrel with his lordship of the Talvelai. She wished merely to live at peace on the Issho estate. He had a house built for her behind the orchard, near the place of her sisters' and her mother's graves. During the day she sewed and spun, and walked through the orchard. It gave her great pleasure to be able to walk beneath the sun and smell the growing things of earth. In the evening she sat beside her doorway, watching night descend. Sometimes the old musician came to visit with her. He alone knew where she had been for fifty years. His knowledge did not trouble her, for she knew that her mother had trusted him. He played the songs that once she had asked him to play; "The Riddle Song" and other songs of childhood. He had grown to be both courtly and wise, and she liked to talk with him. She grew to be quite fond of him, and she blessed her mother's wisdom.

In the autumn after her return the old musician caught a cold, and died. The night after his funeral Kai Talvela wept into her pillow. She loved Issho. But now there was no one to talk to, no one who knew her. The other Talvelai avoided her, and their children scurried from her path as if she were a ghost. Her proper life had been taken away.

For the first time she thought, *I should not have come home. I should have stayed with Sedi.* The full Moon shining through her window seemed to mock her pain.

Suddenly she recalled Sedi's hands cupped around a mirror, and her whispered instructions. Kai ran to her chest and dug beneath the silks. The mirror was still there. Holding it carefully, she took it to the window and positioned it till the moonlight filled its silver face. She said the words Sedi had told her to say. The mirror grew. The moon swelled within it. It grew till it was tall as Kai. Then it trembled, like still water when a pebble strikes it. Out from the ripples of light stepped Sedi. The Moon smiled, and held out her arms. "Have you missed me?" she said. They embraced.

That night Kai's bed was warm. But at dawn Sedi left. "Will you come back?" Kai said.

"I will come when you call me," promised the elemental. Every month on the night of the full Moon Kai held the mirror to the light, and said the words. And every month Sedi returned.

But elementals are fickle, and they are not human, though they may take human shape. One night Sedi did not come. Kai Talvela waited long hours by the window. Years had passed since her return to Issho. She was no longer the woman of twenty who had emerged like a butterfly from the Moon's cave. Yet she was still beautiful, and her spirit was strong as it had ever been. When at last the sunlight came, she rose from her chair. Picking up the mirror from its place, she broke it over her knee.

It seemed to the Talvelai then that she grew old swiftly, aging a year in the space of a day. But her back did not bend, nor did her hair whiten. It remained as black as it had been in her youth. The storytellers say that she never spoke to anyone of her journey. But she must have broken silence one time, or else we would not know this story. Perhaps she spoke as she lay dying. She died on the night of the full Moon, in spring. At dawn some of her vigor returned, and she insisted that her attendants carry her to the window, and dress her in red silk, and lay her sword across her lap. She wore around her neck a piece of broken mirror on a silver chain. And the tale goes on to say that as she died her face brightened to near youthful beauty, and she lifted her arms to the light and cried, "Sedi!"

They buried Kai Talvela beside her mother and her sisters, and then forgot her. Fickleness is also a human trait. But some years later there was war in Issho county. The soldiers of the Talvelai were outnumbered. Doggedly they struggled, as the orchards burned around them. Their enemies backed them as far as the manor gate. It was dusk. They were losing. Suddenly a horn blew, and a woman in bright armor rode from out of nowhere, her mount a black stallion. She swung a shining sword in one fist. "Talvela soldiers, follow me!" she called. At her indomitable manner, the enemy was struck with terror. They dropped their swords and fled into the night. Those soldiers who were closest to the apparition swore that the woman was tall and raven-haired, as the women of the Talvelai are still. They swore also that the sword, as it cut the air, hummed a note so pure that you could almost say it sang.

That was the first appearance of Kai Talvela's shade. Sometimes she comes unarmored, dressed in red silk, gliding through the halls of the Issho estate. When she comes in this guise, she wears a pendant: a broken mirror on a silver chain. When she appears she brings courage to the Talvelai, and fear to their enemies. In the farms and the cities they call her the Mirror Ghost, because of the mirror pendant and because of her brilliant armor. But the folks of the estate know her by name. She is Kai Talvela, the warrior woman of Issho, who loved and fought the Moon, and was loved by her in return.

The daughters of the Talvelai never tire of the story. They ask for it again and again.